Apache Nights

by Sheri WhiteFeather

"I hate being attracted to you."

Kyle's gaze stormed hers, as fierce as a silent war cry.

Joyce struggled to contain her emotions, to stop herself from tasting every inch of him. "Then get off me."

"I don't want to." He traced her top, running his fingers along the neckline. He moved lower, righting her clothes, respecting her in a way she'd never imagined. "And you don't want me to, either."

Like a heart-pounding fool, she let him stay there, body to body, breath to breath. Even so, she fought the urge to put her arms around him, to hold him. She'd known him for eight months, almost long enough to have a baby.

That alone scared the death out of her. Her biological clock wouldn't stop ticking.

"We're in trouble."

Beyond Business
by Rochelle Alers

ﭢﭯﭯﭢ

"You think people will believe I'm carrying your baby?"

Sheldon moved closer to where Renee stood. "I'm certain some people will believe that."

"Oh, Sheldon, what are we going to do?"

"You could let me take care of you," Sheldon said without hesitation.

Renee's mind spun in bewilderment. "What exactly are you saying?"

"You could live with me and be my hostess."

Renee's emotions churned out of control as she tried to make sense of his proposition.

"But you're my boss," she said, shaking her head in confusion. "Are you proposing some sort of business arrangement?"

Sheldon studied Renee thoughtfully for a moment. "And if I weren't your boss?"

Tilting her chin defiantly, Renee gave Sheldon a challenging look. "You didn't answer my question, Mr Blackstone. Would our arrangement be for business or pleasure?"

Sheldon leaned close to her, close enough for his breath to caress her cheek. "That decision would be up to you, Miss Wilson."

Available in October 2006 from Silhouette Desire

Apache Nights
SHERI WHITEFEATHER

Beyond Business
ROCHELLE ALERS

*First published in Great Britain 2006
Silhouette Books, Eton House, 18-24 Paradise Road,
Richmond, Surrey TW9 1SR*

The publisher acknowledges the copyright holders of the
individual works as follows:

Apache Nights © Sheree Henry-WhiteFeather 2005
Beyond Business © Rochelle Alers 2005

*ISBN-13: 978 0 373 60329 9
ISBN-10: 0 373 60329 0*

51-1006

*Printed and bound in Spain
by Litografia Rosés S.A., Barcelona*

APACHE NIGHTS

by
Sheri WhiteFeather

SHERI WHITEFEATHER

lives in Southern California and enjoys ethnic dining, attending powwows and visiting art galleries and vintage clothing stores near the beach. Since her one true passion is writing, she is thrilled to be part of the Silhouette Desire line. When she isn't writing, she often reads until the wee hours of the morning.

Sheri's husband, a member of the Muscogee Creek Nation, inspires many of her stories. They have a son, a daughter and a trio of cats—domestic and wild. She loves to hear from her readers. You may write to her at: PO Box 17146, Anaheim, California 92817, USA.

Visit her website at www.SheriWhiteFeather.com.

To the readers who noticed Kyle in
Always Look Twice and asked if I was going to
write his story, this book is for you.

One

Where in the hell was he?

Joyce Riggs waited at the locked gate in front of Kyle Prescott's obscure seven-acre dwelling, with an irate rottweiler snarling at her through the chain-link fence.

The guard dog fit Kyle to a T, but so did the other pooch, a miniature dachshund, keeping the rotten rotty company.

How many people would pair a rottweiler and an itty-bitty wiener dog together in the same yard?

And speaking of the yard…

Scattered car parts. Old lawn furniture. Playground equipment. Wagon wheels. A cast-iron stove.

She blinked, deciding it was impossible to itemize everything. Kyle was, after all, a junk dealer. Or at least that was his legitimate profession, his cover, the work he claimed on his income tax returns.

She knew he was a militant who trained other militants, a Native American activist who kept the authorities guessing. And to make matters worse, she had a crush on him, an irritating attraction that had been nipping at her heels since they'd both decided nearly eight months ago that they despised each other.

She blew out a rough breath and did her damnedest to ignore the salivating rotty. But it wasn't easy. The domineering beast was getting angrier by the second. The wiener dog, on the other hand, was grinning at her like a sweet little goon.

Finally a banging sound caught her attention. The snap of a heavy wooden door, no doubt. Both dogs reacted, and like a muscle-bound mirage, Kyle appeared in the distance, descending the porch steps of his ancient home.

He lived in an isolated section of the high desert where Charles Manson and his merry band of murderers had been rumored to spend time, a place that still seemed like *Helter Skelter* to the average fear-abiding citizen.

Kyle moved closer, and Joyce squinted at him, wishing he didn't make her pulse flip and flutter.

It took a while, but he reached the gate, emphasizing his long, lazy strides. And then he smirked, giving her a roguish, Rhett Butler-type look. The rottweiler was still baring his fangs, growling in the name of his gorgeous master. She could tell the dog was male. She could see his I'm-a-boy testes.

Fiddle-dee-dee, she thought. Supposedly Kyle had quite a pair, too. Not to mention the body part that went with them. She'd heard he was hung like a Trojan horse.

Not that she cared.

"Detective Riggs," he said. "What a surprise."

"I called and told you to expect me."

"And I told you not to bother."

"Aren't you the least bit curious why I'm here?" she baited.

He angled his head. As usual, his razor-sharp shoulder length hair was held in place with a cloth headband, reminiscent of the Geronimo era in Apache history. At six-four, he was a tall, dark half-blood, a man who carried his heritage like a nine-teenth-century rifle.

He wore a blue T-shirt, button-fly jeans and knee-high moccasins. He was thirty-six, the same age as Joyce, but they didn't have anything in common, nothing but an unyielding attraction.

He shifted his stance, and the sandy soil settled around his feet. "If this is official police business then you'll have to get a warrant."

"Why?" The October wind snapped like a whip, stinging her face. "Did you kill someone?"

His smirk faded. Kyle was a highly decorated Desert Storm soldier, a full-blown war hero. He didn't take death lightly. But neither did she. Joyce was a homicide detective.

For an instant, they simply stared at each other, trapped in a challenging moment. Then she glanced at the rottweiler. He remained on teeth-gnashing alert. "Will you call off that damn dog?"

The smile returned, the crisscross pattern on the fence distorting Kyle's handsome features. "He doesn't like cops."

"I doubt he likes anyone."

"He likes Olivia."

Trust Kyle to bring up his former lover. Olivia was a mutual friend, a psychic who assisted the LAPD and the FBI and every other law enforcement agency Kyle claimed to hate.

But Olivia was also a beautiful, strong-willed woman who trained with Kyle in his private compound, something Joyce was hoping to do.

Especially now, while she was desperate to piece her shattered emotions back together.

"I'm willing to pay you," she said.

That caught his attention. He gave the dog a subtle command, and it stopped snarling. He'd spoken in what sounded like a foreign language. Not anything Joyce recognized. Most likely, he'd trained his rotty to respond to Apache.

"Pay me for what?" he asked.

"For your sessions. Hand to hand combat. War games. Everything you offer here."

"I don't train cops."

"Then I'll be your first."

He gave her a suspicious glare. "Why?"

"Because I'm going through a tough time, some personal issues I can't seem to resolve." She didn't like revealing herself to him, but she wasn't going to unearth every little detail. Joyce's biological clock was ready to explode, something she couldn't begin to understand, something that was spinning out of control. "I need to blow off some steam. Get physical. Take my mind off my problems."

"Then go to the police range and fire your gun. Do whatever your kind do."

"My kind?" She wanted to kick him through the fence, but she knew the rottweiler would go nuts if she staged an attack. "Quit hiding behind your dog and let me in."

"Nice try, Detective. But I'm not macho enough to fall for that."

Yeah, right. He was as macho as a modern-day warrior could get. "Olivia told me all about you, Kyle. Everything."

He had the gall to grin. "So you know I'm good

in bed. So what?" He paused, looked her up and down. "Is that why you're really here, Detective? To bang my brains out?"

She roamed her gaze over him, giving him a taste of his own chauvinistic medicine. "What brains?"

He almost laughed. Almost. But not quite.

As for her, she was used to sparring with hard-edged men, with criminals, with other detectives. Being a woman in a male-dominated environment made her stronger.

But sometimes it made her lonely, too.

A second later, Kyle surprised her by unlocking the gate. "You can come in if you want to."

She motioned to the rottweiler. "What about him?"

"Clyde won't hurt you. Not unless I tell him to."

Clyde. She glanced at the sturdy black and tan canine. He didn't move a well-toned muscle. He sat like a statue at his master's feet. She scanned the grounds for the dachshund and couldn't help but smile. The little wiener dog was wiggling like a ballpark frank trying to escape from a bun.

"What's that one's name?" she asked.

Kyle's lips quirked. "Bonnie."

She raised her eyebrows. Bonnie and Clyde. He'd named his dogs after bank robbers.

He rattled the gate. "Are you coming in or not?"

Suddenly a voice in her head told her to go home, to stay away from Kyle Prescott. But the need to fight her way out of her problems, to train with him, kept her grounded.

Besides, he didn't have a record. And although his activities often bordered on the suspicious, Joyce wanted to believe that when the chips were down, he could be trusted. On the day they'd met, he'd helped the LAPD apprehend a killer, a case that involved Native witchcraft. Of course, he'd only done that for Olivia, for a woman who'd fallen in love with someone else. Not that Olivia had ever been in love with Kyle. She'd claimed he was a bit too bizarre to make her feel secure.

Nonetheless, Joyce took a chance and stepped onto his property. Instantly he moved forward and snapped the padlock back into place, locking her into his domain, telling her, without words, that it was too late to turn tail and run.

As if he could scare her off. She wouldn't dream of chickening out, even if the rational voice in her head was calling her an idiot.

When he turned away from her, she noticed the small-of-the-back holster attached to his belt. She glanced at the semiautomatic SIG and wondered if he armed himself every morning. She knew darn well that Kyle didn't have a permit to carry a gun, open or concealed, but he was on his own property and that put him within the limits of the law.

"Expecting some bad guys to show up?" she asked.

"Just a bad girl." He caught sight of her holstered gun, too. "But she's already here."

"Touché."

"It was your idea to invade my world." He motioned to his house. "Want some coffee?"

"As long as you don't poison it."

"My coffee *is* poison."

And so were his pheromones, she thought. The sparks he sent flying, the sexual energy that made him seem like a predator.

She walked beside him, and Clyde fell into step. She could tell the rotty was aware of everything she did. But so was Kyle.

Refusing to give the males too much attention, she focused on Bonnie. The sweet little thing tagged along, her low-slung belly nearly dragging on the ground.

As they continued toward the house, as Bonnie skirted around salvage items that got in her way, Joyce studied the outbuildings on Kyle's property.

"Is that where you store the rest of your merchandise?" she asked.

He followed her line of sight, then nodded. "Furniture, collectables, memorabilia. Things you'd find in trading posts and antique stores. I've got some nice pieces for sale." He paused. "Do you like vintage stuff?"

"Yes." She loved browsing in charming old stores,

shopping for rare finds. "But atmosphere is important to me, too."

He made a grand gesture. "You don't think my place has atmosphere?"

Was he joking? She couldn't quite tell. "Your airplane hangar has appeal." The enormous structure sat behind everything else, taking up ten thousand square feet of space. She knew the building had been modified to support a highly sophisticated laser tag course, a compound she was anxious to see. But he still hadn't agreed to train her.

To help her with her cause.

To battle the emotions that threatened to swallow her.

Kyle slanted the lady cop a sideways glance. He intended to grill her, to figure out if she was on the level. For all he knew, she'd heard about his upcoming mission and wanted to poke her investigator's nose into his business.

He studied her profile, the chin-length sweep of blond hair, the simple curve of feminine eyelashes. This wasn't a case for a homicide detective. He didn't plan on hurting anyone—no guns, no knives, no weapons of choice. But what he intended to do was still illegal, and Joyce could easily turn him over to one of her peers.

But as far as he was concerned, his mission was

sacred, a spiritual issue, something that was worth going to jail for. Even dying for, if it came down to that.

Of course, neither of those risks appealed to him. And neither did Joyce involving herself in his affairs.

Within minutes, they reached his house. After taking the weather-beaten steps, he opened the front door, gesturing for her to enter. She went inside, the dogs trailing after her.

She glanced around his living room and made a face. "Olivia warned me that you weren't much of a housekeeper. But this looks like somebody ransacked the place."

Typical, he thought. Females always grumbled about the clutter in which he lived, including his former bedmate, a woman who'd accused him of being the biggest slob on the planet.

But he didn't care. He'd decorated with an eclectic style of furniture, with vintage pieces from different eras. And yeah, it was messy, with books, magazines and old clothes littering almost every surface. But he liked it that way. It kept his lovers from getting domestic ideas about him.

"Are you ready to get grossed out by my kitchen?" he asked.

"Is it that bad?"

"You'll probably think so."

Sure enough, she did. When they rounded the corner, the dogs in silent pursuit, she wrinkled her nose. "This is beyond gross."

Kyle merely shrugged. The food-encrusted plates in the sink were probably growing mold. But he had lots of extra dinnerware, boxes and boxes of second-hand stuff. When his dishes got too disgusting, he threw them away and started over. The same with pots, pans, glasses and flatware. The whole shebang.

"Is the coffeepot clean?" she asked.

"It's new." He plugged in the reconditioned unit and set about to make a dark, Colombian brew. He kept hundreds of preowned machines on hand. "Or sort of new. I've never used it before."

"Thank God."

He spared her a quick glance. He suspected that she lived in a tidy West L.A apartment, with silk flowers and a concrete balcony. Pretty but practical. Just like her.

While the coffee brewed, he leaned against the counter and took the time to check her out, to analyze her appearance. Neatly styled hair, blue eyes, noteworthy bone structure and minimal makeup. As for her clothes, she'd chosen an average white blouse, a lightweight blazer and black slacks.

Conservative, he thought. Coplike.

But damn if she didn't have a stimulating body, toned and athletic. Her mouth aroused him, too. The pillowy fullness, the insatiable, go-down-on-a-guy shape. He'd heard that she had a teasing nature. That she flirted for the fun of it. Of course, he'd never seen that side of her.

He wondered how she would look in a push-up bra, smoky eyeliner and stiletto heels. Incredible, he decided.

She glared at him. "Cut it out."

"Cut what out?"

"Looking at me like that."

"Like what?"

"A Cro-Magnon."

Amused, he bit back a smile. Clyde was watching her with guard dog awareness, and Bonnie was sniffing at her nondescript shoes. "Cro-Magnon men were capable hunters and food gatherers. Artistic cave painters, too."

"You know darn well I was referring to their sexual habits."

"Dragging womenfolk off by their hair? It's a fascinating theory, but I don't think it's true. Homo sapiens weren't dim-witted brutes. They were much more sophisticated than—"

She cut him off, and Bonnie scampered away. "Are you denying that you were getting hot and bothered over me?"

"No." He wasn't denying anything. "I was picturing you as a femme fatale." He gave her clothes an unappreciative wave. "You could use a makeover."

"Really?" She gave his duds the same distasteful treatment. "Well, so could you." She tilted her head, as if she were recreating him in her mind. "I guess that means I'll have to picture you in a suit and tie."

Kyle cringed, then turned to pour the coffee. He wouldn't be caught dead in a suit. If his family buried him in one, he would come back to haunt them. "You date corporate guys?"

"They're the type I prefer." She glanced at the cup he'd given her. "Do you have sugar?"

"No."

"Cream? Milk?"

"Milk. But I'm not willing to share. There's only a little bit left and I'm saving it for my cereal, for tomorrow's breakfast."

She returned the coffee. "You're a terrible host."

He pushed the cup back at her, maneuvering the pitch-black drink between them. "I never offered you anything but poison. Besides you deserve it for trying to dress me in a suit."

"And what do you deserve for trying to put me in a G-string and thigh-high hose?"

"Not bad, Detective." She'd almost got it right. "But it was a padded bra and spiked heels."

"I wasn't wearing a skimpy thong?"

"No." He leveled his gaze. "You weren't wearing anything down there."

The coffee sloshed over the side of her cup, nearly

burning both of their hands. She flinched, but he didn't move. He'd just taken control. He'd rattled her senses.

She regained her composure. "I should drag you off by your hair. Pull it out of that perverted skull of yours."

"Now that I'd like to see." He stood right where he was, challenging her to make the first move. She glanced at the rottweiler, and Kyle gave her a half-cocked smile. She would pay hell to get past his dog. Or him for that matter. She might be a highly effective cop, a Special Section detective who tracked serial killers and worked on high profile cases, but she'd come to him for training, for force-on-force drills, for the fight that was supposedly raging in her blood. No matter what, they both knew his tactical skills outmatched hers. His specialty was close-quarter combat, battlefield techniques perfected by the U.S. Special Forces, U.S. Army Rangers and U.S. Marine Corps.

"Is that spiel you gave me true?" he asked.

"What spiel?"

He set her coffee on the counter. "That bit about you going through a tough time. About having personal problems you can't resolve."

"I wasn't lying."

Although she glanced away, something flashed in her eyes. Confusion, he thought. She appeared to be at war with herself.

Were her problems real? Or was she a skilled actress?

He pushed her further, looking for answers. "Did someone hurt you? Is that what's wrong?"

"No."

"You didn't get in too deep with some guy? With some jerk who screwed you over?" He knew there were men who took advantage, who made promises they didn't keep. But Kyle wasn't one of them. His relationships never went beyond sex, beyond raw, honest urges.

"There's no one," she told him. "It isn't like that."

"Then what's going on?"

"Nothing I care to talk about." Her chest rose and fell, her breathing accelerated, just a little, just enough for him to notice.

She wasn't acting, he decided. She was putting herself on the line, something he doubted she did very often. He couldn't imagine what kinds of problems a tough-willed detective like her couldn't resolve. It made him hungry to kiss her, to taste her confusion, to let her seduce him. But he wasn't about to break his self-imposed code.

He didn't sleep with white women.

Of course that didn't mean he wasn't going to help her. Joyce had come to him for a legitimate reason.

He turned away. "I'll get the milk for your coffee."

She blinked. "Are you calling a truce?"

"I'm just trying to be a halfway decent host." He went to the refrigerator, removed the carton and gave Clyde a silent signal, letting the dog know the upcoming threat wouldn't be real. "I'm going to train you."

"You are?" She accepted the milk and poured it into her cup. "What's your schedule like?"

"I'll have to check my calendar."

She glanced up. "I've got time off this week. Or is that too soon for you?"

"I'll try to work something out," he told her, even though he'd already worked it out.

She stirred her coffee, and he curbed a carnivorous smile.

Joyce's first session and the surprise attack that went with it was about to begin.

Two

Joyce sipped her coffee. It was strong, but it was far from poisonous. "This is actually pretty good."

"Glad you think so." He came forward, taking the hot drink from her hand. "Too bad you won't get to finish it."

"What you are doing?"

"This." He set her cup on the counter and moved even closer.

Too close, she thought. She could smell the soap on his skin. An outdoorsy scent, a blend of lavender and sage, of man and nature.

She met his gaze and noticed the brown and gold pattern. Tiger's-eye, she thought. Like the quartz stone Roman soldiers used to wear to protect them in battle.

He moistened his lips, and her pulse went haywire. Was he going to kiss her?

She knew she shouldn't let him. But she was curious to taste him. One long, lingering jolt. One forbidden flavor.

When he pinned her against the counter, she lifted her chin, daring him to do it, to take her mouth with his.

But he didn't. He grabbed her gun instead.

Son of a bitch.

She tried to stop him, but within seconds he'd confiscated her 9mm and ditched it, right along with the SIG he carried. Both guns went sliding across the vinyl floor, out of sight and out of reach. This wasn't an armed battle. This was street fighting, a down-and-dirty brawl.

Only he wasn't hurting her. If anything, she was simply being restrained.

She knew how to punch, how to kick, how land well-aimed blows. But her moves didn't work on him.

Joyce gritted her teeth and attempted a stomp that was supposed to bring down a giant, someone as big as Kyle.

For all the good it did.

He took her down instead. "You're blowing it, Detective."

He landed on top of her, nailing her to the floor.

He kept her there, under him, his tiger's-eye eyes boring into hers. She couldn't move her arms; she couldn't even lift her pelvis a fraction.

But the weight of his body felt good.

Much too good.

"Get off me, Kyle."

He didn't listen. He continued looking at her. Was this another trick? At this point, she still wanted him to kiss her. Softly. Gently. Yet she wanted to shred his clothes, too. To snap and bite and leave marks on his soap-scented skin.

Nothing in her brain made any sense.

"Tell me what's wrong." He climbed off her, ending the exercise, freeing her from his bond. "Tell me what's going on in your life."

Caught off guard, she sat up and noticed he was sitting on the floor, too. "We already discussed that."

"And you didn't tell me a thing."

"It's personal." She wasn't about to admit that her biological clock was ticking like a bomb. For Joyce, it wasn't a natural feeling. She hated the nesting urges inside her, the marriage/baby lust interfering with her job, with everything that used to make her happy. Being a wife and mother had never been part of her agenda. Yet it had begun to take over, like a horror-movie body snatcher.

"Are you sure it's something you can fight your way out of?" he asked.

"Yes." It had to be, she thought. Because she didn't intend to let those urges destroy her. Nor did she intend to cater to them, to marry the first romantic bonehead that came along and have his babies.

Speaking of boneheads…

Kyle stretched his legs and tapped the soles of her shoes with his. "Are you impressed?"

"With what?" She pushed back, pressing on his knee-high moccasins. They held no adornment. No fringe, no tiny beading, no colorful paint. "You?"

"I stole your gun, cop-girl."

"And you can return it now, cheater-boy."

"I didn't cheat."

Joyce couldn't believe they were playing footsies, flirting like a couple of middle school kids. She tried to quit, but he continued, so she did too, kicking him a little harder. "You pretended you were going to kiss me."

"It's not my fault you fell for that."

No, it was hers. And she wouldn't let it happen again.

Suddenly he stopped moving and said something in what she assumed was Apache. She frowned at him, then realized he was talking to Clyde. The dog came forward and dropped her gun in her lap.

She glanced at the handle of the 9mm. The rotty had slobbered all over it. "Gee, thanks."

Kyle grinned. "Wanna know where mine is?"

"Up your butt?" she asked and made him chuckle.

"It's in my holster. Right where it should be." He attacked her soles again. "Tricky, aren't I?"

Joyce couldn't decide if he was a militant or a magician. She moved her feet away from his, then wiped the handle of her gun with her blouse. "That was a lousy training session. All you did was show off."

"I was assessing your skills."

"Fine. Whatever." She wasn't about to throw in the towel. "I better get more out of the next session."

"You will." He stood and offered her hand. "Come by tomorrow around noon."

"You better be worth the money." She refused his hand, hating that he'd bested her. Not in a fight. But in that nonexistent kiss.

The strategy he'd used against her.

After Joyce left, Kyle drove his Jeep to Olivia's downtown loft. He didn't like going to other people for help, but he didn't have a choice. Besides, Olivia was a friend, or as close to a friend as a female could get.

Women were a strange breed. He appreciated their bodies. He considered them the Creator's most compelling work of art, but he didn't understand their minds. And Joyce was no exception. She baffled the hell out of him.

Edgy, he sat on Olivia's sofa. She was perched on

the chair across from him, waiting for him to speak. He used to call her Liv, but he'd decided to stop using the nickname, to stop being overly familiar with her, especially now that she was sleeping with someone else.

She crossed her legs, and he noticed her short black skirt and fishnet stockings. Olivia had always dressed like a dominatrix. Her naughty style is what had attracted him to her. That, and her Lakota/Apache blood.

"Do you know what's going on with Joyce?" he asked.

She ran her hand through her hair. She wore it short and choppy. Her lips were a bold shade of red and her eyes were rimmed in a smudgy kohl liner. "Going on how?"

"With her personal life."

"She doesn't confide in me."

"No girl talk?"

"No."

He blew out an irritated-sounding breath, letting his former lover know that he didn't believe her. He'd always heard that women stuck together. That they chattered like gossip-addicted magpies. "You told her stuff about me."

"So?"

"So did you tell her I was hot in bed?" He sure as hell hoped so, or else he would look like a fool, considering he'd already bragged to Joyce and accused her of wanting him.

"Of course I did. It's the only thing you're good at."

He wasn't flattered, not completely. He took pride in other aspects of his life, in the Warrior Society that dictated his missions. "I'm good at other things."

"You were a lousy boyfriend."

Okay, so she had him there. He hadn't mastered the art of romance, of wining and dining. And he totally sucked at the emotional stuff. But he'd never claimed to be polished or poetic.

"Who cares?" he said.

"Apparently you do or you wouldn't be asking me about Joyce."

"I was asking about her personal problems." The mystery of why she was troubled was driving him crazy. "She came to me for training. She wants to fight her way out of her dilemma."

"I know. She told me."

"Right." He gave Olivia a hard stare. "During the conversation that wasn't girl talk." To him, evaluating a man's performance in bed was as girly as a discussion could get, even if the man in question was grateful for it. "I can't believe she didn't go into more detail. That she didn't admit what's bothering her. "

"Well, she didn't."

They both fell silent. Frustrated, Kyle looked around the loft. The walls were decorated with a mural Olivia's sister had painted, with fantasy creatures that included an armor-clad knight and a fire-breathing dragon.

He squinted at the knight and wondered if there was a damsel in distress waiting in the wings somewhere.

If women like Olivia and Joyce ruled the world, they would be slaying the dragon. Not that Kyle didn't respect ass-kicking females. They totally turned him on. But he appreciated their softer sides, too. The vulnerability that made them women. Which, he supposed, was why Joyce's secret was chipping away at him.

He picked up a decorative pillow and fussed with the froufrou tassel, flicking the gold fringe. "Why didn't you try to zap into Joyce's mind and pick her brain? Why didn't you try to find out what's going on?"

Olivia glanced at the front door. "I wasn't going to invade her privacy. That wouldn't have been right."

Right, smight. Kyle wished he were psychic.

Just then, the door opened and a dark-haired man in a black suit entered the trendy building and set his briefcase down. Olivia must have sensed his presence.

Special Agent Ian West. Her FBI lover. She stood and West came toward her. They didn't say anything. They locked lips instead, sweet and slow, as if they hadn't seen each other for a thousand years. But that wasn't the case. They worked together as often as they could, and whenever the hotshot profiler was in town, he crashed at her place.

When the other man deepened the kiss, Kyle made a disgusted face. "Knock it off."

They separated, and West raised his eyebrows. "What's the matter, Prescott? Are you jealous?"

"Hardly." He was glad Olivia had met her match. That West was taking her for a heartfelt ride. But that didn't mean he wanted to watch them swap spit.

"Kyle came here to talk about Joyce," Olivia said, straightening West's tie.

"Really?" The fed seemed intrigued. "She used to have a thing for me."

Now Kyle was jealous. "She did not." He turned to Olivia. "Did she?"

"She thought he was hot when she first met him. But that was before we hooked up."

"I guess there's no accounting for taste. Not that it matters." He rose from the sofa, ditching the stupid pillow. "I'm not interested in her."

West and Olivia exchanged an oh-sure look.

"I'm not," he reiterated.

Olivia walked him to the door. "You want to sleep with her."

"That's doesn't mean I'm going to."

She shook her head, as if she didn't believe him, as if he didn't have the slightest bit of willpower.

As if a blue-eyed blonde, a cop no less, could bring him to his knees.

The following day, Joyce prepared for the silent war churning inside her. Her personal fight. And the battle she intended to wage against Kyle. There was more than one way to skin a cat, to strip a tiger down to the bone. This time, she was going to dupe him.

She glanced around, surprised by what she saw. His basement had been converted into a gym, and unlike the rest of his house, the room was spotless. Every piece of machinery gleamed.

Finally she met his gaze. He stood across from her on a sparring mat. He wasn't armed. No holster. No semiautomatic weapon. He wore standard gray sweatpants and a ribbed tank top.

He looked dangerous, tall and strong and strapped with muscle. His hair was secured in the usual manner, with a cotton cloth tied around his head.

He moved closer, and she withheld a triumphant smile. He couldn't keep his eyes off her cleavage, off her scooped neckline.

"You're staring," she said.

"Because that's not proper attire."

"These pants are made for working out. Lycra stretches."

"I was talking about that skimpy top," he said, even though her skintight capris had caught his attention, too.

"I didn't know there was a dress code. Besides, I'm wearing a push-up bra."

His gaze drifted again. "I noticed."

"I wore it for you. For your fantasy."

"Don't mess with me, Joyce."

"Is that what I'm doing?" She batted her lashes, poking fun at their attraction.

He rolled his eyes, and she laughed, breaking the tension, the male-female heat that crackled in the air.

But she was just getting started, letting him think she wasn't a threat. That she wasn't clever enough to outsmart him.

"Good thing I didn't wear spiked heels," she told him. "Or no panties."

He merely blinked.

"Are you ready?" she asked.

He didn't answer.

"Kyle?" she pressed.

"Of course I'm ready." He copped a macho stance, widening his legs and planting his feet in a solid position. "I'm not going to fall for your little game."

She glanced at his tank top. His nipples were erect. Hers were, too. They protruded like .45 caliber bullets, jutting against the silky fabric of her bra. A condition that didn't go unnoticed.

He was already falling for her game.

She tucked her hair behind her ears and told herself there was no such thing as a dumb blonde. Women who used their sexuality knew exactly what they were doing.

Not that she was going to seduce him. The idea was to set him up, to divert his attention. The way he'd done to her when he'd faked that kiss.

The session began, with Kyle pointing out the mistakes she'd made yesterday, explaining why her moves hadn't been effective on him. According to him, she'd been trained properly in the past, but she wasn't using her knowledge to her best advantage.

She stepped back and watched him demonstrate his style, his techniques. He reminded her of Tarzan. Fluid, natural. A man who'd been born to bend his body, to kick, to spin, to conquer the jungle.

When they began sparring, she went after his vulnerable areas. He blocked her, of course. He wasn't going to let her crush his Adam's apple or knee his kidneys. But he commended her anyway.

For a moment, she wondered if she should cut her losses and forget about the way he'd tricked her. But then she caught him looking down her top, stealing peeks between all those muscular moves.

Tarzan was getting turned on.

They kept sparring, making physical contact. She worked hard, concentrating on the lesson. She listened to his instructions. She followed his advice.

He was a damn good instructor. But that didn't mean she was going to let him win.

By the time they took a break, her skin was damp and warm.

He walked over to a minifridge in the corner, removed two bottles of water and handed her one.

"Thanks." She sipped, and he guzzled, like the Cro-Magnon he was. She wasn't buying his story that his predecessors didn't drag women off by their hair.

He wasn't swigging from thirst. He hadn't even broken a sweat. If anything, he was trying to temper his overactive libido.

Time to go for the gold, she thought. To get her revenge. With as much drama as she could muster, she poured some water down her top, letting it trail between her breasts.

He gaped at her. "What are you doing?"

"Cooling off."

"This isn't a wet T-shirt contest."

"I'd have to take my bra off for that."

"You better not."

She almost laughed. He was angry. Ticked that she was toying with him. Big, primordial ape.

He moved closer. "Cut the crap, Joyce."

"I'm just having a little fun."

"And I already told you that I wasn't going to fall for your game."

She glanced at his groin. She wanted to give him a swift kick, but she knew he was wearing a cup. Men like Kyle didn't spar without protection.

She tugged at her water-misted top. "Maybe I will take off my bra. It's starting to itch."

"Do whatever you want. It's not going to make a difference."

Oh, yes it would. She reached back and unfastened the hooks. But as she maneuvered the garment under her top, she pretended that she was having trouble. That she couldn't get the straps down.

He chuckled under his breath. And better yet, he moved even closer, letting down his guard.

"You're a hell of a seductress, Detective."

She played up her dilemma, giving him a slapstick show. She kept flailing her arms. He was too tall to punch in the nose, so she raised her fist and surprised him with an uppercut, catching his jaw, hitting him as hard as she could.

Score one for the cop. His head snapped on his neck.

Her big bad trainer wasn't chuckling anymore.

"Damn." He rubbed his chin, scraping his hand across the surface of his skin. "You got me good."

She took his unexpected compliment to heart. Her knuckles throbbed like crazy, but it was worth it. "Thanks."

"Want to smack me again?"

While he was primed and ready? Fat chance of that. "That's okay. We can just call it even."

"Like hell we can." He locked his foot around her ankle and tripped her. No fancy moves. No spins, no kicks. Just a smart-aleck trip.

She landed on the mat with a thud. He laughed, and

she grabbed his leg and pulled him down, too. They attacked each other, wrestling like a couple of kids.

The horseplay continued, back and forth. She yanked on his headband and tried to blindfold him with it. He faked a blow to her chin, teasing her for socking him in the jaw.

Then he rolled on top of her. Two hundred pounds of testosterone. Within an instant, her body was pinned beneath his, a lot like yesterday. "You're on a power trip, Prescott."

He smiled. "You think?"

"Yeah, I do." She noticed he gave her more rein this time, enough to fight back if she wanted to.

Suddenly he stopped smiling. "You're even prettier up close."

Her heart zapped her chest, a lightning effect that charged her like Frankenstein's monster. She flinched, warning herself to be careful.

His voice turned rough. "I don't like it any more than you do."

"Me being pretty?" She cursed the ragged feeling, the fire-hazard risk. "Actually I'm okay with it."

"I was talking about you and me." His gaze stormed hers, as fierce as a silent war cry, as the ghost of a warrior howling in the wind. "I hate being attracted to you."

She struggled to contain her emotions, to stop herself from shoving her tongue down his throat, from tasting every inch of him. "Then get off me."

"I don't want to." He traced her top, running his fingers along the neckline. Finally he moved lower, untangling the twisted straps of her bra, where they were falling down her shoulders. "And you don't want me to, either."

She'd forgotten about her unhooked bra, about being half-naked under her shirt. No wonder she looked pretty to him. "Maybe I should force you off of me."

"Maybe you should," he told her, without the slightest trace of malice. He was still touching her, still righting her mangled clothes, respecting her in a way she'd never imagined.

Like a heart-pounding fool, she let him stay there, body to body, breath to breath. But even so, she fought the urge to put her arms around him, to hold him. She'd known him for eight months, almost long enough to have a baby.

That alone scared the death out of her.

Her biological clock wouldn't quit ticking.

"We're in trouble," he said.

Joyce didn't argue. She looked into his eyes, knowing he was going to kiss her.

As softly as they both could endure.

Three

Kyle studied Joyce's expression. She was waiting for his lips to touch hers, for the confusing tenderness they both craved.

He smoothed a strand of her hair. She looked delicate, vulnerable, so unlike the tough-girl cop he knew her to be.

His willpower sucked, he thought, as he lowered his head and closed his eyes.

Their mouths met, and the flavor swirled in his mind. He tasted lipstick and spearmint, a combination that made his head spin.

She ran her hands along his spine. A touch so light, so tentative, he barely knew it was happening.

Wanting more, he used his tongue, taking the kiss to the next level.

She reciprocated, making pleasured sounds. Then she lifted the hem of his tank top and rolled it up a little, just enough to create a shiver.

Fingertips and bare flesh.

He wanted to lift her shirt, too.

Anxious, he positioned himself between her legs, then cursed the metal cup he was wearing, the barrier that kept him from straddling her, from rubbing his body against hers.

He pulled back and opened his eyes.

Silent, she gazed at him, as well.

There she was, all soft and blonde, with her bra still undone and her top slightly skewed. Earlier, he'd tried to fix her clothes and now he wanted to peel them right off. Along with his tank, his sweatpants and the jockstrap that had brought him to his senses.

"You don't have to stop," she said.

"Yes, I do."

"It was just a kiss."

"It was more than that." It was foreplay, he thought. An explosion just waiting to happen. "I don't do this kind of thing. Not with—" He stalled and got to his feet.

"Not with what?" She sat up and struggled to hook her bra. But she was careful not to lift her top, at least not in front.

Kyle thought her cautious manner made her seem vulnerable again.

"Not with what?" she repeated, frowning at him. She still hadn't fastened her bra.

"With women like you," he admitted. "I don't get involved with white women."

Her jaw all but dropped. "That's what this is about? My race? The color of my skin?"

He didn't know how to respond, how to explain why it mattered. She was looking at him as if he were some sort of monster. "I've never been drawn to white women. You're the first one I've ever kissed. Or ever wanted to sleep with."

She ignored her bra and stood up. When she did, the straps peeked out from under her top, falling down her shoulders, the way they'd done earlier. "And that's why you hate being attracted to me? Do you know how offensive that is?"

"It doesn't help that you're a cop."

"Screw you, Kyle. On both counts."

He wanted to move closer, to touch her, to stop her from being so angry, but he kept his hands to himself. "You're making a bigger deal out of this than it is."

"Am I?" She rounded on him. "You're part white. So what does that say about you?"

He wasn't about to answer her question. He didn't want to discuss his childhood with her. Or his adulthood, for that matter. Being a half-blood wasn't easy, not then and not now. "Drop it, Joyce. Let it go."

"Why? Because you don't want to admit that you're a bigot? Do you know how many hate crimes are committed in this country? People bashing other people because—"

"I'm not committing a hate crime. I'm not hurting anyone." As soon as those words spilled out of his mouth, he wanted to take them back. He'd just hurt her. He could see it in her eyes.

Blue eyes. White eyes, as his ancestors used to say.

"Why do you hate being attracted to me?" he asked, turning the tables on her.

"Not because you're Apache. I don't let someone's race get in the way."

"Then what is it?"

"I'm not sure. Maybe it's the way you make me feel. All hot and jumbled. Not like myself."

"You do that to me, too."

"I know." She grabbed her gym bag. "But I'm not interested in training with you anymore."

"So that's it? We're done?" He shouldn't care. It shouldn't matter. But it did. The thought of losing her clenched his gut. He didn't want her to disappear.

Yet when she left, when she walked away, he let her go, unable to admit that the choice he'd made was based on prejudice.

* * *

At 9:00 p.m. Kyle walked through the courtyard of Joyce's apartment building. She lived in a large complex, with flourishing flower beds, lush green-belts and winding hardscape.

He approached the sidewalk that led to her stair-well and frowned at the path in front of him. He'd called Olivia and asked her for Joyce's address, and now he was taking reluctant steps to her door.

He'd never apologized to a woman before and the notion of saying "I'm sorry" was making him squeamish. He'd rather be tortured, stretched on a medieval rack with metal thumbscrews on his hands and an iron mask on his face.

Then what was he doing here?

He ignored the question and started up the stairs. Her unit, D-2, was on the right. On the left was D-4. Both doors displayed Halloween decorations. Joyce had chosen a glow-in-the-dark skeleton, a friendly looking fellow who mocked him with a toothy grin.

He knocked on D-2 and waited for her to answer. She didn't respond. So he knocked again, harder this time. He knew she was home. He'd seen her car in the parking structure and if he listened close enough, he could hear strains of one of those crime scene in-vestigation shows on her TV.

As if she didn't get enough of that in real life.

Finally footsteps sounded. But she didn't open

the door. He assumed she was peering through the peephole to see who was standing on her second-story stoop.

He made a face, letting her know that he felt like a fool, keeping company with a plastic skeleton. Lucky for him, the Halloween decoration wasn't obstructing her view.

Or maybe it was unlucky. She still didn't answer.

"Come on, Joyce. Let me in."

Nothing. *Nada.*

"I didn't even bring a gun." He stepped back and turned in a small circle.

Still nothing.

He cursed and removed the skeleton. "Check this out." He waltzed with the bony creature, making its legs dangle. "I bet you didn't know I could dance."

Suddenly a door opened. But it wasn't Joyce. Still romancing the skeleton, he turned around and made eye contact with her neighbors, an elderly couple staring at him as if he'd lost his mind.

"Evening," he said, switching to a tango and dipping the neon bag of bones.

They continued gaping at him. The old man was as bald as a billiard ball and his wife had a neck like a turkey. Kyle figured they'd been married for at least a hundred years.

"What are you doing?" the man finally asked.

"Trying to make Detective Riggs swoon." He used

the skeleton's hand to gesture to his loose-fitting shirt, snug jeans and battered moccasins. "Can't you tell? I'm a regular Romeo."

"He's crazy," the woman murmured.

"I'll bet he's an undercover cop." The husband gave his six-foot-four frame a serious gander. "He's just the type."

Without another word, they closed the door in his face, assuming he was one of Joyce's offbeat peers. Kyle didn't know whether to laugh or defend his own pathetic honor.

"I see you met Mr. and Mrs. Winkler."

He spun around. Joyce had managed to open her door without him knowing it. So much for his warrior skills. She was holding a pistol on him, too.

Him and the skeleton.

"What's going on?" he asked.

"As if you don't know." She closed her door and came outside, instructing him to assume the frisk position.

He couldn't help but grin. "Is this a sexual thing?"

"Don't get cute."

"Yes, ma'am." He decided it might be fun to let a lady cop pat him down. He hung the skeleton back on its nail, spread his legs and pressed his palms against her door. The only problem was that he'd lied about not being armed. He had his favorite SIG shoved in the waistband of his pants, aimed at the family jewels and covered by his shirt.

Good thing the safety was on.

She searched him, getting familiar in all the right places. "Just what I figured." She confiscated the semiautomatic, grazing his abdomen in the process. "Where's your CCW license, Kyle?"

"I don't have one." He'd never bothered to apply for a permit to carry a concealed weapon. Mostly because he knew he'd never get one. California was stingy that way. He turned around, his stomach muscles jumping. Her hands on his body had felt damn good. "Are you going to bust me?"

She motioned with the barrel of his gun. She'd already holstered hers. "Get inside."

He entered her apartment, wondering if she liked cartoons. Quick Draw McGraw had been one of his favorites when he was a kid.

She followed him into the living room, closed the door and removed the magazine from his weapon. Then she retrieved a metal pistol box, put his unloaded SIG inside and locked it. Only then, did she return his now useless gun.

He frowned at her. She hadn't given him the key. Or the magazine. He set the locked box on a nearby table. "I ought to file a complaint against you. Illegal search and seizure. Or sexual harassment or something."

Her smile was brief. Faint. Barely there. By now, she'd stored her pistol, too, keeping it away from him. "You do have nice abs."

"Oh, yeah?" He moved closer, attempting to touch her hair. As much as he hated to admit it, the pale yellow color fascinated him. "So it *was* a sexual thing."

She stepped out of range. "You wish." Her TV played in the background. "What are you doing here?"

"Aside from annoying your neighbors and getting felt up by you? I came to—" he paused to wince "—apologize."

"And I can see that it hurts."

"Groveling is hard for me."

"Then you should do it more often."

"I'm sorry." This time, he managed to get close enough to reach her hair, to let it slide through his fingers. "I'm not a bigot, Joyce. I swear, I'm not."

"Then what are you?" she asked, snaring his gaze, challenging him to delve into his soul.

"A mixed-up mixed-blood, I guess."

After that, he quit touching her. He dropped his hand, trying to look more casual than he felt.

She waited for him to continue. "Aren't you going to tell me why you're mixed up?"

While she was staring at him? Hanging on his every word? "Maybe later." He broke eye contact and glanced around her apartment.

He noticed that she favored dark woods and feminine colors. Her floral-printed sofa reminded him of rainbow sherbet, and the ceramic bowl on her mahogany coffee table was mint green. Just as he'd suspected, she didn't have any living plants, nothing to water or fuss over. The flowers on her dinette set were silk.

He opened the sliding glass door in the living room and walked onto her balcony. It was nothing more than a slab of concrete, but she'd dressed it up with a café table. He envisioned her drinking coffee there, stealing a few quiet moments before she left for work each morning, the calm before the storm that made up her day.

Her footsteps sounded behind him. "What are you doing, Kyle?"

"Analyzing your life." He turned to look at her. She wasn't wearing the same skimpy top she'd had on earlier. The push-up bra was gone, too. She'd donned an oversize T-shirt, tan leggings and thick socks.

"My life?" She leaned against the rail. "You're supposed to be telling me about yours."

"My problem with getting involved with white women?" He knew he owed her an explanation, even if he had to share his jumbled emotions with her. "My parents' relationship influenced me. The interracial difficulties they had."

"Where did you grow up?"

"In New Mexico on the Mescalero Reservation. The Mescalero, Lipan and Chiricahua Apache are there. My mom was Chiricahua, and my father was a teacher on the rez. A white man living out of his element."

She sat at the table. "But he married your mom?"

"She got pregnant with me. It wasn't a match made in Heaven." Kyle didn't sit. He remained standing on the balcony. "They're both dead now."

"I'm sorry."

"I still have family on the rez. Some family in L.A., too. This is where my dad was originally from." He pulled his hand through his hair, removing his headband and stuffing it in his pocket. His hair was thick and dark, like his mom's used to be. "I look like both of my parents. I got his stature and her features. My skin color is somewhere in between. It's obvious to most people that I'm a mixed-blood."

She watched him through soft blue eyes. "You're a handsome man."

"Thanks." He shrugged and pushed the headband farther into his pocket. "Being handsome didn't help when I was growing up. I was part white, and I got a lot of flack for that. Mostly because my dad didn't appreciate Native ways. In those days, a lot of reservation teachers were like that. They were still trying to tame the savages."

"So the other kids took it out on you?"

He nodded. "I did everything I could to seem more Indian, to prove that I wasn't like my dad. All I wanted was to drain the white blood from my veins."

"But you can't, Kyle. It's part of who you are."

"I know. But it only got worse. After my parents got divorced, I stayed on the rez with my mother, and my father went back to L.A. It should have been okay then, but Mom died soon after that." He blew out the breath he was holding. "She was my salvation. The parent who understood me. And then she was gone."

Joyce left her chain and stood next to him, searching his gaze. "What happened? Were you forced to move to L.A. with your dad?"

"He was my legal guardian. He got custody of me after Mom died. And he was bound and determined to teach me to live in his world."

"How old were you?"

"Fourteen." He smiled a little, recalling how rebellious he'd been. "I fought him every step of the way. I became the biggest, baddest urban skin you ever saw."

"Skin?"

"Indian."

"Big and bad." She opened her hands, gesturing to him. "Like the man you are today."

"Pretty much. I got involved in the American Indian Movement. To my dad, that's the worse thing I could have done. AIM was the anti-Christ to him."

"A bunch of hotheaded Natives campaigning for their rights?"

"Exactly. He didn't respect our values, the changes we were trying to make. That's the sort of behavior he'd been trying to tame on the rez. He was backward in that way."

"And it rubbed off on you," she said catching his attention, making him frown.

"My so-called bigotry?"

"You reversed his prejudice. You turned it around to make it work for you."

"I told you I was mixed up."

"You don't have to be. You don't have to avoid non-Native relationships. If you're attracted to someone, it shouldn't matter."

"I know. It shouldn't. But it does. And not just because of my dad. I'm not actively involved in AIM anymore, but I'm part of a Warrior Society, a militant group. I'm a full-force activist, Joyce."

She looked him straight in the eye. "I know who you are."

Of course she did. She was a cop. The lady who'd confiscated his gun. "How would it look for a half-blood who fights Native causes to date non-Native women? Especially white women?"

She heaved an audible sigh. "So you're living by an image? By what's expected of you?"

"Yeah. I guess I am." And the revelation hit him like a fist, hard and deep, right in the solar plexus. "That sucks, doesn't it? The big bad skin worrying about what other people think?"

"It's keeping you out of my bed," she said, walking into the house and leaving him alone on the balcony.

He simply stood there, for at least five minutes, staring after her. What the hell was that? A make-him-suffer rebuff? A slap in the face?

Screw this, he thought. He followed her, catching her in the kitchen, where she was preparing to make a cup of herbal tea. How frigging refined of her.

"Do you want some?" she asked.

"No." He crowded her.

"Back off." She tried to nudge him out of her way.

"Don't act like all of this is my fault. If push came to shove, you wouldn't be seen with a guy like me. Not publicly."

She turned on the stove and the flame ignited, a bit like her temper. "Is that your answer to everything? Blaming other people?"

He ground his teeth. He wanted to grab her and kiss her, shut her up with his tongue. "You're avoiding my accusation."

"This is about sex, Kyle. Neither of us is looking for anything beyond an affair."

How was he supposed to know what she was looking for? Women never made any sense. How many times did they say one thing, then do another? "I thought you weren't interested in banging my brains out. I thought you came to me for training. To fight your way out of your problems, not to fu—"

"Don't talk to me like that." She cut him off before he could get too crude. "It's offensive."

He watched her remove a jar of honey from the cabinet above her head. It bothered him that she was still being pissy. That she hadn't let him off the hook. "Will you go on a date with me?"

She nearly dropped the honey. "What?"

"You heard me."

She pressed the bear-shaped jar against her chest. "When?"

"Tomorrow night. We'll go to a strip club or something."

"Very funny."

"Fine." He refused to smile. "We'll have dinner."

She removed the near-boiling water from the stove and poured it into her cup. She wasn't smiling, either. "Will you wear a suit?"

"Get real." He bumped her arm and made her spill the water.

She rounded on him. "You did that on purpose."

He stood his ground. She knew better than to try to fight him. "Are you going to go out with me or not?"

"I suppose I could."

"Such enthusiasm." He turned to leave. "You better heat some more water."

"Just get out of here."

"Be glad to."

Before he walked out of the kitchen, she stopped him. "What time are you picking me up tomorrow?"

"Seven."

She refilled the pot. "Don't be late."

"You, either." He went into the living room and wondered what he'd just gotten himself into.

He reached for the metal box with his SIG and decided to pick the lock. While Joyce made tea, he poked around for a paperclip on her rolltop desk, found one and opened the box. Then he located the magazine, loaded the gun and shoved it in the waistband of his pants.

"I'm leaving," he called out to her, deciding she would think twice about disarming him again.

Four

Joyce sat across from Kyle in a restaurant in Universal Studios CityWalk. It wasn't a quiet eatery, considering it boasted three mechanical bulls, three full bars, an outdoor dance floor and stage, live music, karaoke, video monitors and diagonal big screens.

He'd taken her to a tourist attraction for their date.

"Interesting choice," she said.

"We can't avoid the public here."

No kidding. The steak house was centrally located between the entrance of CityWalk and a Universal Studios tour bus parking lot, where the foot traffic was horrendous.

Kyle gestured to a nearby bull. Wooden tables, including theirs, surrounded the pen that housed it. "Want to go for a ride later?"

"Not on your life."

"They give women easy rides." He leaned forward. "Slow and sexy."

She ignored the chill that sleeked up her spine. "With all these people watching. No way."

"I'll do it if you will."

She wasn't about to fall for his bait, to let him talk her into it. "You'd probably kick butt. It's probably right up your alley."

"I'm always up for trying something new."

She raised her eyebrows. "Like dating me?"

"You're my worst nightmare." He flashed a naughty smile. "But damn if you don't look hot."

"Thanks." She wore a slim black dress and classic pumps. "Can you imagine me on the bull in this?"

"Yeah, I can." He took a swig of his beer and settled his gaze on her décolleté. "I totally can."

She fussed with the gold chain around her neck. He was looking at her as if he wanted her to ride him instead. But what did she expect? She'd made good use of the push-up bra, something that was bound to capture his attention.

The waitress brought their meals, and Joyce told herself to relax. She tracked serial killers for a living. Having dinner with Kyle was no big deal.

Then why wouldn't her heart quit pounding?

He was dressed in jeans and a button-down shirt. His jacket was leather. She imagined that was as formal as he got. As for his hair, he'd pulled it into a ponytail, leaving the hard, handsome angles of his face unframed.

She glanced at their plates. She'd ordered a center cut of New York, and Kyle had gone for a twenty-two ounce porterhouse, the biggest steak on the menu. He assaulted it the way he attacked the world. He liked his meat blood red, but that didn't surprise her.

She shifted her gaze, studying his fingers, the way he held his fork. "How did you pick that lock?"

He looked up. "What lock? Oh, you mean the pistol box at your house?"

"The very one." She knew he hadn't found the key. She'd secured that in her pocket.

"I used a paper clip."

She clamped her jaw before it fell. "I paid eighty bucks for that case."

"Then you got ripped off. Either that or I'm a damn good thief."

"What about tonight?" It was impossible to tell what he had going on under his jacket. "Are you armed?"

"No, but if you want proof, you can pat me down. I wouldn't mind a repeat performance."

"I'll bet." She wielded her knife. Her heart was still

pounding, still thumping in her chest. Finally she cut into her steak. It was well-done, the opposite of his.

"Do you think your fellow officers will think you've gone native?" he asked. "Or aren't you going to tell them you're seeing me?"

"I haven't decided." Going native meant police burnout, a cop suffering a mental breakdown, drinking too much, doing drugs, carousing. "Clever play on words." In this case, going native meant keeping company with a lust-driven Apache.

They both fell silent, and she wondered if he was going to tell his Indian comrades about her. Somehow, she envisioned him keeping quiet.

"This is a good start," she said. "I'm glad you brought me here."

His gaze drilled hers. "Are you?"

"Yes. This place is perfect." It was loud and raunchy, but the tourists made it seem normal. They were regular people, not L.A. hipsters.

Proving Joyce's point, a fifty-something woman in polyester pants and a lightweight sweater climbed onto the mechanical bull. Her ride was slow, but far from sexy. Yet that hardly mattered. Her family was cheering her on.

Kyle watched the activity. "Looks like they're having fun."

"Yes, it does." She felt a pang of familiarity. The woman's husband was giving her pointers, and the people Joyce assumed were her children were young adults, probably with chaotic lives of their own, but the bond was there, the undeniable connection. "My family is like that."

"Your mom would come here and ride a bull?"

That made her laugh. Her mother was an old-fashioned, sweetly behaved homemaker. "No. But she's our foundation. She holds all of us together."

"All of you?" He sat back and examined her. "Do you come from a big family?"

"Six girls."

"Damn. I'll bet your dad went crazy. All that hairspray and perfume in one house." He made a face. "Not to mention PMS six times a month." He paused, pondering the situation. "Seven if you include your mom."

Joyce shook her head. Kyle never failed to express his chauvinist views. She balled up an extra napkin and threw it at him. He shrugged and tossed it back at her.

The woman's ride ended. She walked over to her family, where good cheer erupted. Her husband gave her a playful swat on the bottom.

The pang of familiarity returned. Joyce's dad did that to her mom, too. "My father is a retired police officer."

Kyle frowned a little. "Is he the one who influenced you?"

"I always loved hearing about his job." To her, it

had seemed far more exciting than her mom's station in life. But now she didn't know what to think. Those baby urges were messing with her brain.

"Are any of your sisters cops?"

"No." They all had a career of some kind, and they all had husbands and kids, but no one, not even their husbands were in law enforcement. "They worry about me the way they used to worry about Dad."

"That's understandable. It's human nature, I guess. We live in violent times."

She gave him a pointed look. "With men who carry guns. Men who aren't supposed to."

He came forward in his chair. "Then your sisters have a lot to worry about, don't they?"

"I should have busted you."

He smiled. "Yeah, but you went out with me instead." He saluted her with his empty beer. "The girl's got guts."

She smiled, too. "Or mush for brains."

They finished dinner, and he insisted on dessert. Not that Joyce was opposed to a hunk of chocolate cake. She just imagined it going to her hips. Still, it didn't take much to persuade her.

"Do you want to dance later?" he asked. "The band comes on around eleven."

She dived into her cake, knowing she would have to hit the gym first thing in the morning. "Dance?"

"Did you think I was goofing around with the skeleton? Those were some serious moves."

She bit back a smile, recalling the way her neighbors had gaped at him. "Very serious. Debonair, too."

"Damn straight."

She glanced at her watch. Eleven o'clock was still an hour away. "What should we do in the meantime?" Her dessert was nearly gone. His, too. He'd practically inhaled it. But he probably worked out for at least four hours a day, loving every excruciating minute of it. For that, she wanted to kick him.

"We could browse around like everyone else," he said.

"Are you suggesting that we behave like tourists?"

"Why not? There's a slew of specialty stores. There's even a gothic shop. An entire building filled with creepy collectibles."

"Just what every homicide detective needs. More gore." She ate the last of her cake and decided that being a tourist sounded fun. She couldn't remember the last time she'd shopped in nonsensical stores. And never with a man like Kyle.

To Kyle, CityWalk was like Disneyland, Hollywood Boulevard and the set of a blockbuster movie all rolled into one. Where else could you find a crashed flying saucer protruding from the roof of a sci-fi store? Or how about a rock and roll bowling alley? Music madness and retail mayhem, he thought. It didn't get any better than this.

A stroke of marketing genius, CityWalk catered to over eight million people a year. Kyle and Joyce became two in a crowd.

The first store they wandered into was a place that specialized in wind-up toys. Kyle felt like a kid in a pineapple under the sea. He found a SpongeBob Squarepants boat he was dying to have.

He showed it to Joyce. "It drives around in circles."

She angled her head. "So?"

"So, I'm buying it."

"For who?"

"Myself."

She clucked her tongue. "Seriously?"

"Would I lie about my favorite cartoon character?"

"No. I suppose not. My nieces and nephews like him, too. But they're a lot younger than you." She removed the boat from his hand and examined it. "Is this for the tub?"

"Yeah." He moved closer, stealing a perverted peek down the front of her dress. "Want to soak with me later? We can test it out."

She held the wind-up toy between them. "Not without bubble bath."

Was she kidding? He would buy her a gallon of whatever tripped her fancy.

He paid for the boat, then escorted her outside,

where they returned to the shopping walk. He kept his eye open for girly stores, retailers that might sell bath and body products. He had no idea if Joyce was teasing him, but he was willing to take a chance.

He spotted a shop with pretty things in the window. They went inside, and sure enough, there was a collection of bubbly items on a glass display.

"Pick out what you want," he said.

"I never said I wanted anything."

"Humor me," he told her. "Give me a thrill."

She couldn't decide. She looked at everything, fingering all the festive bottles and shrink-wrapped baskets. Finally she chose a bubble bath with an oceanic scent.

Kyle wasn't sure what that meant. "It doesn't smell like saltwater, does it? That might be okay for SpongeBob, but—"

She laughed and popped the cap, waving the bottle under his nose. The fragrance was crisp and sensual, breezy and fresh. It made him want to strip her where she stood.

He took the bubble bath to the front counter and noticed a package of little pots advertised as lip sugar.

He glanced at Joyce. She stood next to him in line, her stretchy black dress capturing her breasts and flowing to her ankles. He decided that lip sugar was just what they needed.

In or out of the tub.

He grabbed the shimmering pots, and she slanted him a curious look. He read the package. "They're flavored. Cranberry, papaya, watermelon and mango. Just imagine what we can do with this stuff."

She leaned against him, pressing her mouth to his ear. "This isn't a sex shop, Kyle."

It might as well have been. He turned his head and kissed her, fast and furious, leaving her breathless when he was done. He didn't care how many people were in the store.

Joyce righted her clothes afterward, smoothing the front of her dress and wobbling on her pointed-toe pumps. Kyle hadn't touched her dress or her shoes. But apparently he'd made her feel sexually skewed.

What could be more perfect than that?

He paid for the items and gave her the bag. She smacked him with it, and they both laughed. He wondered if she'd brought her gun, if it was stuffed in her purse with a classy compact and a pair of police-issued handcuffs.

Lord, he hoped so.

They continued shopping, killing time and driving each other crazy. He bought a Wolf Man doll in the gothic place and made it attack a shelf of Barbie dolls in the regular toy store.

"Stop it." Joyce repositioned the Barbies he'd knocked over. "You're going to get us in trouble."

"We've been in trouble since we met." He removed Wolfy from the box, figuring the hairy guy could have more fun that way. "Did you play with Barbie when you were young?"

"Of course I did." She grabbed Wolf Man, stopping him from destroying another display. "I had her house, her car, the whole bit. So did my sisters."

"What about Ken?"

"What about him?"

"He always seemed like a wuss to me. They should have given her a stud like G.I. Joe." He hunted around for Barbie's latest car and discovered that she had all sorts of vehicles. The Happy Family Volvo fascinated him, so he decided to buy it for Wolf Man.

"This is big enough for Frankenstein and Dracula, too. I have them at home. Just imagine the road trip they can go on."

She looked at him as if he'd gone mad. "Maybe they can tow SpongeBob's boat while they're at it."

"Don't get smart. You and all of your Barbie accessories. Girls get everything."

"And boys like you make girls like me run the other way." She blew out an exaggerated breath. "Olivia told me you were bizarre."

Kyle shrugged. Most women couldn't get past his quirks, but he could tell that Joyce was enjoying his company, even if she thought he was strange. "That's not all Olivia told you."

She shook her head, and he merely gazed at her. There was no point in denying that he'd confirmed what had been discussed. He was the first to admit that he was a sexual egomaniac.

She held Wolf Man like a baby, cradling him against her breast. "What am I going to do with you, Kyle?"

He reached out and touched her cheek. Her skin was the color of honey and cream and candlelit ivory. "You can do whatever you want."

She released a shaky breath. Only this time she wasn't faking it. "Wanting you this badly scares me."

"Sometimes being afraid is good." He kissed her, tasting her fear, her passion, the forbidden urges driving her into his arms.

Their bodies bumped. He was too tall for her, but with heels, she made an erotic fit. He liked the way she felt next to him. Warm and womanly, with her pulse battering his. "Are you ready to dance?"

She nodded. "I'm ready."

They separated, and he took her hand. Damn if he wasn't aroused, if her anxiety didn't excite him.

They walked to the parking lot and put their packages in his SUV, then returned to the restaurant, where the nightlife thrived.

The band played a variety of music, songs that went from slow to fast to somewhere in between. Some riffs were twangy, some were sleek and sensual.

Kyle guided Joyce onto the dance floor and they

found the rhythm. They moved, hip to hip, rocking back and forth. There wasn't a lot of space. Other couples crowded them, forcing them toward the edge of the stage.

Then suddenly she slid her hands inside his jacket.

Talk about getting turned on. "Are you frisking me?"

She went lower. "You told me you wouldn't mind a repeat performance." She grazed the front of his pants, but there was no SIG, no semiautomatic weapon to bust him for. The hardness was him.

He wanted to haul her against his fly, to make damn sure she felt it. He wanted to pull down the front of her dress, too. Right here, right now. His mind was spinning, going in lethal directions. "Maybe you better be careful."

"Me?" She backed him against a wall, where the music vibrated. They weren't on the dance floor anymore. They were in a darkened corner. "I have the law on my side."

"And I'm bigger than you. Stronger." He switched places, pinning her against the wall. "If I go home with you tonight, your badge won't matter." He snared her wrists, holding them above her head. "It won't mean a thing."

She didn't fight him off. But she didn't submit, either. She challenged him instead, looking into his eyes. "Who says I'm letting you come home with me?"

"No one. I'm just giving you fair warning." He re-leased her. "You were afraid earlier."

"And you said that sometimes being afraid can be good."

"It can. As long as it brings out a person's survival skills." He smoothed her hair. "I still don't know what's going on in your life. If you can survive what's happening between us."

She barely blinked. "I already told you that I wasn't looking for anything beyond an affair."

Yeah, she'd told him. Last night. While she'd been on the defense. He wasn't sure if that counted. "What if you're too confused to know what you want?"

"I'm not going to get attached, not to a guy like you." She batted his hand away from her hair. "That's not what scares me."

"Then what is it?"

"Edgy sex. I'm afraid I'll do things to you that I've never done before. That I'll let you do even kinkier stuff to me."

His heart struck his chest. "Really?"

"Really."

"In that case." He grabbed her and kissed her, and when she reacted like a black widow, nearly swallow-ing him whole, he gave up the fight, dragging her against his body. If she wanted to eat him alive, he would let her.

But he didn't know if she was going to take the

next step, if she would actually invite him to her bed. Kyle didn't take anything for granted.

Especially women.

Five

After their date ended, Kyle and Joyce arrived at her apartment building. He pulled into a guest-parking stall and killed the engine.

Joyce didn't know what to say, what to do. If she asked him to come upstairs with her, it wouldn't be for a nightcap. They were beyond that point.

It was sex or nothing at all.

He turned to look at her, and her pulse went crazy, electrifying every part of her body.

"Have you ever done it in a car?" he asked.

She tried to maintain her composure. She'd never met anyone quite like him. "No. Have you?"

"Are you kidding?" He shot her a teasing grin.

"Me?" He reached over and opened the glove compartment. "Check out the condoms."

Sure enough, there was a variety pack crammed into the tight space. "You're not supposed to store them where they can be exposed to heat. It will damage the latex."

"I know. But I don't keep them here for extended periods of time. I'm careful about that. I replace them as often as I can."

"It's indecent exposure," she said, itching to riffle through the box.

"What is?"

"Having sex in a car."

"That's what makes it so fun."

She gave in and grabbed the condoms. She poked through the box, raising her eyebrows at him when she came across a glow-in-the-dark style.

He shrugged and then laughed. "They're phosphorous."

"Only a man like you would use his penis for a night-light."

He laughed again. "I'm a novelty kind of guy." He moved closer to her, leaning across the center console. "These are my favorite." He removed several packages that had *warm sensations* written on them. "They're lubricated with this stuff that makes both partners feel warm and tingly."

Joyce was already feeling warm and tingly. His

face was only inches from hers. He was close enough
to kiss, to taste, to tempt, to tease.

They stared at each other, and then his eyes, his
tiger's gaze, made a predator's sweep, moving up and
down. She couldn't help it. Her nipples went hard.

"I want you to take off your dress," he said.

So did she. She wanted to strip down to her panties and bra and climb in his lap. But if they got
caught, her job would be on the line. Law-abiding detectives didn't have sex in cars, in public places
where they could be seen.

He whispered against her ear. "You're thinking
about it, aren't you?"

"Yes."

"Then do it."

"I can't."

"Then let me do it."

She shook her head. "You're trying to corrupt me."

"Then tell me to go home. Send me away."

"I can't do that, either." She traced the angles of
his face, the sculpted edges, the hollow ridges, the
untamed beauty. "I want you to stay."

His lips formed a sensual slant, exposing a flash
of teeth. "Now *you're* trying to corrupt *me*."

"I don't think that's possible."

"Yes, it is. You, with your pretty blond hair and
cop-girl ways. I shouldn't be with a lady like you."

He glanced at her satin handbag. "Do you have handcuffs in your purse?"

"What? No." She tried to calm the pounding in her chest, the runaway beats of her heart. "I don't bring handcuffs on dates."

"Do you have some in your apartment?"

"Yes."

"Can I lock you up with them?" he asked. "Would you trust me to do that?"

"Is this a trick question?"

"No." He slid his hands through her hair, then put a strand a across her mouth. "No trick."

She gripped his shoulders, and he kissed her, sucking on her tongue and her hair. She closed her eyes, loving every second of what he was doing.

When he let her go, she wanted to crawl all over him. But she was nervous, too. The anxiety of being with him hadn't gone away.

"Are you okay?" he asked.

"I'm fine."

"You don't look fine."

She dropped her hand to her knee, curling her fingers around her dress. She didn't know how to explain her feelings, how to tell him what he did to her. "You overwhelm me, Kyle."

"I can't change who I am." He frowned, then smoothed her hair, taming the strand that had been in his mouth. "I'm crude and hard. I'm not good at being romantic."

"I don't care about hearts and flowers." And his touch was gentler than it should have been, much too tender for a man who claimed to be so hard. "That's the last thing I want."

"Maybe so. But most women like that kind of stuff. Why would you be any different?"

"I just am."

"But why?" He pierced her with a ravening gaze, with a look that was becoming all too familiar. "Because you're a cop? Is that what sets you apart?"

"Yes." That and her determination to stop herself from lusting after a husband, from wanting a baby.

"Then get edgy with me, Detective. Make our cravings worthwhile."

"I will. I am." As a surge of adrenaline spiked her veins, she gave herself permission to enjoy him, to take him upstairs, to keep him.

All night long.

Kyle and Joyce entered her apartment, and when she closed the door, he watched her turn the dead bolt and latch the chain, locking them inside.

He'd brought their packages in from the car. He'd brought the entire box of condoms, too, stuffing them into one of the bags. He intended to have a wicked time with Detective Riggs. He couldn't remember wanting a woman so badly.

She didn't say anything, and neither did he. They stood in the living room with two Tiffany-style lamps burning brightly. The mottled glass shades created a prism of color. They were pretty, but they weren't the real thing. Kyle had a hundred year old Tiffany lamp in storage that would probably blow her away. He wondered if she would think he was crazy if he gave it to her.

She clutched her handbag, and he noticed the simple gold clasp. Was she being honest about the hearts-and-flowers thing? Maybe. And maybe not. She still had some issues in her life that she refused to talk about.

"Is sex going to help?" he asked.

She set her purse down. "With what?"

"Your problems."

She managed a risqué smile. "I hope so."

"More than sparring with me? More than our training sessions?"

"I can't spar with you in bed?"

Now it was his turn to smile. "Does it have to happen in bed?" He gestured to her flowery sofa, to the dining room table, to a chair that would probably collapse with their combined weight. "We could attack the rest of your furniture. Or the floor. Or maybe the concrete on the balcony." He watched her eyes go wide. "I'm not picky."

"I want you in bed." She took his arm and led him down the hall.

He didn't complain. He liked being a willing captive. Besides, he took one look around her room and got even more turned on. It was soft and feminine, with a white quilt and lacy sheers. She even had a vanity table with a gilded mirror and perfume bottles on the marble top. A 9mm Glock rested on the vanity, too.

Before he could draw his next breath, she tossed handcuffs onto the bed. Kyle nearly fell to his knees. The double-locking device was even sexier than her gun.

He emptied their shopping bags, where the condoms, lip sugar and bubble bath tumbled onto the quilt. The toys fell out, too.

Suddenly they both laughed.

And then they stared at each other.

"Will you take your dress off for me?" he asked.

She nodded and reached for the zipper. He watched and waited, his skin going warm. The metal teeth made a sliding sound.

Finally she dropped the dress and stepped out of it. She wore a black push-up bra, matching panties and thigh-high hose, the modern kind without garters. The tops were banded in lace, where they stayed up on their own.

"You're beautiful," he told her.

She closed her eyes, held them tightly shut, then opened them. "That sounded romantic."

Damn. "It did?"

"Yes."

"Sorry." He righted the compliment. "You look like one of those girls who jump out of cakes."

She adjusted her bra, exposing more cleavage. "That's better."

He walked over to her. In spite of her bravado, he could tell she was nervous. Earlier, he'd reminded her that he was bigger and stronger. That her badge wouldn't matter. Yet she'd offered him her handcuffs anyway.

Was she regretting her decision?

"I won't hurt you, Joyce."

"I trust you."

"No, you don't. Not completely." But he wanted her to enjoy the experience, to have fun, to let her inhibitions go. "We don't have to do anything that makes you uncomfortable."

"I know, but…"

"But what?"

"Edgy sex scares me." She fussed with her bra again. By now the tops of her areolas were exposed, and her legs were slightly parted, her stance long and lean. "Yet I'm willing to chance it. At least with you."

He wanted to tell her that she was even more beautiful than before, but not at the risk of sounding romantic. "The parts of our brain that control fear, anxiety and arousal are close together." He kept his gaze locked onto hers. "So close that a little bit of nervousness can enhance the pleasure."

"When are you going to do it?"

He knew she was talking about the handcuffs. "Later."

"How much later?"

"After we're both naked." He removed his boots, then bared himself to the waist, leaving his jeans intact. For now, he wanted to focus on her.

Anxious, he moved forward, reached around, unhooked her bra and got rid of it. Her breasts spilled into his hands. She made a sweet sound, and he thumbed her nipples. Pink and pearled, they stood out against the whiteness of her skin. She was so different from him, so soft and fair.

Fascinated, he went lower, moving to her stomach. She had an athletic body, perfect for a man's greedy touch. Next he toyed with the waistband of her panties. She quivered, and he slipped his hand inside, then used two fingers, plunging deep.

Quick and hard.

He barely gave her time to think. She gasped, and he smiled. "Surprise attack."

She gripped his shoulders. "You're good at that."

"Glad you think so." Kyle pulled her panties down, and her knees nearly buckled. He caught her before she fell, stumbling to the bed, taking her with him.

He pushed the toys, bubble bath, condoms and handcuffs to the edge of the mattress, leaving the flavored gloss at his disposable.

He opened the shimmering pots, then handed her the watermelon flavor. "Are you ready to play, Detective?"

Her voice vibrated. "Yes."

"Then be bad for me," he said, challenging her to take control, to lead them both into temptation. "As naughty as you can get."

Joyce couldn't believe what she was doing. Messing around with a man she barely knew. Getting caught up in sinful games, in the thrill of dangerous sex.

She took the gloss and painted it around her belly button, then drew a line downward, stopping before she reached her pubis.

"Do it there," he said.

Her pulse skipped. She wasn't ready. She needed more time. More courage. "Not yet."

She put a dollop inside her navel, then went in the other direction, dabbing the gloss onto her nipples, moving in tiny circles, encouraging him to follow her path.

He did, every step of the way. He licked; he sucked; he sent erotic chills up and down her spine.

When he lifted his head, they kissed, slick and sweet and carnal. And then they rolled over the bed, knocking the condom box onto the floor. She could see the colorful packets spill onto the carpet, scattering like a pirate's treasure. The toys and bubble bath fell onto the floor, too.

Somewhere in the back of her mind, the handcuffs clanked, reminding her of what was yet to come. She'd left both sets of keys on the nightstand, where they remained at Kyle's disposal.

Was she crazy?

Sexually insane?

Her heartbeat staggered, and he pushed another container of gloss into her palm, closing her fingers around it.

"I don't want to wait anymore," he said. "Put this between your legs. Make me taste it."

Heaven help her. She sat up and looked at him. He was looking at her, too. Suddenly she felt like the most desirable woman in the world. He overflowed with lust. She glanced down, shifting the gloss in her hand. "Mango."

His voice turned rough. "Lip sugar."

Much too aroused, she opened her thighs and smeared the sticky cosmetic between her legs. And like the seductress she'd become, she still wore the lace-topped hose and black high heels.

He watched her, and she realized she was touching herself for him. But she didn't care. She liked the excitement, the anticipation, the raw, ragged pleasure.

Joyce scooted closer to him, and he lifted her legs onto his shoulders. She closed her eyes, and he made love to her with his mouth. Deep and dark and hungry. He was like a tiger feasting on his favorite meal, on the prey he'd captured.

She tugged her hands through his hair and opened her eyes. "Kyle."

He glanced up, and their gazes locked.

The intimacy hit her like a fist. She clenched her body to sustain the impact, the force of climaxing all over him, of thrashing through shuddering waves.

When it was over, when she could breathe again, she touched his face. He was still there, between her thighs, watching her.

"That was incredible," she said.

"For me, too." He lowered her legs from his shoulders and removed her stockings and shoes, making her more comfortable. Then he took her in his arms, holding her close.

She rested her head against his chest, telling herself this wasn't romance. But before things got too cozy, she slid her hand to his fly and unzipped his pants. "Are you as big as Olivia says?"

His eyebrows shot up. "You two talked about—"

"Yep." She tugged at his jeans, pulling them and

his boxers down, just enough to see him. He sprang free, granite-hard and porn-star huge.

She sucked in a staggering breath.

He grinned, and she wrestled with his pants, stripping him down to his birthday suit. And then she grabbed the cranberry gloss and rubbed it onto his skin, stroking him with the shiny sweetness.

He opened his legs, surrendering to her ministrations. "You're going to drive me crazy."

"That's the idea." She went down on him, using her tongue, flicking it over the tip.

He shivered, and she settled between his thighs. She couldn't take all of him, but she took as much as she could, making every inch count.

He lifted his hips, getting more and more aroused.

She was excited, too. Thrilled to please him, to suck and nuzzle and make him moan. In the past, she'd found fellatio tedious, something she'd done out of obligation. But with Kyle, it seemed hot and sexy.

She liked the shape of him, the silky hardness, the masculine girth. She even like the way he tasted, the earthy flavor, the primal saltiness.

Giving was as good as receiving.

When he cursed and fisted the sheets, she stopped to gulp some air. "Should I keep going?"

"Yes. No. Damn you." He dragged her up and crushed her mouth with his. The kiss was desperate, rough and insatiable, tongues mating, teeth clashing.

Beneath her hands, his muscles hardened like steel. She traced his abs, enthralled by his nakedness, by the power of how she'd made him feel.

But in the heat of the moment, he stole her victory, proving how big and strong he really was. He grabbed the handcuffs, and her world turned upside down. He didn't chain her to the headboard. He didn't attach her to an inanimate object.

He locked her to him instead, binding their wrists, making them both prisoners.

The lady cop and her lover.

Six

Joyce's heart thundered with every beat. Kyle rolled on top of her with a wicked smile on his face. The handcuffs rattled between them, where his right hand was shackled to her left.

"You tricked me," she said.

"No, I didn't. This is what I had in mind all along."

"Then you should have told me."

"And spoil the fun? Besides, this is perfect for our first time."

She took a labored breath. He made them sound like virgins. "You've never done this before?"

"I've used handcuffs, but I've never attached myself to someone else."

Great. Just great. She couldn't escape his charm. Literally and figuratively.

And that was scarier than what she'd imagined him doing with the handcuffs. In her mind, bondage wasn't nearly this intimate.

"We're going to sleep like this," he said.

"What if I have to get up to go to the bathroom?"

"Then I'll go with you. You're stuck with me, Detective. I already hid the keys."

She glanced at the nightstand. Sure enough, they were gone. He was clever that way: a militant, a magician, a thief.

Kyle snared her gaze, and Joyce shook her head. He was so handsome, so thrilling, so downright domineering, she wanted to knock him on his butt. But she wanted to make hard, hot love with him, too. He was still enormously aroused, his erection pressed against her stomach. She picked up the last pot of gloss—papaya—and waved it under his nose. "We haven't used this one yet."

Aggressive as ever, he took it from her, smeared it all over her lips and pushed his tongue down her throat.

Sultry sex and half-starved sin.

She clawed his shoulders, and they went mad, tumbling over the bed, kissing and biting and battling pheromones.

Within seconds, he went after the condoms on the

floor. Grabbing a fistful, he sorted through them, tossing the rejected packets like confetti.

He tore open a *warm sensation* style, using both of his hands. The motion dragged her chained hand along, too.

"Help me put it on," he said.

She smoothed the latex over him, and he watched her. His stomach muscles jumped, and she realized how anxious he was. His body was taut, waiting for hers. His chest rose and fell.

"You're my captive," she said.

"And you're mine." He nudged her legs apart. "Forbidden lovers."

She lifted her hips. "Dark fantasies."

"Mindless games." He thrust into her, and she caught her breath.

She'd never had anyone as determined, as powerful, as provocative as Kyle. He pumped himself in and out of her, using her for his pleasure.

But she used him, too. She took everything he gave, every low, primal groan, every passionate demand. She met him, stroke for stroke, letting him fill the void, the need that clawed at her soul.

He slid his hand between their bodies and touched her, rubbing and teasing, intensifying the heat, the undeniable wetness. He used the hand that was bound to hers, making her part of his ploy. Suddenly she was touching herself, too, the cold steel grazing her skin.

"I like it when you do that," he said.

"I can tell." His eyes, that catlike gaze, had gone hazy. She was hypnotizing him.

But that didn't stop him from making ruthless love to her. She wrapped her legs around him, grateful for the untamed feeling, for the slick, sliding motion, for the warm, tingling sensation.

"Come for me," he whispered. "Come like you did when I was licking you."

Softly spoken words and a heart-hammering rhythm. She climaxed on command, the naughty sentiment pushing her over the edge.

He kissed her while it happened, and the room started to spin. For her, for him, for both of them. She could feel his need, his hunger, his orgasm threatening to burst.

When it was over, he held her while she quivered beneath him, while she jangled the relentless handcuffs and fell prey to the comfort of his arms.

Kyle nuzzled Joyce's neck. He knew that most women liked to cuddle after sex, so he tried to make it a habit. Of course for him, it was tough to lie still. Cuddling made him want to nibble and kiss and do it all over again.

She shifted in his arms, and he rubbed his cheek against her hair. He liked the feathery softness.

"Don't go to sleep," he told her.

"Why not?"

He bumped his groin against hers. "Because I have to get rid of this condom."

"So get rid of it."

"The trash can is in your bathroom."

She squinted at him. Their faces were just inches apart. "Which means I have to get out of bed, too."

"'Fraid so. You and I are a team."

"You're a pain in the butt, Kyle."

"So are you." He pulled her up, using his chained arm. She made a sour face, and he stole a quick kiss. "But you're a hell of a lay."

"Gee, thanks."

He chuckled and grabbed the bubble bath and toy boat off the floor. "As long as we're in there, we might as well soak in the tub."

She shook the metals cuffs. "In these?"

"Yep. In these. I'm not letting you go until morning."

"Lucky me."

"Don't get snide." He hauled her into the bathroom and discarded the used condom. "I'm the best you'll ever have. You'll never want another guy after me."

"Such ego." She leaned over him while he filled the tub. Then she nibbled his bare shoulder.

He smiled and poured the bubble bath into the water. Having her as a lover was better than he'd imagined.

His first cop. His first Caucasian.

He enjoyed her tough-girl attitude. But he appreciated her dreamy side, too. The lady who'd slipped into his arms after he'd banged her breathless.

"That's enough," she said.

He turned to look at her. "What?"

She grabbed the oceanic liquid from him. "You're not supposed to use the whole bottle."

"Spoilsport." He lowered the boat into the frothing foam. "SpongeBob wanted lots of bubbles."

"You and SpongeBob are weird."

"So are you." He scooped her up, and she squealed like a teenager. He wanted to drop her into the bubbles, but he couldn't, not while they were attached. Holding her was awkward enough. So he climbed into the tub and plopped down, making a dramatic splash and positioning her in front of him.

The tub was too small for both of them, but he didn't care. He opened his legs and bent his knees to make room for her. She leaned back and cozied her butt against him, shifting and moving and driving him to distraction. He moaned, and she laughed.

"You're evil, Detective Riggs."

She wiggled her rear again. "I try."

"No kidding." He wound up the boat, and they watched it drive around in goofy little circles.

He put his free arm around her. "Can you imagine what conjoined twins feel like? Being connected to each other all the time?"

"It's all they know."

"Unless a team of doctors separates them."

She relaxed against him. "I'll bet that's even harder than being together. They probably miss each other afterward."

He rewound the boat when it stopped moving. "Probably."

Her voice turned soft. "Was it lonely for you being an only child?"

The toy bumped his knee, a reminder of his mixed-up youth, of spinning in circles. "Maybe it would have been easier if I had brothers and sisters. They could have suffered with me." He gave the boat a gentle push, away from his knee. "Misery loves company."

When Joyce moved her head, her hair tickled his chest. "Sometimes I used to yearn for privacy, but I wouldn't trade my family for anything."

"Where do you fit in?" he asked. "Are you the oldest? The youngest? Or are you one of the middle kids?"

"I'm the oldest." She heaved a barely audible sigh. "And I used to think I was the wisest. But I don't think so anymore."

"Because of what's going on in your life?"

"I'm my own worst enemy."

He contemplated her response. "You're creating your own turmoil?"

"Yes." She angled her shoulders, turning, trying

to look back at him. Between the cramped quarters and the handcuffs, her mobility was limited. "It's my own fault."

Kyle was as confused as ever, but he didn't expect to understand her. "I've never been able to figure women out. You're such a baffling breed."

She pinched his thigh. "Breed?"

"Gender." He nibbled the side of her neck, tasting soap and skin. "Are you ready to go back to bed?"

"If you are."

"I'm always ready to mess around."

"Oh, I see. Is that why we're going back to bed?"

"Definitely." He stood, giving her no choice but to stand, too. "You can be on top this time."

She nudged him toward the towel rack. "You're such a gentleman."

He knew she was kidding, teasing him for being so blatant, for saying whatever came to mind. He wrapped her in terry cloth, drying her off. He used another towel on himself and dropped both of them onto the floor.

Squeaky clean and warm from the tub, they tumbled into bed. Only this time, they ditched the virgin-white quilt and made use of her pastel-colored sheets.

They didn't bother with foreplay, at least not to the degree of building up the sexual tension. Kyle was already aroused. Just thinking about being with her again made him hard. Joyce seemed just as anxious.

While he leaned against the headboard, she chose a ribbed condom, fitted him with it and climbed onto his lap.

"I like how big you are," she told him, impaling herself with a warm, wet thrust.

Kyle's breath rushed out. "Then go deeper. Take more."

"This much?" She sank onto him again, riding him the way he'd imagined her riding the bull.

"Yeah. That much." He didn't need to lean forward to kiss her. They were already as close as humanly possibly, courtesy of the police-issued handcuffs. "These are better than the sex-shop kind."

She moved up and down, milking every inch. "They're not a toy."

"They are now." He studied her, compelled by her beauty, by the shape of her breasts, the flatness of her stomach, the flare of her hips. He shifted his gaze even lower, mesmerized by the V between her legs.

"You're watching us," she said.

"So are you." He noticed that her head was bent, too. She kept watching. "It's sexy."

"Totally." Intercourse, he thought. Copulation. The visual effect was driving him half-mad. "Do you like dirty movies?"

She looked up. *"Kyle."*

He stared at her. "Do you?"

She bit down on her bottom lip. "No."

"Liar. You like everything I like."

"No, I don't."

"Yes, you do." He took a chance and whispered something lewd in her ear, something gentlemen didn't say, something ladies shouldn't hear.

She reacted.

Violently.

She called him a bastard, drove her nails into his skin, and then kissed him, nearly devouring his mouth in one fell swoop.

He pushed her down, switching positions so he was on top, so he could pound her into the bed. She wrapped her legs around him, thrashing their shackled wrists.

And then he felt it. The feminine fire. The hot-blooded moisture. The pretty blond cop coming like a call girl.

The edgy sex, the kinky stuff she'd been worried about, was nothing more than a few strategic words. But it didn't matter. Kyle felt as if he'd just scaled a mountain. He loved sex. He always had. But with her, it was even better.

He tugged her head back, using her hair, behaving like the caveman she'd accused him of being. Then he caught himself.

Cursing his stupidity, he released her. "I'm sorry. I wasn't supposed to hurt you."

"Don't apologize." She squeezed her thighs to-gether, tightening her grip, locking him between her legs. "I'm going to hurt you, too."

His heart slammed against his chest. "You are?"

"Without a doubt." This time when she clawed his skin, she drew blood, leaving marks down his chest.

Hard and deep and steeped in pain. They made love like maniacs, and Kyle went off like a six-foot-four rocket.

But he didn't stop when it was over.

He got his second wind and corrupted her, and himself, all over again.

At dawn, Joyce woke up alone. Daylight streamed through the sheers, spilling lavender hues across the bed. She sat up and dragged the sheet against her naked body.

Kyle had left? Just walked out without even say-ing goodbye? She shouldn't care. But she did.

She glanced at the nightstand. The handcuffs and both sets of keys were there. She peered over the bed and noticed everything that belonged to him was gone, including the confetti of condoms.

He'd taken his protection and hightailed it out of her apartment before she could fix him breakfast or seduce him or kick him out of bed herself.

Damn him anyway.

She stole a panicked glance at the vanity table

just to be sure her gun wasn't missing. Thank goodness. He hadn't disappeared with her Glock.

Joyce slipped on her robe and went into the bathroom. She looked around and noticed that Kyle had tidied up. He'd put the towels he'd dropped on the floor last night in the hamper. Of course, his travel-size toothbrush, which he'd conveniently brought with him, was gone. And so was the SpongeBob boat.

For a man who lived like a slob, he was excruciatingly neat in someone else's home. But that hardly mattered. She would have preferred that he'd said goodbye.

Who cared if—

Suddenly she heard footsteps sounding down the hall. She exited the bathroom, and her heart tripped, just once, before Kyle rounded the corner and nearly bumped into her.

"I was just coming to check on you," he said.

Joyce didn't respond. There he was, half dressed with his hair loose and his ruggedly square jaw in need of a shave.

Finally she found her voice. "Where are the rest of your clothes?"

He made a face at her. "In the closet."

"What about the toy car and Wolf Man?"

"They're in the living room. I was playing with them."

She refused to soften her emotions, to imagine

him pushing around Barbie's Volvo with a werewolf behind the wheel. The man was too damn weird for his own good. "Where are the condoms, the boat and your toothbrush?"

"In there." He gestured to the bathroom.

"They are not."

"Yes, they are. I put everything in the cabinet under the sink. I didn't want you yelling at me for leaving my stuff sitting around."

"You should have told me."

"You were asleep." He made another face. "What's wrong with you? Did you start your period or something?"

She smacked his bare shoulder. He was obsessed with PMS. "No, you big baboon. I thought you ditched me."

A grin crawled across his handsome face. "Before we did it again? Are you kidding? What kind of guy walks out on great sex?" He tugged on her robe. "Are you naked under that ugly thing?"

She glared at him. She wanted to kiss him silly, but she hated to seem too anxious. "My robe isn't ugly."

"Oh, yeah? My grandmother has one just like it."

"Then your grandmother has taste." She tightened the belt on the conservative terry-cloth wrap. "Go make some coffee while I get dressed."

"Only if you promise to have sex with me. Today," he added. "Before I go home."

"We'll see." She turned her back on him and heard him grumble. But he left to brew the coffee anyway.

Joyce brushed her teeth, washed her face and combed her hair, wishing he wasn't so charming.

She climbed into her clothes, wondering if she should make him wait a day or two. Just to prove that she wasn't an easy lay. Of course, that would mean depriving herself, too.

First things first, she decided. Coffee and breakfast.

She entered the kitchen and found Kyle watching the dark liquid brew.

He turned around, and she glanced at his chest. He wasn't wearing a shirt, and his jeans were barely fastened.

He removed two cups from the cabinet and handed her one, making himself at home in her kitchen. "Do you still think I'm a big baboon?"

"No." She poured herself some coffee, adding cream and sugar to it. "I think you're a big, gorgeous baboon."

He laughed and stole a quick kiss. He tasted like mint, like her toothpaste. But so did she.

"What do you want to eat?" she asked. When he shot her a naughty grin, she bit back a smile. "Besides me, you pervert?"

"In that case, you decide."

"Okay, I will." While she opened the refrigerator, he went into the living room and overhauled the toy car, taking it apart and putting it back together.

She shook her head and arranged the ingredients for Spanish omelets and broiled potato wedges.

By the time breakfast was ready, Kyle came to the table with several small toys.

She sat across from him. "What are those?"

"Car seats. This one is for a little kid and this one is an infant seat. The Volvo came with all sorts of accessories." He frowned. "What should I do with them?"

"How should I know?" She didn't want to consider anything that had to do with children, especially newborn babies.

He kept frowning. "Do Ken and Barbie have kids? Or are these for someone else's kids? Barbie's friends or something?"

She cut into her omelet. "I have no idea."

"You should keep track of this stuff."

"Me? What for?"

"You have nieces and nephews."

"That doesn't make me an authority on their toys."

"If I were you, I'd be an authority on their toys."

"Of course you would." She gripped her fork a little tighter. "You're an overgrown ten-year-old."

"There's nothing wrong with being young at heart. Besides, I like kids. I'm good with them."

Joyce gulped her coffee. The last thing she needed was picturing him as the father of her nameless, faceless nonexistent offspring. "If you like children so much, why don't you have any?"

"Because I'm never getting married." He downed the last of his coffee, too. "My mom loved my dad, and he screwed her over. I don't want someone doing that to me. And I don't want to do that to someone else."

"That's understandable." When he set the infant seat on the table, she reached for it. "My parents have been together for nearly forty years. They have an anniversary coming up."

"That's pretty rare these days."

"Yes, it is." She set down the toy, realizing she shouldn't have picked it up to begin with.

"Given your family history, it seems like you would be more marriage minded." He poured ketchup over his potatoes. "But you're not, are you?"

She smoothed her napkin, keeping herself from fussing with the infant seat again. "No, I'm not," she responded, trying to convince herself that she wasn't lying. "My career has always come first."

"I guess that means you're not mom material."

She snared his gaze. "Do I look like mom material?"

"No." He gave her critical study. "But that robe you had on earlier made you look like grandma material."

"So you said." She changed the subject, and they finished their breakfast engaged in another conversation.

Something that had nothing to do with marriage and babies and the hollow ache inside her womb.

Seven

"Are you okay?" Kyle asked.

"I'm fine." Joyce ran a sponge across the frying pan she'd used to cook the omelets. She hadn't quit thinking about marriage and babies, and she hated herself for being so weak, so longingly maternal. "I'm rinsing the dishes."

"Looks like you're washing them to me."

She didn't turn around. He was standing behind her, nearly breathing down her neck. "I can't put them in the dishwasher if they have food stuck on them."

"Then what's the point of having a dishwasher?"

"Some models clean better than others. This is a cheap one, I guess." She reached for their plates, and he slipped his arms around her waist. To her, the affection seemed husbandly, and that was a dangerous perception.

Extremely dangerous.

She liked the feeling.

He nuzzled her hair. "What are you thinking about?"

"Nothing."

"You seem preoccupied."

"I'm into the dishes."

"And I'm into you." He sent a ripple of air along her skin. "Really into you."

Water splashed over her hands. She was still rinsing their plates, still trying to control her emotions. He felt so big and strong behind her, so perfectly powerful. The kind of husband a female cop should have. "You just want to have sex."

"Can you blame me?" His voice made her shiver. "We're good together."

Too good. She shut off the faucet, but she didn't turn around. Not yet. For now, she liked being pressed against the sink. Snared. Trapped. At his mercy.

Kyle leaned forward and closed his hands over her breasts, rubbing, making her nipples hard. Then he told her to lift her arms, so he could remove her T-shirt.

She let him undress her. After he discarded her top, he tugged on her sweatpants, pulling them down and helping her step out of them.

Finally she turned around. There she stood in her bra and panties while he still wore his jeans.

Joyce couldn't think of anything to say. Her hands were slightly damp from the dishes, and the sun streamed through the window, bathing Kyle in a warm glow.

He took her in his arms and kissed her.

Softly. Gently.

When they separated, she teetered on her feet. Her brain had zapped back into the husband mode. "Did you bring a condom?" she asked, trying to steer her mind in a safer direction.

"Yes. And I brought this, too." He reached into his pocket and removed a black cloth.

"Your headband?"

"I always have one with me."

"What does that have to do with us?"

He moved closer. "I want to blindfold you."

Her breath rushed out.

"Will you let me?" he asked.

Suddenly he didn't seem like her husband anymore. She glanced at the material in his hand. "Have you done this to other women?"

"Yes."

"Has anyone ever done it to you?"

"You almost did."

Confused, she frowned. Then she recalled teasing him during their first training session, pulling his headband over his eyes while they were rolling around on the sparring mats. But that was before they were lovers. "That doesn't count, Kyle."

"Yes, it does. It turned me on."

She bit back a nervous smile. "Everything turns you on."

He dangled the cloth in front of her. "So can I do it?"

"Where?"

"Here." He pinned her against the sink, the way she'd been trapped before. Only this time, she was facing him. "Right now."

She agreed to play his game, to let him seduce her. "My kitchen will never be the same."

His mouth twisted into a wicked grin. "Every time you wash dishes, you'll think of me. Of this."

He covered her eyes, tying the makeshift blindfold in place, and she became aware of the darkness, of the morning light fading from view. There was nothing but the contact of her lover's hands. A man she was still learning to trust.

"Does it make you feel vulnerable?" he asked.

"Yes. But it feels good, too."

"You like the way I'm touching you?"

She nodded. He roamed her body, molding her as if she were made of clay or wax or a substance she couldn't quite name.

When he reached back and unhooked her bra, her senses heightened, goose bumps peppering her skin. He discarded her panties after that, leaving her naked.

And alone.

He wasn't touching her anymore.

She tried to listen, to decipher what came next. "What are you doing?"

"Looking at you."

Now she felt even more vulnerable. "Whatever you do, don't tell me I'm beautiful."

"But you are. It's not fair that I don't get to say it."

She considered removing the cloth from her eyes and grabbing her clothes. "Being naked and blind-folded isn't beautiful."

"Yes, it is." Before she could end his game, he pulled her tight against him, kissing her hard and fast.

There was no time to let her emotions linger, to give into being self-conscious. She kissed him back, devouring his tongue the way he devoured hers.

He used his fingers between her legs, and she squirmed against the pressure.

"Are you going to take off your jeans?" she asked.

"No."

"Can I take them off of you?"

"No," he responded again.

She gulped the air in her lungs. "Now who's being unfair?"

"Me." He dropped to his knees and put his mouth all over her.

Joyce feared she would lose her mind. She nearly melted on the spot. She couldn't see him. She couldn't watch. But she could feel every warm, spiraling sensation.

She slid her hands through his hair, tangling the thick, straight strands. She wanted more, so much more. By the time it was over, she wanted him inside her.

Dizzy, she leaned against the sink to keep herself steady.

He stood up. She could hear him unzipping his pants and pulling them down. Then the sound of the condom packet being torn open reverberated in her ears. She waited, assuming he was putting on the protection.

What was taking him so long? The seconds seemed like hours.

"I'm too tall for you," he said.

"No, you're not."

"Yes, I am. It will be easier if we—" He stopped talking and lowered her onto the floor, opening her legs to accommodate him.

Finally—*finally*—he entered her, deep and slow. The closeness, the roughness, almost made her weep.

He hadn't removed his clothes, not completely. The texture of his jeans abraded her, but she didn't care. Being blindfolded *was* beautiful, especially when Kyle was inside her.

He made erotic love to her, pushing toward his release. She realized she was on top of her clothes, with her sweatpants cushioning her head.

His climax triggered hers, and for the second time that morning, she burst like a water fountain.

He collapsed on top of her, his body hitting hers with the force of dead weight. But she liked it. She liked the connection.

Maybe too much.

"You're heavy," she said.

He didn't budge. "I am?"

"You know you are." And besides that, he had her arms pinned. She couldn't remove the blindfold. "Come on, Kyle."

"I already did."

"What?"

"Come."

"Very funny." She pushed against him.

A smile sounded in his voice. "That feels good."

"You're insufferable." But she smiled, too.

He stole a quick kiss—something he kept taking the liberty of doing—and removed the blindfold. She met his gaze, struck by his gold-flecked eyes.

Finally he let her go, lifting his body from hers.

While she sat on the floor and gathered her clothes, he stood up and disposed of the condom, wrapping it in a paper towel and throwing it away in the trash can under the sink. Then he zipped his jeans. She climbed to her feet and got dressed.

"Are you going to get mad if I go home?" he asked.

She adjusted her top and smoothed her hair. "No."

"Are you sure?"

"Yes." In some small way, she *was* angry. Yet in another small way, she wanted him to leave, to quit seducing her.

He shoved the black cloth into his pocket. "I have a training session this afternoon."

"With who?"

"No one you know." He watched her tie the drawstring on her sweatpants. "Are you on vacation for the rest of the week?"

She nodded. "I go back to work next Monday."

"Do you want to come over tomorrow? We can hang out with the dogs or something."

She tried to find an excuse not to drive to the desert, to be with him. "Clyde doesn't like me."

"He'll get used to you." Kyle swooped, pulling her into his arms. "And I want to make the most of what's happening between us."

Her pulse pounded out of control. "What is happening?"

"I don't know, but it's fun. We might as well enjoy it while it lasts."

Yes, she told herself. *While it lasts.* They both knew they wouldn't be sleeping together forever. She took a moment to lean into his embrace, to nuzzle, to kiss. Then she pulled away. "Go home and I'll see you tomorrow."

"Sounds good." He collected his belongings and within no time, he was gone.

The only things he left behind were the toy car seats. Joyce contemplated throwing them away, but she couldn't bring herself to do it.

Instead she tucked them away in a rarely used drawer in her dresser.

Out of sight and out of mind.

Fifteen minutes later, the doorbell sounded. Joyce answered the summons and found her youngest sister, Jessica, on the other side. Accompanying Jessica were her two children. Five-year-old Owen had spiky blond hair, ruddy cheeks and a boyish grin. His baby sister, seven-month-old Gail rested on their mama's hip. Gail, the little gremlin, as Joyce called her, was grinning, too.

"Aunt Joy?" Owen gave her a perplexed look. "How come your Halloween guy looks like that?"

"Like what?"

The child pointed to the door. "Like that."

She poked her head around and saw that Kyle had blindfolded the plastic skeleton before he'd left. Good grief. "One of my friends was goofing around."

"It's funny," the boy said.

"I have funny friends." She lifted the black cloth and changed it to a headband. Owen thought that was amusing, too. A second later, she glanced at her sister. "It's great to see all of you."

"I'm glad you think so. I was worried about in-
truding on your time off." Jessica transferred Gail
into Joyce's arms. "I have to get her playpen. She's
been a monster today."

Gail giggled like the gremlin she was. Joyce
rubbed her cheek against the baby's hair, her maternal yearnings kicking into high gear.

"Will you watch these two while I go to the car?"
Jessica asked.

"Of course I will. But I can help you. We can all
go together."

"It'll be easier if I do it alone." Jessica leaned in
close. At twenty-six, she hadn't outgrown her long
blond hair or her high-school-type rebellions. She
hung the diaper bag over Joyce's shoulder. "I'm
dying for a cigarette."

"You're supposed to be quitting."

"I know. And that's why I don't want them to see
me. Owen will tattle on me. He'll tell his daddy."

Jessica disappeared, and Joyce brought her niece
and nephew into the apartment. Owen showed her his
latest toy police car. He had a collection of them. He
liked officers of the law. He'd been taught they were his
friends, and he was old enough to appreciate that Joyce
was a cop and that his grandpa used to be one, too.

Joyce sat on the couch, with an overly active Gail
on her lap and Owen pushing his black-and-white
cruiser around the living room. She thought about
Kyle and decided Owen would like him.

When Jessica returned, she barreled into the doorway. In spite of the playpen she'd lugged up the stairs, she had a nicotine-satisfied look on her face.

Jessica would probably like Kyle, too. She used to date bad boys in high school, something that had disturbed the hell out of their dad.

Luckily she'd married a proper young man. Of course she had to sneak a smoke now and then. But her accountant husband adored her.

Jessica opened the playpen and confined Gail. Then she gave her daughter a bundle of soft, squeaky, chewy toys. The gremlin amused herself by tossing them around her cushy cage. Joyce's heartstrings tugged a bit too hard. She wanted a baby just like Gail. She wanted a gremlin, too.

Her sister sat beside her on the couch. "Tom was hoping to set you up with his boss. I know how you detest blind dates, but he thinks you two would get along great."

She merely blinked. Tom was Jessica's husband, and she suspected that his boss was a recently divorced CPA, probably the man who managed the corporate accounting firm. "I'm already seeing someone."

"You are?" The younger woman sent her a suspicious glare. "Since when?"

Joyce sighed. She had been dodging her family's blind date attempts for years. "Yesterday."

"How convenient."

"It's true. We went out last night."

Another suspicious glare. "What's his name and how did you meet him?"

"Kyle Prescott, and he's a friend of a friend."

"What does he do?"

Uh-oh, she thought. Here comes the tricky part. "He's a junk dealer."

"Yeah, right. Now I know you're lying."

"I am not." Joyce looked over at Owen. He was still driving his police car, adding engine noises to go along with it. "That's his main source of income."

"Main source? What else does he do?"

"He teaches close-quarter combat."

Jessica's jaw all but dropped. "That kill-or-be-killed stuff?"

"It's designed to cause permanent damage."

"I'll say. I can't decide if Dad is going to love or hate this guy."

Joyce ignored the glint in her sister's eye. "Dad isn't going to meet him."

"Sure he is. You're going to bring Kyle to Mom and Dad's anniversary party." Jessica scooted to the edge of her seat. "If you don't, I'm going to tell Tom to invite his boss."

"That's blackmail."

"Call it what you will."

"You still don't believe me, do you? You think I'm making Kyle up."

"No, I don't. I think he's the 'funny' friend who blindfolded your skeleton." Jessica lowered her voice. "He is, isn't he?"

Joyce sucked in a breath. "Yes."

"Is he as dangerous as he seems?"

"Of course not," she lied, not wanting to admit to her sister that she was caught up in a thrill-seeking affair. Or worse yet, that every so often, she would envision being married to Kyle. "That was a joke."

"A naughty joke, I'll bet."

Joyce didn't respond. How could she? At this stage, she wondered if she was getting in over her head. If Kyle *was* as dangerous as he seemed.

Eight

The following afternoon, Joyce decided to investigate her lover. She already knew his sexual appetite made him dangerous. But what about the rest of his life? The Warrior Society he belonged to? The Indian activists that kept the authorities guessing?

Needing answers, she shared a scarred wooden table with Special Agent West. He'd agreed to meet her at the Mockingbird, a downtown bar and a cop-patronized watering hole that boasted a jukebox in front and a billiard table in back.

As West nursed a beer, he dipped into a bowl of peanuts. Joyce considered the special agent a friend, and since he was Olivia's boyfriend, he knew Kyle, as well.

At this point, she wanted to talk to the FBI, and West fit the bill. She picked up her drink, a lemon-lime soda, and took a sip. The maraschino cherry had sunk to the bottom of the glass. She could only imagine what Kyle would do with her cherry.

West angled his head, and she frowned. This wasn't the time to be thinking about Kyle's erotic games.

She shifted her attention to the special agent. He wore a black suit, a pale shirt and a narrow tie. His hair was thick and dark, and his eyes were an alarming shade of gray. He was a hell of a profiler, a man who knew what made violent criminals tick.

At the moment, he was analyzing her.

"What's going on?" he asked.

"I want to discuss Kyle with you."

"That's what I figured." He went after another handful of peanuts. "He got you into bed, didn't he?"

"So? Olivia did that to you."

"Yes, but she and I are on the same side. She assists law enforcement agencies." He sat back and gave her an obvious study. "You're worried that Kyle is engaged in illegal activity."

She wasn't about to skirt around the issue, even if Kyle had assisted on a case she and West had worked on. They both knew he didn't lend his skills on a regular basis. "I know he doesn't have a record, but are the feds keeping an eye on him? Or his Warrior Society?"

West dusted the salt from his fingers. "There's a file on the society and Kyle's name is in it."

She scooted to the edge of her chair. "Has he or anyone else been linked to any crimes?"

"Nothing that can be proven."

"But there's speculation?"

"Yes."

"What kind of speculation?" she asked.

West blew out a rough breath. "If you want to know what Kyle is up to, then you should ask him."

She merely blinked. Suddenly the special agent was snubbing her, refusing to share information. "You're protecting him from me? *You,* of all people."

"He helped when I was sick."

"I helped, too." Frustrated, she put down her drink. Although some people would find it hard to believe, West had been infected with an object-intrusion spell, a Native American witchcraft tool that had nearly killed him. But that was eight months ago, and he was well now. "When did you check to see if there was a file on him?" she asked. "Before or after he helped you?"

"After. But I was curious about him before."

"And now I'm curious."

"That's understandable." West finished his beer. "But I'm not going to betray him. Not with the woman he's sleeping with."

"How noble of you. How male. How Indian," she added, lacing her voice with sarcasm.

"Don't even go there, Riggs. I'm not that kind of Indian."

"Aren't you?" Although he wasn't an activist like Kyle, he was a mixed-blood registered with his tribe. And on top of that, Olivia probably influenced him. She'd done her fair share of fighting for Native causes.

"You know damn well I'm not," he countered.

Joyce didn't respond. West had never touted his heritage in front of her. By most people's standards, he didn't even look Indian. But sitting across from him now, he made her feel white.

"Ask Kyle," he pressed. "Talk to him about this."

She reached for her drink and plucked the cherry out of it, placing it on the cocktail napkin beside her. "Fine. But do you really think he is going to be honest with me?"

"If he cares about you, he will," West said, leaving her with a lump in the back of her throat.

"I was getting worried," Kyle told Joyce as he unlocked the gate that led to his property. "I expected you before now."

"We never specified a time." She glanced at his companions. Clyde stood patiently, and Bonnie danced around Joyce's feet. She knelt to pet the wiener dog, then looked up at Kyle.

He wore varying shades of denim and a battered fringe jacket reminiscent of the Vietnam War era. A slight breeze tousled his hair.

"I fixed lunch," he said.

Her heart made a foolish flutter. This wasn't the time to get girlish over him. Yesterday they'd agreed to spend some casual time together, but today she had an ulterior motive. "You cooked for me?"

"I made sandwiches. For a picnic," he added.

"Really?" She hadn't pegged him for the picnic type. "Where?"

"In the laser tag compound."

"That sounds fun." And it made her feel guilty, even if she knew she had the right to question him about his Warrior Society activities.

They walked to his house, and he retrieved their late-day lunch. From there, they took his Jeep to the airplane hangar that supported the laser tag course. The dogs came with them.

Once they went inside, Joyce marveled at the genius of the structure. The building was equipped with a variety of movie props and set changes, including lifelike audio tracks and devices that scented the air and altered the weather.

She glanced up. At the moment, the painted sky was sunny and the temperature was warm.

"I can make it rain," Kyle said.

"At a picnic?"

"We could huddle in a cave." He gestured to a stone path that led to a mountainlike formation.

Indoor rain sounded sexy, but she wasn't sure if it was a good idea. Sooner or later, she was going to ask him if he was involved in criminal activity, and a sunny day seemed safer somehow.

"I'd prefer a dry picnic," she said.

He removed his jacket. "Then come with me."

She walked beside him with the dogs in tow. They crossed a small bridge and stopped in an area that was designed to look like a meadow. Faux flowers colored the grasslike ground, creating an alluring effect.

Bonnie ran ahead of them, and Joyce laughed. Clyde was too macho to make mad dash for the fake foliage, but he watched his canine friend kick up her heels.

Joyce and Kyle sat in the middle of the floral field. An electronic bird winged above their heads, and she admired its realistic flight.

"That's part of the magic," he told her.

Strange magic, she thought. She knew he played war games here. "I'll bet it's booby-trapped."

"Could be." He spread his jacket on the ground and setup their picnic, removing items from a duffel bag.

He'd packed more than sandwiches. She noticed cheese and crackers, too. And containers filled with various fruits and salads. For their beverage, he'd brought bottled water.

Joyce tasted her sandwich, a hearty roll with roast beef, avocado, tomato and lettuce. "This is good."

"Just because I hate to clean my kitchen doesn't mean I can't fix a halfway decent meal." He scooped one of the salads onto a paper plate for her. "Try the pasta."

She took a bite, impressed by the raw vegetables and spicy Italian dressing he'd added to the curly noodles. "A man of many talents."

"That's me." He leaned forward to kiss her, planting a chaste peck on her lips.

She wanted to kiss him for real, but her guilt had kicked in again, so she pretended that she wasn't craving more. Or that she wasn't stalling, stopping herself from asking him about his Warrior Society.

When he sat back, Bonnie climbed onto his lap. He petted the tiny pooch, then set her on her feet. As for Kyle's feet, Joyce noticed that he was wearing his moccasins.

She gestured with her fork. "Did someone make those for you?"

"Someone? Like who?"

"A female relative," she suggested. "Or an old lover."

"I made them. I'm crafty that way. Domestic slob that I am."

He was more than crafty, she thought. He was a loner. A man who'd learned to cook and sew to prove that he didn't need a woman tending to his needs.

As for cleaning...

"You should hire a housekeeper," she told him.

"My grandmother thinks I should find a wife."

Joyce sucked in a breath. Like the troubled woman she was, her mind strayed in a husbandly direction. Why did it matter how Kyle lived his life? She'd known he was a suspicious character when she'd first met him.

"The grandmother with the robe like mine?" she asked.

"Yep, that's her." He flashed a silly smile. "Grandma Ugly Robe."

She looked at him, her emotions still acting up. Why did his lifestyle matter? Because she was sleeping with him. And because in her own stupid way, she was getting attached.

"My baby sister thinks I should invite you to our parents' anniversary party," she said, wanting to clear the air, to admit that she'd told someone in her family about him.

"Really? So are you going to invite me?"

"It depends on how honest you are."

"About what?"

"Criminal activity."

For a moment, he merely stared at her. "What the hell is that supposed to mean?"

"Don't play dumb, Kyle. The FBI has a file on your Warrior Society."

"Of course they do." A muscle twitched in his jaw, and his faithful rottweiler sat down beside him, aware of his agitation. "The feds don't trust guys like me."

"Then why should I trust you?"

He stared at her once again. "I never claimed you should."

She held his gaze. "Is that an admission of guilt?"

"No."

"The FBI has been speculating about your activities."

He wrapped up his half-eaten sandwich and shoved it into the duffel bag. "Who told you that?"

"Special Agent West. But before you start cursing him, he wouldn't tell me what those speculations are."

Kyle crossed his arms. "Why? What's his agenda?"

"I don't think he has one. Other than not wanting to betray you to the woman you're sleeping with." She glanced at the spray of rainbow flowers, wishing they were real, wishing they could give her comfort. "He also thinks that if you cared about me, you'd tell me the truth."

"That's not right." He looked around the fake meadow, too. Avoiding her gaze. Avoiding the discomfort between them. "West shouldn't have said that."

"No, I suppose he shouldn't have." But he did, and the words made her ache. As foolish as it was, she wanted Kyle to care about her.

* * *

Kyle couldn't sleep. He sat up in bed and glanced at the clock: 2:24. He picked up the phone, then set it down. He couldn't call Joyce at this hour. Could he?

He got up, went down the hall to the bathroom and splashed some water on his face. He looked like hell, like a man haunted by a woman.

When he returned to his room, the clock said 2:25.

Screw it. He climbed back into bed and grabbed the phone again. He was going to call her. With a frown, he punched out the numbers.

The ringing on the other end of the line made his stomach jolt. Finally she answered.

"Hello?" She sounded anxious, as if she were expecting an emergency. Or a homicide-oriented call, something related to her job.

Which wasn't that far off the mark. She would probably want to kill him for interrupting her sleep.

"It's me," he told her.

"Kyle? Do you know what time it is?"

He stole another glance at the clock: 2:27 and counting. "Yes."

"And?" she pressed, waiting for him to explain.

He envisioned her sitting up in bed, too. Only her bed was soft and scented, with pastel sheets and a virginal quilt. He wished he were there, nuzzling her naked body. "Can I come over?"

She blew out an annoyed breath. "No."

"Why not?"

"Because I'm not giving in every time you have a sexual whim."

"Why not?"

"Kyle."

A slight laugh sounded in her voice, and he smiled. He liked making her laugh. He liked making love to her, too. But that wasn't why he'd called. "I am starting to care about you, Joyce."

Silence. Then, "You are?"

"Of course I am. I wouldn't be spending all this time with you if I wasn't." He kicked away the covers. "Are you starting to care about me?"

"Yes."

"Enough to let me come over?"

She turned suspicious. "What for?"

"To talk." His stomach jolted again, just a little, just enough to prove how she affected him. "Would it matter if I cared about you in the way West suggested?"

"Of course it would." Her voice perked up. "Are you offering to come clean? To discuss the Warrior Society?"

He made a face, hoping he wasn't going to regret this decision. That she wouldn't turn on him like the cop she was. "Yes, but you have to promise to come clean, too. To talk about your personal problems."

She stalled, sighing into the phone. "I never expected you to strike a bargain."

"Too bad. Take it or leave it."

Another sigh. "That's going to be difficult for me."

"And me opening up to a detective isn't?" Once he spilled his guts, she could hang him out to dry. Screw him over but good. "I'm not giving you something for nothing. Either we trust each other or we don't."

"This is scary," she said.

No kidding, he thought. "Are you game?"

When she cleared her throat and said, "Yes," he reached for his clothes and told her he would be over in about an hour. The drive would take him at least that long.

Kyle arrived at Joyce's apartment wearing a pair of jeans, an old sweatshirt and the moccasins he'd made. His hair was loose and getting in his eyes. He noticed the skeleton on the door was no longer blindfolded. The fabric was tied around its head instead.

Joyce opened the door before Kyle could knock or ring the bell.

"Hi," she said.

"Hi." He entered her living room. She was wearing her ugly robe and a nightgown beneath it. He'd assumed that she slept naked when she was alone, but apparently he was wrong. It didn't matter, he supposed. He liked the satiny nightgown, even if he couldn't see all of it.

They gazed at each other, and he hated how awkward this was.

"Where do you want to talk?" she asked.

"In bed. But we can keep our clothes on," he added, reminding her that this wasn't about sex.

She agreed, and he followed her to her room.

It looked as inviting as he remembered. The lights burned low, and the perfume bottles on her vanity table glinted with cut-glass allure, the shapes and see-through colors catching his eye. Her gun was there, too. Just like last time.

He turned to look at her, and she tucked her hair behind her ears. She seemed nervous, but he knew this was more intimate than sex. More revealing. They'd just agreed to confide in each other, to unearth their secrets.

Kyle waited for her to shed her robe and climb into bed. Once she did, he removed his moccasins and took the spot next to her.

By now, it was nearly four in the morning.

"I'm glad you don't have to work tomorrow," he said, wondering if the nature of her job ever chilled her in the middle of the night, if she saw murder victims in her sleep. "It's good that you have time off."

Her eyes locked onto his. "It's turning into a strange vacation."

"Because of me?"

She nodded. "You're deeper than I thought you were. More complex."

"So are you." He was itching to touch her, but he kept his hands to himself.

"You have to go first, Kyle."

"I know." He felt as though they were playing a soul-searching game of Truth or Dare, and they'd both picked Truth. "Maybe you should ask me some questions. Get the ball rolling that way."

"Fine." She took an audible breath. "Do you know what the FBI is speculating about you? About your Warrior Society?"

He turned to face her. "They probably think we steal."

She frowned at him. "And do you?"

"That depends on a person's perceptive." He watched her adjust the quilt. They were both leaning against the headboard. "We've been known to retrieve sacred objects and return them to their rightful owners."

"Why don't the rightful owners have legal possession of these objects? There are laws to protect them. Federal and state enactments."

"Yes, but it's not as simple as it sounds. I know of a tribe, here in California, who spent five years, back and forth with the federal government, trying to re-obtain something from a university that's sacred to their Nation. Something the university considered research material."

"So what are you saying? That in these types of situations the Warrior Society offers to help? To steal back what belongs to them?"

"Yes, but most Nations don't take us up on our offer. Not when a tribal council is involved."

"Because they're smart," she said. "They know better than to get involved in illegal activity."

He shrugged. "It doesn't matter. We've got enough missions to keep us busy. Mostly we focus on private collectors who claim that they don't have items that are supposed to be returned. Collectors who manage to elude the law altogether, who are keeping things that were robbed from graves."

"That's a noble cause, Kyle. But you can't just go around breaking into people's homes, looking for funerary objects."

"Why not? Someone stole them to begin with."

"Then do whatever you can to prove your case," she argued. "To expose these collectors and reobtain the objects legally." She paused, frowned a little. "Even if it takes years."

"We've tried that in the past, and the investigations have gone nowhere."

"So instead, you put yourself in the position of getting arrested for breaking and entering? Or getting shot and killed during a robbery attempt?"

"Yes," he responded honestly.

She sighed, and he could see that she didn't understand. That she didn't think the crime was worth the consequence.

He snared her gaze. "Do you think it's right that someone should disrespect a little girl's bones, that her skeleton should be hidden somewhere?"

"No. Of course not."

"We'll that's my current mission," he told her. "There's a private collector, an older man with tons of money, who we believe has the skeleton of an Indian child."

Joyce fussed with the quilt, and he could see that he'd unnerved her.

"I know the child's name," he said. "I know what century she was born in and when she died. And now I want to return her to her descendents, so she can be buried. So she can find peace."

"Then let me help you. We can discuss it with Agent West. We can—"

"No." He stopped her before she could continue. "I'm doing this my way. No paperwork. No red tape. No federal raids that turn up nothing."

She shook her head. "You don't have any faith in law enforcement."

He squinted at her. "Does that offend you?"

"It makes me worry. I don't want you to do something that will get you in trouble." She searched his gaze. "Will you promise me something?"

He didn't respond. Instead he waited for her to continue.

She did, only a second later. "Promise that you won't steal anything while we're still dating. No breaking and entering. No crimes."

Damn, he thought. Talk about getting screwed. "That's asking a lot, Detective."

"I can't condone what you do. I can't be with a man who's breaking the law."

"I just want to bring a little girl's remains home."

"I know. And I understand how you feel. But it's not the moral issue that concerns me. It's you getting busted. Or hurt. Or hurting someone else."

"I'd never participate in an armed robbery."

"You don't need a weapon," she countered. "You're an expert at unarmed combat."

"I would never hurt anyone. That's not what my missions are about."

She glared at him. "Either make the promise or say no."

Kyle knew this was his fault for admitting the truth, for telling a cop his secrets. But he was willing to accept responsibility, at least for while. "Fine. No crimes, not while I'm with you." He wasn't ready for their relationship to end. Not yet. "But later, when this thing between us is over, I'm doing whatever I want."

"Go ahead. But if you get busted, don't come crying to me."

He relaxed a little. Apparently she wasn't going to turn him in, run to the feds with the information he'd given her. "Now you can tell me about your personal problems. You can come clean."

Suddenly her expression changed. She made a face, then fussed with the quilt again. "Can it wait?"

He gauged the anxiety in her gestures. She was on overload, he thought. They both were. "Until when?"

"Until we get some sleep." She glanced at the clock. "We've been up all night."

Like an idiot, he caved in. "I suppose a few more hours won't make a difference." He wanted to know what was going on in her life, but he wanted to hold her, too. To let the moment settle, to let their emotions slip into slumber.

She fluffed her pillow, getting ready to lie down. "Thank you, Kyle."

"For what?" He removed his sweatshirt, but decided to leave his jeans on.

"Everything," she responded.

He accepted her answer. In his heart, he knew how important his honesty had been to her.

Together, they adjusted the covers. And when she closed her eyes, he reached for her, and she snuggled against him. They were a strange couple, he thought. But for now, he liked being with her, even if they were as mismatched as two people could get.

Nine

Joyce woke up beside Kyle. She turned on her side to look at him. He was still asleep, with his hair partially covering his face and the sheet draped around his waist.

She wanted to run her hand along his chest and down his stomach, but this wasn't the time to get sexual. She'd promised to talk about her problems.

She sat up, her nerves jangling. It was foolish to be worried. Her secret wasn't as damaging as his. He'd admitted that he was involved in illegal activity. All she was going to do was admit that she was longing to get married and have a baby. That was a far cry from telling a detective that you steal.

Kyle never ceased to amaze her. He'd offered information about himself that very few people would entrust to a cop. Which meant what? That the bond between them was growing stronger? That he wanted her to know what he was willing to risk his freedom for?

A little girl's bones, she thought. A child's remains.

Joyce tried not to get attached to the dead, to the victims associated with her job. But sometimes she did. Sometimes her emotions got in the way. Apparently Kyle had become attached to "his" little girl, a child that had probably been born over a hundred years ago.

She gave in and touched him, placing her hand against his chest, against the warm, steady beats of his heart. Then she slipped lower, brushing the waistband of his jeans.

He opened his eyes, squinting at her, and she flinched. Guilty pleasure, she thought. She'd gotten caught with her hand in the cookie jar.

Well, not *in* the cookie jar. But darn close.

"What are you doing?" he asked.

"Nothing." She took her hand away.

His lips quirked. "It felt like something to me."

She changed the subject. "Do you want some coffee? I'm going to make a pot."

"Sure." He sat up and smoothed his hair. "Did you know that I left some condoms in your bathroom from last time?"

"You did? Where?"

"Under the sink, behind your tampons."

Good grief. "We don't need them right now."

He grinned. "The tampons?"

She couldn't find the will to laugh. "The condoms." She got out of bed, her nerves jumping like frogs in a pond. "You didn't come over to have sex, remember?"

"Yeah, I remember." His grin faded. "Are you okay, Joyce?"

"I'm fine." Just fretful about telling him her secret. In her own anxiety-ridden way, she wanted to make love with him before she spilled the beans, before she started talking about babies. But she knew that would be cheating. The true test of their affair would come after she told him. After he knew her biological clock was ticking.

Not that he was going to offer to give her a baby. No, she thought. He would never do that. If anything, he would panic and consider running for the door.

Of course she had no business imagining him as the father of her unborn children.

None whatsoever.

Joyce left to make the coffee, and he waited for her. When she returned with two steaming cups, she handed Kyle his, knowing he liked it black.

"Thanks." He scooted over so she could rejoin him in bed.

She took her designated spot and sipped the hot brew. The quiet laziness appealed to her. And so did having a big, rugged, rumpled male next to her.

"You're going to think I'm crazy," she said, getting ready to tell him her story.

He shrugged, then smiled. "All cops are crazy."

"Not like me." She blew out the breath she'd been holding, expanding her lungs. "I keep freaking out about wanting a baby."

His smile disappeared. Just like that. It was gone. "Is this a joke?"

"No."

"That's why you wanted to train with me? To stop yourself from hungering after a kid?"

She winced. Then abandoned her coffee. Her stomach had begun to burn. "And a husband. I want to get married, as well."

He winced, too. But kept his coffee. "You are crazy."

"I told you."

"We sparred over your domestic urges?" He gulped the caffeine-laced beverage, swallowing a bit too loudly. "That makes me feel weird."

She could see the panic setting in. He even glanced at the door, as if he wanted to bolt. "I'm pushing forty, Kyle. These things happen to women."

"These things?"

"Biological-clock issues. Besides, remember what

you said the other morning? That given my family history, you expected me to be more marriage-minded?"

"Maybe so. But I didn't think that was the trauma in your life." His eyebrows furrowed, working into a frown. "I made a promise to you last night, and now you have to make one to me."

She angled her head. "What?"

"That you don't start caring about me too much."

Pride kicked her square in the gut, a swift blow, a wallop she couldn't deny. And on top of that, a strap on her nightgown had begun to slip. She pushed it back into place, wishing she wasn't wearing such a girly garment. "What's that supposed to mean? That you think I'm dumb enough to fall in love with you?"

"I'm not that bad. That unlovable." He seemed irritated, too. "I have my moments."

"You could have fooled me."

"Yeah, listen to you. You're hot for me."

She narrowed her eyes. "No hotter than you are for me."

"Okay. Whatever." He accepted their attraction on equal ground. "How about if we both agree not to fall in love? Not to make more of this than it is?"

She wasn't about to argue. She didn't want to fall for Kyle any more than he wanted to fall for her. "That's fine with me."

"Do you want to shake on it?" he asked.

She gave him a stupefied look. "This isn't a business arrangement."

"You're right. There's no point in going overboard." He set his cup on the nightstand. "Shaking hands would be kind of goofy. Maybe we could mess around to seal the deal."

Suddenly she forgot about being annoyed with him. She laughed instead, enjoying his offbeat charm. "Is that all you think about?"

He laughed, too. "It seems like it, huh? It must be your effect on me."

And his effect on her, she thought. She feared that getting him out of her system wouldn't be as easy as it sounded.

He flopped onto his pillow and took her hand. She put her head on her pillow, too. And for a while, they didn't speak.

Nothing. No words. No jokes. No sexual innuendos. Just a closeness they weren't supposed to share.

Finally he turned to face her. He was still holding her hand. "You're going to find the right guy someday."

Something inside her ached. Horribly. "You think so?"

"Yeah, I do. You'll be married with a baby before you turn forty."

"I don't know. At this point, I'd rather fight off those feelings."

"And tie yourself up in knots. That's not worth it, Joyce. Just let it happen when it's meant to."

It was good advice, she thought. Sound. Kind. Everything she needed to hear. He was a levelheaded man. Or he could be, when the mood struck him. "I can't imagine why Olivia's sister thinks you're dumb."

"What?" The change of topic threw him.

"Olivia's sister, Allie. She thinks you're dumb."

"No, she doesn't. Not anymore. I've been training her for nearly a year. She knows now how brilliant I am." He chuckled. "She's the airhead. Addle-brain Allie."

Joyce took her hand away and pinched him. "You're not supposed to call her that."

"Even if it's true?"

She rolled her eyes. The first disagreement they'd ever had was about his nickname for Allie. And that was on the day they'd met. Eight months ago, she thought. And now here she was, in bed with him.

Better her than Olivia. Or Allie. Or any other woman he was associated with.

She moved closer, snuggling against him, against the warmth of his flesh, the roughness of his jeans. "I think we're going to need those condoms you left in the bathroom."

He guided her hand to his pocket. "I already snagged one when you were in the kitchen. Just in case."

"What a cheater." She dug into the denim, bumping his fly in the process. "A sexy cheater." She secured the packet and glanced at the ridge beneath his zipper. "Did I do that?"

"You know damn well you did." He toyed with her nightgown, fingering the silky trim. Then he removed it, slowly, sensually, baring her breasts and exposing her panties.

When the air hit her skin, her nipples turned hard. He kissed her, then cupped her breasts, making them ache. She closed her eyes and let him put his hands all over her.

He was gentler than she expected, gentler than any man who'd ever touched her. She wanted to tell him to stop being so loving, so caring, but she didn't think he realized what he was doing.

She opened her eyes, and he discarded her panties. They were pink, like cotton candy, and she could have sworn they'd melted into thin air.

He undressed himself and pressed his nakedness against hers. The sensation made her shiver. All she wanted to do was hold him, keep him close.

They rolled over the bed, the covers bunching beneath them. Colors swirled in her mind, as pale and pastel as the sheets.

"Will you give me a key to your apartment?" he asked.

She blinked. "Why?"

"For when you go back to work. So I can come

over when you're not home and wait for you." He straddled her, nudging her thighs apart. "I'll give it back when we're not together anymore."

She agreed to give him a key. At this point, she would deny him nothing.

He used the protection, and they made warm, syrupy love. She gripped his shoulders and felt the moisture between her legs, the stimulation of each and every stroke. He penetrated her even deeper, and she lost her breath.

He filled her so fully, so completely, the lines between them blurred.

And when they climaxed at the same moment, at the very same instant, the rest of the world seemed to disappear, fading into nothingness.

Like the edges of a dream.

Kyle and Joyce spent the rest of the afternoon together. They took a shower, soaping each other down, then got dressed and headed to Santa Monica. Kyle loved the sand and the surf. The weather was overcast, bordering on drizzly, but that made it even better. To him, the beach was prettier in the fall and winter months of the year.

They stood on the pier and looked out at Pacific Park, with its oceanview Ferris wheel and other family-entertainment rides. The park was closed, but this was a weekday during an off-season.

He glanced down. The boardwalk itself was separated into two distinct sections. Part of it was made of wood, and the other part offered a long, asphalt surface, where a few locals were fishing. Overall, there weren't a lot of people around.

As Kyle and Joyce walked past the police pier substation, he slanted her an amused look. "I can't seem to get away from cops."

"No, you can't, can't you?" She took his hand, and they continued their stroll.

Suddenly he realized the magnitude of their relationship. He'd agreed to halt his upcoming mission—albeit temporarily—for her.

He frowned, and she turned to look at him. "What's wrong?" she asked.

"Nothing." He stopped to watch the wind blow her hair around her face. She looked pretty in the cloudy light. "Nothing I can't deal with later." He paused, inhaling the moisture in the air. "Do you want go down to the beach? Maybe walk on the sand?"

She nodded. "Sure."

They took a set of cement stairs and reached the bottom, where Mother Earth presented a close-up view of the Pacific Ocean. The sand felt right beneath Kyle's moccasins. He wore the same clothes he'd worn to Joyce's apartment last night. She was dressed in a similar way, with jeans and a sweatshirt. Her shoes were lace-up boots.

"I used to come here when I was a teenager," he said. "When I got stuck living with my dad. But I always came here on cold days or at night. I didn't like it as much when it was sunny and crowded."

"What about now?"

"I still prefer it when there's less people around."

"I like the beach either way," she said. "Summer days can be fun, too. The street performers, the hot dogs, the lemonade, music blaring from boom boxes."

He led her along an endless stretch of land, close to the shore, but far enough away not to get their feet wet. "I'd probably come here in the summer if I had a family. It'd be fun to haul my kids to the beach. To teach them to build sand castles or something."

She stopped walking. "I thought you didn't want to get married and have children."

"I don't." He noticed how blue her eyes were, how they reflected the ocean. "I was just saying it hypothetically."

She seemed to be focused on his eyes, too. "I wish you wanted kids."

He tried not to react, but his pulse made a disconcerting leap. "Why?"

"So you would understand how I feel."

"I do understand. I said you were going to find the right guy someday. Someday in the near future," he added.

"Before I'm forty." She laughed a little. "Everyone seems to worry about the big four-oh. Especially single women." She considered him. "How do you know that I'm going to find the right guy? You're not psychic."

"No, but I have common sense. You're beautiful and tough and sexy. A lot of men would want to settle down with a lady like you."

She shrugged and turned away to look at the ocean. He wasn't sure if she believed him.

"Maybe I should ask Olivia," he said.

She spun back around. "Ask her what?"

"When you're going to find the guy of your dreams."

"Don't you dare," she warned. "Don't you dare ask her."

"Why not? She's a damn good psychic. If anyone would know—"

"Don't do it, Kyle. Don't involve her in my petty problems."

"They're not petty, Joyce. This baby-thing is tearing you apart."

"I'm learning to cope." She grazed the side of his face, skimming her fingers along his jaw. "And you're helping me. My diversion. My sparring partner. My roll-in-the-hay lover."

He smiled at her. Her touch felt good, soft and sweet. "We haven't done it in a hay loft."

"So we'll find a barn somewhere."

"Yeah, right." He couldn't help but scoff. "As if you'd be willing to do it someplace where we could get caught."

"Okay, so maybe we'll have to skip the hay." She leaned in to kiss him, to make the moment warm and sensual.

He put his arms around her, and they held each other, with the wind blowing and the sea crashing in foamy waves. She nuzzled his neck, and he breathed in her perfume, a floral fragrance from her vanity table. He couldn't remember the name of it, but he'd watched her spray it on earlier that day.

When they separated, he was strangely aroused. More emotionally than sexually, something he didn't quite understand.

"Are you going to invite me to your parents' anniversary party?" he asked.

She gave him a surprised look. "I wasn't sure if you'd want to go."

"I'm curious to meet your family. But if you're uncomfortable taking me—"

"No. I'd like you to be there. Besides, if I don't bring you, I'll get roped into a blind date. My youngest sister threatened to set me up with her husband's boss."

A snap of masculine rivalry lashed across his chest, across his annoyed heart. He didn't want her dating anyone else, not while she was sleeping with him. "Some corporate dude, I'll bet."

"The suit-and-tie type." She bumped his arm. "Jealous?"

"No."

She seemed disappointed. "Not even a little?"

"I don't know. Maybe." He bumped her right back. "You're supposed to be mine for a while. At least until Halloween."

"Why Halloween?"

"So we can hand out candy together. At your apartment. No one trick or treats at my house."

"With the locked fence and the big, black guard dog? Gee, I can't imagine why."

"Smart aleck." He dug his moccasins into the sand. "When is the anniversary party?"

"It's on the Saturday before Halloween."

"Then it's perfect timing. I can come in costume. I can be an Indian. A big, bad Apache."

"Very funny." She grabbed his waist and pulled him tight against her, initiating a kiss.

For now, he thought, they owned the beach: the sea, the grainy soil, the shells scattered upon the shore. This was their moment, their forbidden romance, their affair.

She tasted like heaven, like everything he wanted, everything he needed. But it wasn't meant to last.

They'd both agreed not to fall in love.

Ten

Two weeks later, Kyle got ready for the anniversary shindig. He'd agreed to meet Joyce at the party because she'd gone early to help with the food and whatnot.

And now he was stressed out about arriving alone, about being judged by her family, about why he'd persuaded her to invite him in the first place.

His affection for her was getting the best of him.

After her vacation had ended and she returned to her job, he started missing her. She worked long, grueling hours. They barely got to spend any time together, just a few stolen hours, a few late-night lovemaking sessions.

And at the moment, it didn't seem like enough.

He glanced at Clyde. The rottweiler was sitting on the bedroom floor, watching him. Bonnie was there, too.

"I should know better," he said out loud.

The dogs, of course, didn't answer. They merely let him talk, let him vent in front of the mirror, where he tucked his shirt into his pants.

"She's all I think about. Me, hooked on a cop." He turned to address his companions. "How stupid is that?"

Clyde didn't react, but Bonnie perked her ears.

Kyle blew out an anxious breath, then finished getting dressed. He'd already pulled his hair into a ponytail because he thought it made him look more respectable, more reserved, if that were possible.

He went outside to get in his Jeep, and the dogs followed him to the yard, where they stayed to protect the property. Bonnie seemed to think her teeny-weeny presence made a difference. Kyle didn't have the heart to tell her otherwise.

He drove to the San Fernando Valley, where Joyce's parents lived. Their house was a two-story structure with a manicured lawn, several shady trees and a brick flowerbed.

As he neared the front door, he could hear jovial sounds of the party in progress. Luckily it wasn't a formal affair. But it wasn't a barbecue, either. It was somewhere in between, or at least that was what Joyce had told him.

He knocked, and a young woman answered. She was blonde, cute and curious. He noticed her checking him out.

"You must be Kyle," she said.

And she must be the baby of the family, he thought. The one who had threatened to set Joyce up with the corporate dude.

He nodded, affirming who he was. "It's obvious, I guess."

"Completely." She extended a greeting. "I'm Jessica, Joyce's sister. There are six of us altogether. All 'J' names." She paused to look him over again. "You're not Joyce's usual type."

"I know. She prefers a suit and tie." He met her gaze. "Or she used to. I think she prefers me now."

"You're right. She does. She would never admit it, but she's been chomping at the bit for you to show up."

Good, he thought. "Is your husband's boss here?" he asked, letting Jessica know that he'd heard about the other man.

"No." She sent him an impish grin. "But I'm glad it matters to you."

He didn't deny her claim. For now, it did matter. The lady cop was his lover, and he wasn't ready to give her up. He should be, but he wasn't.

Jessica linked her arm through his. "Come on. I'll take you to Joyce and she can introduce you around."

She led him inside, and he caught sight of a spacious living room, a colorful kitchen and a glass sunroom. The other guests were everywhere, socializing with drinks and appetizers.

He didn't have to glance around to know that quite a few people had taken notice of him. He was big and tall. He always made an impression.

Suddenly he saw Joyce. There she was, surrounded by family and friends, talking and smiling. She sat in a wicker chair in the sunroom, bouncing a baby on her lap. He couldn't tell how old the child was, but a pink headband bow and frilly dress gave away her gender.

Joyce glanced up and noticed him from across the room. As they stared at each other, the afternoon sun streaked between them, making the glass enclosure seem even brighter.

"Dang," Jessica said. "You two are intense."

Embarrassed, Kyle broke the trance. He'd forgotten the younger woman was still standing beside him.

Joyce left her chair and came toward him, taking the baby girl with her.

"I'm glad you finally made it," she said, when they were only inches apart.

"I didn't mean to be late." He glanced at the child, and she gave him a slurpy smile. He couldn't help but smile back at her.

"That's my daughter," Jessica told him. "Her name is Gail."

"How old is she?" he asked.

"Seven months. Do you want to hold her?" Before he could respond, Joyce's sister reached for the baby and plunked her in his arms. "She loves everybody."

No kidding, he thought. Gail latched onto him, like a monkey to a tree, reaching around to grab his ponytail.

"Be good," her mamma said. "Don't pull his hair."

Gail didn't listen. She tugged on it, like she was yanking his chain. Then she put her head on his shoulder and cozied up to him.

Joyce watched him with the baby, a tender look in her eyes. "She's got your number."

He tried not to make too much of it. He'd already told Joyce that he appreciated kids. "She's just like her aunt." He smoothed Gail's ruffled dress. "Feisty one minute and sweet the next."

The lady cop smiled, and they stared at each other again. He knew half the people in the room were watching them, wondering who Joyce's new lover was, but he didn't care. For now, they were still a couple.

Soon the little girl in his arms nodded off, using him as a pillow. Jessica took her daughter, leaving him and Joyce alone.

"Are you ready to meet my parents?" she asked.

He wanted to say no, but he couldn't avoid the guests of honor. This party was for them. "Sure. Why not?"

She introduced him to her mom first, who was hanging out in the kitchen with a group of older women, where a buffet-style meal was being prepared.

"Mom, this is Kyle Prescott. Kyle, this is Alice Riggs, the saint who raised six girls and put up with my dad for forty years."

"Then I'm honored," he said, grateful for Joyce's wit.

Alice, a slightly plump blonde in her sixties, laughed and shook his hand, welcoming him with genuine warmth.

When he moved closer to Joyce, the older woman seemed pleased by his affection for her daughter. He felt a bit guilty, knowing he and Joyce had agreed not to fall in love. He didn't think Alice would understand a sex-only affair.

He met some of the other ladies in the kitchen and they were warm and friendly, too. But coming face-to-face with Joyce's father wasn't so easy.

They found him in the garage, where he and his cronies gathered around a vintage car.

Joyce made the introduction, but she didn't crack a joke, not this time. "Kyle, this is my father, Brock Riggs. Dad, this is Kyle Prescott."

The men shook hands. Brock stood about six feet, with good-size shoulders and short gray hair. He had steely blue eyes and a moustache, one that reminded Kyle of a parody of a seventies cop. All he needed was a pair of mirrored shades to go with it.

Joyce's dad was stuck in a time warp.

Amused, Kyle shifted his stance. He wanted to smile, but he didn't dare. Brock was giving him a critical study.

"My daughter told me you're a Desert Storm veteran."

Joyce had mentioned him? No doubt trying to soften the blow. "Yes, sir."

"She said you're highly decorated."

"I believe in serving my country."

Brock merely nodded. "I respect that."

"Thank you." He wanted to breathe a sigh of relief.

Or salute. Or get the hell out of here and never come back.

But then Brock offered him a beer, and he figured he'd passed the test. A second later, as Joyce's dad walked over to the ice chest, she slanted Kyle a grin that made him feel like they were in high school. He gave in and grinned, too.

Brock turned around and caught them.

The older man's moustache twitched, but that was as close as his lips came to forming a smile. But for Kyle, it was enough. More than he'd expected from a retired cop who seemed hell-bent on protecting his only unmarried daughter.

* * *

After the party, Joyce dropped off her car at her apartment, changed into comfy clothes and packed a small bag. Kyle had invited her to spend the night with him, and she couldn't resist. Especially since he claimed that he had a surprise for her.

She sat next to him in his Jeep, analyzing the way he'd interacted with her family. Her parents accepted him, and her sisters and their husbands seemed to like him, too. But most of all, her nieces and nephews adored him. He'd played video games with the older kids, while the little ones had approached him with awe, bringing him their toys.

No wonder Joyce had slipped back into the marriage/baby mode. She had it bad. And it was Kyle's fault.

Of course he hadn't done it purposely. She couldn't hold her emotions against him.

He slanted her a quick glance. "I had a good time. Better than I thought I would."

"I'm glad you were there." And sad that sooner or later, he would disappear from her life. "So what's my surprise?"

He changed lanes, getting ready to exit the freeway. "If I told you, it wouldn't be a surprise. Besides, it's not that big of a deal. Just one of my whims."

"I'll bet you cleaned your house."

"Then you're going to be disappointed." He took the off-ramp that led to a desert highway. "It's still a mess."

She sat back in her seat, unable to figure out what he was up to. She supposed that was one of things she enjoyed about him. No one could call him predictable.

When they arrived at his house, he unlocked the vehicle-entry gate and drove straight to the airplane hangar.

"My surprise is in there?" she asked.

He smiled. "You're awfully curious, Detective."

"That's precisely why I'm a detective." She unbuckled her seat belt. "My inquisitive nature."

They entered the laser tag course, which at the moment, was pitch black. Joyce nearly bumped into Kyle, and he chuckled.

He flipped on the lights, but nothing spectacular happened. From her vantage point, everything looked the same as it had on the day of the picnic. Then again, in a building this big, she couldn't be sure.

"Let's go for a walk," he said. "We'll take this path."

She looked around, wondering if he'd turned the hangar into a haunted house. "Is it going to start raining? Or snowing?" She moved cautiously. "Or are the lights going to go out? Is something spooky going to jump out and grab me?"

He shook his head. "Ye of little faith. I would

never try to scare a woman who looks at pictures of dead people all day."

"I do more than that."

"Oh, that's right. You go to autopsies, too."

"That's not funny." Even if she had puked her guts up the first time she'd smelled a rotting corpse. "I help put killers behind bars."

"I know." He stopped walking. "And you work endless hours to do it."

She met his gaze. By now, they were near the faux-flower meadow. "I have tomorrow off."

"Which is why I intend to hold onto you tonight. To keep you for as long as I can."

"Oh." She softened her voice, touched by the tender possessiveness in his. "I guess that means you've been missing me."

"You have no idea." He took her hand and guided her around a fake wall.

And that was when she saw the hayloft. Instantly she knew it was her surprise.

"My roll-in-the-hay lover." She turned to smile at him. "You put that up for me."

"It gave me something to do while you were working all that overtime." He gestured to the enclosure. "Want to try it out?"

"Absolutely." She started up the stairs first. The entire structure was made of spruce logs, giving it a rustic quality. "Did you build this yourself?"

"Yes." He climbed the steps behind her. "I usually buy or lease the props in here, but I wanted to make this one."

To her, it was more than a prop. It was a heartfelt gift, something she would never forget.

Once they reached the top, they both dived into the scratchy bedding. Although it was warm and absorbent, it grazed their skin, clinging to their hair and clothes.

They looked at each other and laughed.

"This isn't what horses eat," he said. "This is what they sleep on."

"I know." She lifted a handful of the golden stalks, letting it flutter like rain. "I'm not that much of a city girl. I know the difference between hay and straw." She paused to contemplate her situation. "I guess this makes you my roll-in-the-straw lover."

Her leaned over her. "I guess it does."

She lay beneath him, studying the handsome angles of his face. "Did you really miss me that much?"

He nodded. "It frustrates me. Thinking about a woman when she isn't around."

"You don't seem frustrated now."

"Because you're here." He closed his hand over her blouse. "And I can touch you."

"You're good at that."

One by one, he released her buttons. He seemed so intense, so completely absorbed in what he was doing. He removed her tennis shoes and tugged on her jeans, determined to undress her.

When she was naked, he kissed her. A kiss so warm, so compelling, she wondered how she was ever going to replace him.

She undressed him, too. She wanted to explore his body, to roam his muscles, to skim his scars, the healed-over bullet wounds that marred his skin. She'd noticed them before, but she hadn't focused on them until now.

But tonight, everything seemed different.

More powerful. More real.

She circled the scar on his chest. "Is this from the war?"

He nodded.

"And this one?" She gestured to his leg. She knew Olivia had accidentally shot him.

"That was nothing, just a scratch." He studied her expression, her sneaky smile. "But apparently you already know that."

"Sorry, I couldn't help it." She removed a piece of straw from his hair. "Olivia told me about it."

"We've told each other things, too."

"You and her?"

He shook his head. "You and me. I've never confided in anyone like I have with you."

"Me, neither." Her pulse tripped and stumbled. Here she was in a makeshift hayloft with a man who'd become more than her playmate. He'd also become her dearest, most treasured friend.

"Are you ready for me?" he asked, holding her close, his body warm against hers.

"Yes." She knew he was talking about sex, about a physical joining. But for her, it was more than that.

Suddenly Joyce knew exactly what was happening.

She was losing her heart.

To a man she'd vowed not to love.

Eleven

On Wednesday afternoon Kyle conducted a training session with Allie Whirlwind, Olivia's younger sister. He and Allie stood on a sparring mat in his gym, with barely any communication between them.

Kyle couldn't concentrate on the lesson.

"You're not paying attention," Allie said.

"Yes, I am," he lied.

"No, you're not." Peeved, she put her hands on her hips.

Kyle analyzed Allie. She was tall and lean with waist-length hair and striking features. He used to think she was hot, but over time she'd become like a little sister to him. He'd quit noticing her in a male-female sense. Not that she'd ever noticed him that way. Allie used to think he was dumb.

He squinted at her. Maybe he was dumb, at least dumb enough to keep lusting after a cop. Joyce was working today, putting in long hours, as usual.

And he couldn't quit thinking about her.

"What's wrong with you?" Allie asked.

"Nothing." He walked over to the mini fridge and removed two bottled waters, handing her one.

She frowned at the offering. "I'm not thirsty."

"Too bad. We're taking a break. Besides, you need to drink water during a session. I've told you that before. Getting dehydrated is a health risk."

She uncapped the bottle and took a small sip. "Maybe we should spar outside today. You're always going on and on about environmental training. New challenges. A change of scenery and all that."

"I don't want to go outside."

"Fine." She plopped down on the mat, sitting cross-legged, scowling at him.

Kyle wondered if he should end the session early, if he was wasting her time.

Suddenly she quit sulking. In an instant, her mood turned chipper. "I just figured out what's bugging you."

Great. Now he had to listen to one of her addle-brained theories. He adored Allie, but her constant chatter got on his nerves.

Her dark eyes lit up. "You're falling in love with Detective Riggs."

Kyle's breath rushed out. No way was he going to let Allie mess with his emotions, not about Joyce. Not about the pact they'd made. "You're full of crap."

"Yeah, right. It's written all over your face, lover boy."

"Keep it up and I'm going to knock you on your butt."

She lifted her hind-end a smidgen, raising one cheek in the air. "I'm already on my butt. And you're just getting ticked off because you know it's true."

He crossed his arms. "I made a promise to Joyce, and she made one to me. We agreed not to let it happen."

"That's ridiculous." She shook her head. "I'll bet Joyce has already figured out how she feels."

"No way."

"Yes, way. She's a detective. It's her nature to solve crimes." She grinned a little. "And her being in love with you is a crime. You're a terrible catch."

"I am not. I—" He stopped. He wasn't about to let her trick him into some sort of half-cocked admission. He was sexually obsessed with Joyce. She'd gotten under his skin. But that wasn't the same as being in love. "You're wrong, and I'm going to prove it." He grabbed her hand and dragged her up. "We're going to your house to talk to your sister. Olivia will set this straight."

"Why? Because she's psychic? I knew she was in love with West before she did. And I knew he loved her, too."

"It's different with Joyce and me." He nudged Allie toward the basement door, practically pushing her up the stairs. "There's another man in Joyce's future."

An hour later, Kyle and Allie sat across from Olivia in the loft where both women lived. To him, the mystic décor only intensified the moment: the velvet sofa, the fantasy mural, the scented candles.

"I don't like to delve into people's lives without their permission," Olivia said, denying his request.

"That's bull," Kyle retorted. "You do readings for police work all the time."

"Joyce isn't under investigation," she informed him.

"No, but your pain-in-the-carcass sister is claiming that Joyce and I are in love, and Joyce would hate that worse than an unauthorized reading."

Olivia sighed. "Why don't I do one on you instead?"

"Fine." He glanced at Allie, irked by the smug look on her face. "I've got nothing to hide."

Olivia left her chair and scooted between him and Allie on the couch. She took Kyle's hand and held it. He didn't say anything. He knew it was easier for her to get an accurate reading if she was touching someone. Of course, she could draw information from photographs, too. Or simply from her mind. Olivia was clairvoyant, clairaudient and empathic. In addition to having visions, she heard voices and sounds in her head. But her strongest gift was feeling other people's emotions.

She tilted her head, her expression difficult to discern. Her short, choppy hair fell in multiple layers, spiking around her face. Her psychic energy came from her ancestors. All of the women in her family, aside from her and Allie, were witches—a disgrace in their culture. But she and Allie had managed to overcome it.

Finally Olivia released his hand.

"Well?" he said.

She kept her expression blank. "You're the man Joyce is meant to be with."

He cursed, using the crudest word he could think of. "You're just saying that to side with Allie."

"No. I'm not. You're going to have a baby with her. A little girl."

"She's pregnant?" His stomach tensed, fear clawing at his gut. "But we used protection. We were careful. We—"

Olivia interrupted. "This baby hasn't been conceived yet. It isn't happening now. But it's part of your future." Her voice turned soft. "And Joyce is going to be an incredible mother."

He stood up, fighting the air in his lungs, struggling to breathe. He hadn't told Olivia about Joyce's secret. He hadn't told anyone.

"Is he going to be a good dad?" Allie asked her sister, while Kyle's knees nearly gave out.

"I don't know," the psychic answered. "My feelings didn't go in that direction."

"Hmm." Allie considered the situation. "I'll bet he will be. He's weird, but he—"

"Stop talking about me as if I'm not here." He rounded on both women, not surprised that their ancestors were witches. "You cooked up this little scheme, didn't you? You put your evil heads together and came up with a plan to coerce me into marrying Joyce."

Olivia rose to her feet, looking him in the eye. "Don't be such an imbecile. I have better things to do with my time."

"I told you he's always been a bit dense," Allie interjected. "But deep down he knows better. He's just scared, the way you were when you fell in love with West."

"I can't handle this." He couldn't picture himself as a husband and father. But worse yet, he couldn't imagine being married to an officer of the law, to a woman who would force him to conform, to change who and what he was. "I have to go."

"Where?" Allie called out after him. By now, he was halfway to the door.

To end his relationship with Joyce, he thought. To talk to her as soon as she got home. To stop Olivia's prediction from coming true.

After an exhausting day, Joyce walked into her apartment to find Kyle waiting for her. Surprised to see him, she set her belongings on a nearby end table. This was the first time he'd used the key she'd given him.

He rose from the couch and turned to look at her. Joyce's pulse zigzagged. Just knowing that she loved him made her nervous. Sweetly, strangely excited.

He blew out a rough breath, and she realized that he seemed anxious, too. But not in a good way. And in addition to that, he was wearing the kind of T-shirt and sweatpants he normally sparred in, which seemed odd.

"Did you come here to fight?" she asked.

He shook his head. "To talk. I've been here for hours."

Which meant he had something important on his mind. And instinct told her what it was. She didn't have to be a genius to figure it out, to read the expression on his face. "You don't want to be with me anymore, do you?"

He closed his eyes, squeezing them shut. Then he opened them. "Can we go outside? Maybe go for a walk so I can explain why?"

"Yes, of course." She prayed that she could keep

her emotions intact, that her eyes didn't water, that her voice didn't crack.

They left the apartment and headed down the stairs. From there, they took a cement path that cut across a greenbelt.

Dusk had fallen, leaving the October sky with a deep lavender hue. Joyce was dressed in black slacks and a matching blazer, and although the weather was mild, she fought a chill.

She glanced at Kyle and noticed his frown. She didn't have the courage to admit that she loved him. Not now. Not like this.

"I had a panic attack today," he said.

She stopped walking. "You did. Why?"

"Because of something Olivia said." He pulled a hand through his unbound hair. It flowed to his shoulders, rain-straight and as dark as the night. "I went to see her because I was trying to prove Allie wrong. Allie thinks the pact you and I made is stupid and that we're already in love."

Joyce struggled to respond. Suddenly everything inside her ached. "Allie has always been a dreamer."

"I know. And that's why I wanted Olivia to set her straight."

She buttoned her jacket, warding off another chill. "So what did Olivia say?"

"She did a reading on me. And—" He stalled, fidgeting with his hands, as if he didn't know what to do with them. His sweats didn't have pockets. "She messed with my mind. She told me that I was going to be the father of your baby. That we were going to have a little girl."

Joyce nearly swayed on her feet. "There's no way I'm pregnant. My menstrual cycle was on time."

"This little girl is supposed to be part of our future, a baby that hasn't been conceived yet." He stepped back. "Can you imagine us getting married? Raising a kid? You, a cop. Me, a guy who carries an illegal firearm and plots robberies. It would be insane."

She knew he was right, that as a couple they made no sense. But that didn't stop her from loving him, from wishing that he loved her, too.

"What if Olivia wasn't pulling a scam?" he said. "What if her prediction was real? What if you and I keep sleeping together and we make a baby?" He kept his distance, not standing too close. "I wouldn't know how to provide for a family, to be that stable. You should be with someone else."

Joyce didn't want anyone else. She wanted him. But she'd seen enough destruction to know that life didn't always give you want you wanted.

Still, she battled the hurt, the loneliness, the pain-wrenching loss. In her mind's eye, she could see the wedding they would never have, the mixed-blood daughter they would never conceive.

"I didn't even tell Olivia that you wanted kids." He

dropped his arms to his sides, and suddenly he seemed sad. "But she said you'd make an incredible mom. She didn't know if I'd make a good dad. That wasn't part of the reading."

She resisted the urge to cradle her womb, to clutch her middle. "Of course you would."

"Allie thinks so, too. Me and all my goofy toys, I guess." He took a step toward her, just one small, cautious step. "Do you understand why we shouldn't keep seeing each other, Joyce?"

She nodded, and her eyes filled with the tears she wasn't supposed to cry. Unsure of what else to do, she blinked, trying to will them away, trying to look strong and steady.

He reached out to touch her, but dropped his hand instead. "I'm sorry."

"Me, too." Her voice turned fragile, and she cursed her vulnerability. She longed to put her head on his shoulder, to grieve in his arms. But she wouldn't dare. She couldn't bear to fall apart in front of him. "You should go now. There's no point in hanging around."

"Promise me that you'll take care of yourself." He released an audible breath. "That you'll be happy. That you'll find the right guy."

"I will." She swallowed the lump in her throat, knowing she was lying. "Promise me that you won't get arrested. That you won't destroy your future."

He didn't respond. He just stood there.

And as the wind stirred, blowing a soft breeze around her face, she prayed that he would change his mind. That he would tell her that he'd fallen in love with her, that she was worth the risk, that he would alter his choices so he could marry a cop.

But he didn't.

He said goodbye and walked away, leaving her alone in the dark. She watched him until he disappeared, until there was nothing left but the emptiness in her heart.

Two days had passed and Kyle couldn't sleep. So he burned the late-night oil, rummaging through his storage sheds, looking for the Tiffany lamp he'd considered giving to Joyce.

He had no idea what he was going to do once he found the damn thing. Send it to her, he supposed. Along with the key to her apartment that he'd forgotten to return.

He cursed the dust that gathered on boxes, much in the way he'd been cursing himself. His mind had been straying in a dangerous direction. He could almost imagine planting a baby in Joyce's womb, giving her the child she wanted so desperately.

Which meant what? That he could imagine marrying her, too?

Yeah, right. As if he deserved to spend the rest of

his life with her. The sweet, beautiful detective he'd shackled and blindfolded. He sounded like a sado-masochist, not a loving, caring husband.

Finally he came across the carton he was search-ing for. Frustrated, he opened it with a pocketknife and removed the carefully packed object.

Mired in confusion, he stared at the stained-glass motif on the shade. Break a woman's heart, then send her an expensive antique? That made no sense.

He could tell how much he'd hurt Joyce. He'd seen the tears in her eyes. He'd heard the pain in her voice.

Was Allie right? Did Joyce love him? And what about himself? Was he too stubborn to admit that he was in love, too? Or too scared, as Allie had suggested?

He closed his eyes, wondering what he should do. Call Joyce? Go see her? Ask her to forgive him?

He didn't like being enthralled by a woman. It went against his nature, his big, bad macho lifestyle. But worse yet was not being with her at all.

His cell phone rang, jarring him from his thoughts. He checked the readout, hoping it was Joyce. But it wasn't. The display indicated that the caller was Allie.

He answered the summons, and her voice rushed over the line.

"Kyle? I tried your house, but you weren't there."

"I'm in one of my sheds." And it was late for her to be calling him. Almost midnight. "What's going on?"

"Have you seen Joyce? Is she with you?"

"No." Instantly alarmed, his pulse jumped to his throat. "Why? What's wrong?"

"I've been trying to reach her, but she's not answering her phone. Not her home number or her cell." Allie stalled for a second, then said, "I heard on the news that two police officers were shot this evening. I think one of them was a woman. Maybe even a detective."

Oh, God. He took a deep breath, warning himself not to panic. "Are you sure? Are you sure you heard the report correctly?"

"Not really, no. I missed a portion of it. I was in the kitchen and the TV was on in the living room." She paused and made a nervous sound. "But just to be sure, I called the Los Angeles Street Station where Joyce works, but they wouldn't answer any of my questions. They wouldn't tell me anything."

"What about Olivia? What about West? They work with the police, they—"

"My sister and West went out of town on some covert FBI case. I can't reach them, either."

"Hospitals," he said, starting to panic. "Did you try—"

"No, but I doubt they would give me any information. I'm not a relative."

He turned and nearly knocked over the lamp. He wasn't a relative, either. He was nothing to Joyce. Nothing but the man who'd made her cry.

"I'm trying not to overreact, not to think bad thoughts," Allie said. "But it's awful not to know what's going on."

"I'll find out." As soon as he could breathe, as soon as he quit envisioning Joyce with a bullet through her body. If something bad happened to her, he wouldn't survive. He wouldn't make it through another day. "I broke up with her. I walked away."

"Don't beat yourself up. You were just trying to cope with your feelings."

His forced the air from his lungs. "You and Olivia weren't pulling a matchmaking scam. Her prediction was real, wasn't it?"

"As real as a psychic reading can be."

But sometimes Olivia was wrong, he thought. Sometimes she made mistakes. There was no guarantee that what she said would come true.

Not if Joyce was dead, he told himself.

Not if he'd just lost the woman he loved.

Twelve

Kyle went crazy trying to find out if Joyce was safe. The first thing he did was call the network that had reported the shootings to get more information, but the lady who answered in the news department told him that she didn't have the capability of researching the story for him. He would have to call back in the morning when the network was fully staffed.

After that, he drove everywhere, all over the city, looking for answers. He entered the Los Angeles Street Station and inquired about Joyce in person, but the desk sergeant didn't appear to believe that he was Joyce's lover. The other man refused to share any information with him. Instead, the wary sergeant treated him as though he were a criminal stalking a cop.

Kyle tried to locate her partner, a detective he'd met eight months ago when he'd first met Joyce, but that was a dead end, too. There was no one at the station who could vouch for him, who knew he'd helped the police in the past.

From there, he drove to her parents' house, but they weren't home. To him, that was a major red flag. Where would her mom and dad be at this hour? Keeping vigil at their daughter's hospital bed? At the morgue, identifying her body?

There was nothing left to do but check hospitals and morgues himself. He spent hours going from place to place, battling the tightness in his stomach, looking for the lady he loved. But he didn't find her or her family.

He wasn't able to contact Joyce's sisters. He had no idea where they lived or what their phone numbers were. And since all of them were married, he didn't know their last names. Calling the local directory wouldn't help.

At daybreak, he sat in his car, wondering if he'd missed any hospitals. Los Angeles and the surrounding areas were filled with medical centers. He didn't know where the shooting had occurred and what facility the police officers had been taken to, but he'd gone to as many locations as he could.

The morgues he'd visited had left him cold, chilled straight to the bone. If Joyce was laid out on a slab somewhere, he hadn't been directed to her body.

At this point, he was lost, alone and confused. He called Allie to check in with her, then drove to Joyce's apartment.

What else could he do but go to her house and wait? Pray that she came home, that this nightmare was a mistake, that the report Allie had heard was flawed.

He used his key and went inside. The empty apartment gave him a ghostly feeling. He walked from room to room, then remained in her bedroom, where he lifted a perfume bottle from her vanity table.

The familiar fragrance made him ache.

He would do anything to hold her again, to take her in his arms and feel her heart beating next to his. He sat on the edge of her bed. It was neatly made, the pillows fluffed, the white quilt draped like a wedding dress.

Kyle knew he wanted to marry her. He knew, without a doubt, that he wanted her to be his wife.

For all the good it did. If she never came home, then his vow wouldn't matter. All that would be left was the night he'd left her standing alone in the dark.

The night he'd ended their relationship.

Too weary to think straight, he turned on the clock radio. The small black box came alive, sending music into the air. He found a station that was reporting the local news and listened intently, but they didn't mention the shootings.

Nothing. No update.

Exhausted, he turned it off, then flopped down and closed his eyes. If he fell asleep, would Joyce appear in his mind? Kyle wasn't a dream shaman. Even if he saw her in his subconscious, he wouldn't know what it meant.

Still, he wanted to see her. He wanted to be with her, as close as possible. Even if she wasn't real.

For him, it was better than not having her at all.

Butterflies lit upon Kyle's cheek. No, not butterflies. Fingertips. Someone was touching him, but only for a second.

He squinted in the misty morning light and saw the outline of a woman standing over him.

Was this the dream he'd been hoping for? "Joyce?" he said, wondering if she was an angel or a ghost.

"What are you doing here?" she responded.

"Waiting for you." Groggy, he struggled to clear the cobwebs from his mind. Her voice sounded distant, faraway.

His lover. The woman he feared was dead.

By now, his pulse was trembling. He clutched the quilt, afraid the room might spin, that she might disappear.

Confused, he sat up. "Is this actually happening? Are you real?"

"Of course, I am. You're in my apartment. What's going on?"

He took a deep breath, filling his lungs with oxygen. He wanted to grab her and never let go. But she seemed cautious, unsure of him.

"I thought something terrible happened to you." He explained everything, starting with Allie's phone call. "I've been so scared, Joyce. So worried."

She sat next to him. Her hair framed her face and her makeup was slightly mussed. He wanted to kiss her, but he knew it was too soon. She hadn't accepted him yet.

"I'm sorry," she said. "I saw that news report. But those officers weren't shot here. It happened in Northern California."

Which made sense, the reason he couldn't find any answers last night. "Do you know if they're okay?"

"The last I heard, they were both in stable condition." She brushed his knee, a barely there touch. "You look exhausted, Kyle."

"Can you blame me? How would you look if you thought I was dead?" He wished she trusted him enough to keep touching him, to make their connection more real. "Why couldn't I find you? Where were you?"

"I spent the night at Jessica's house. I've been

there for the past few days. My sister is helping me cope with…"

Her words faded into nothingness, but he knew what she meant. Joyce was hurting over their breakup, and he hated himself for what he'd done to her. "Your parents weren't home last night, either."

"They're on a holiday. Dad surprised Mom with an anniversary trip to Hawaii."

"Why didn't you answer your cell phone? Allie left messages and so did I." He paused, unable to clear the emotion from his voice. "I kept calling all night."

She made a troubled face. "I lost my phone. Or Owen lost it, I guess. He was playing 'police radio' with it and it disappeared. It's probably buried in Jessica's yard somewhere."

Suddenly Kyle couldn't help but smile, picturing her nephew leaving her phone in a pile of kid rubble.

A second later, his smile fell. "The cops at your station wouldn't tell me anything. They didn't believe that we dated. That I was your lover."

"I'm sorry. I never told my co-workers about you."

He understood. He hadn't told his Warrior Society about her, either.

In the next instant, they both fell silent. The moment turned awkward, and he didn't know what to say. Their affair seemed like a long, lost memory. Yet they'd made love less than a week ago.

Finally, she spoke. "Maybe you should call Allie. You should tell her I'm safe."

He agreed, using his cell phone, putting Allie's concerns to rest. Afterward, he gazed at Joyce. He was nervous about admitting that he loved her, nervous about saying the words out loud.

"Are you as mixed up as I am?" he asked.

She nodded, and he breathed a sigh of relief, grateful for her honesty. Relationships had never been easy for Kyle. He'd based his life on the mess his parents had made of theirs, on the hurt and pain his mother had endured. He never wanted to do that to a woman.

Never.

But he knew he wouldn't. Not if Joyce would give him a chance.

"I'm in love with you," he said, taking the fear-induced plunge.

She all but blinked at him. "Because you thought I died?"

"Yes. No. Sort of." His nerves kicked in again. He wasn't good at expressing himself, at exposing his heart. "I started figuring out how I felt before Allie called. Before I thought something happened to you."

"Are you sure?" Her voice vibrated. "Are you absolutely sure?"

"I've never been more for sure of anything in my life."

"I'm in love with you, too." Sunlight streamed into the room, making her hair seem more golden, her eyes more blue. "But how can we make it work? We're so different from each other."

"That shouldn't matter, Joyce."

"But it does. You know it does." She stalled for a moment. "Why do you carry a concealed weapon, Kyle?"

Her question caught him off guard. He wasn't armed. He'd left his SIG at home. "It's been my way of rebelling, I guess. Of being a modern-day warrior. But I won't carry a gun anymore." He smiled a little, making a silly joke, hoping to ease the tension. "Not unless you can help me get a permit."

She smiled too, but she didn't seem any calmer than he was. When she folded her hands on her lap, he noticed that some of her fingernails were chipped, splintered, as though she'd torn them purposely, as though it were an anxiety-ridden habit, something she struggled to control.

"I'm willing to make all sorts of changes," he said. "To compromise, to do whatever I have to do for us to be together."

"That's what I wanted you to say on the night you broke up with me. I wanted you to alter your lifestyle for me, but I don't know if that's fair, if it's right." Her eyes locked on his. "You are who you are."

He feared that he was losing her, that she would never marry him, never agree to be his wife. He frowned at her. "I just told you that I wasn't going to carry an illegal firearm anymore. That it isn't important."

"What about your missions? Stealing back stolen antiquities?" She held his gaze. "I could never condone that. Never accept it. But if you gave up your missions, you'd probably resent me for interfering."

"I don't have to give up my missions. I can pursue them legally. And you can help. You and the FBI. You already said you would."

She pushed the issue. "What about the other men in your Warrior Society? How are they going to feel about you being in love with a white cop?"

"They're going to think I'm nuts," he admitted. "But they already think I'm half-crazy anyway. And if they don't accept the woman I love, then they're not my friends. They're not the brotherhood I thought they were." He turned the conversation in her direction. "Maybe this is harder for you than it is for me. You've got your family and your job to consider. What would everyone think if you got engaged to a guy like me? If I became your husband?"

"My husband?" Her breath hitched. "Are you asking me to marry you?"

"Yes." His heart blasted his chest. He'd done it.

He'd just proposed to her. "I want us to have the baby Olivia predicted. I want a future with you."

"I want that, too." She gave into her emotions, letting her eyes water, letting him see what his words meant to her. "I've been fantasizing about you being my husband all along."

He reached for her. "Please tell me that's your way of saying yes."

She fell into his embrace, nearly crying in his arms. "Yes."

He nuzzled her hair. "Are we losing our minds, Detective Riggs?"

"Yes," she said again, making him laugh. "But I'm willing to compromise, too."

"To live with me and all of my junk? To tell your family and your co-workers that you're marrying a big, bad Apache?" He pulled her onto his lap, holding her gently, refusing to let go. "You've got your work cut out for you."

"My family likes you." She put her head on his shoulder. "And my co-workers will learn to accept you. If they don't, I'll kick their law enforcement butts."

"Listen to you. Tough girl."

"I've had a good trainer." She gave him a warm, willing kiss, showing him that she needed him as much as he needed her. "A big, bad Apache who changed my life."

* * *

On Halloween, Joyce and Kyle spent the evening at her apartment. She arranged a mixture of candy in a large glass bowl, and he carved a pumpkin, giving the jack-o-lantern a big, toothy smile.

She moved to stand beside him. There were squash innards all over the kitchen table. "He looks friendly."

"I don't want to scare the little kids who come to the door. And it's a she." He pointed to the marks above the rectangular eyes. "See? Long, pretty lashes."

She studied his handiwork. She couldn't have imagined a more perfect holiday, a more perfect man. He turned to kiss her, and she tugged on his shirt, keeping him close to her heart.

Suddenly Bonnie barked, nabbing their attention, dancing happily at their feet. Joyce picked up the little pooch and nuzzled her. She was dressed like an angel, with a doggie halo Kyle had found at a pet store.

She shifted her gaze to Clyde. The rottweiler wore a set of devil horns. But he didn't seem to mind. If anything, he took it in stride, accepting the silly costume as another aspect of his loyal duties.

She set Bonnie down and went over to Clyde, kneeling to scratch his chin. Now that he realized she was Kyle's lifelong mate, he'd warmed up to her.

Kyle illuminated the jack-o-lantern with a battery-operated device that looked like a candle. He placed the pumpkin outside, preparing for trick or treaters.

When he returned, he smiled at Joyce. "Have you thought of any names?"

She adjusted Clyde's horns. "Names?"

"For our daughter."

Her pulse fluttered. "It's too soon. I'm not anywhere near being pregnant."

"Yeah, but you will be. I threw away the condoms."

"*Kyle.*"

"Don't *Kyle* me. I'm pushing forty, too. If we're going to have kids, then we need to get started."

"Don't you think we should get married first?" she teased, even though they'd been planning their wedding. She wanted a formal ceremony, so he'd agreed to wear a tux, as long as the lapels were beaded with an Apache design. She thought it was a beautiful idea.

"Oh, that's right. I proposed, didn't I?" He walked over to her and removed a plastic container—the kind that held gumball prizes—from his pocket.

She stared at it. "What's that?"

"A ring."

Joyce didn't know what to expect, a real diamond or a fifty-cent treasure. With Kyle, a woman could never be sure.

She cracked open the case and found both: an engagement ring that nearly knocked her off her feet, and a toy ring that looked as hokey as hokey could get.

Dazzled, she leaped into his arms and kissed him breathless. He tasted like dreams and wishes and wild, crazy love.

After they separated, she put a ring on each hand. He checked out the bling-bling effect and grinned.

Heaven help her, but she adored this man and all of his romantic quirkiness. Their children were going to adore him, too.

The doorbell rang, and they answered it together, handing out candy to a group of dressed-up toddlers who'd arrived with their parents.

Bonnie peeked around the corner, making the little ones laugh. Clyde stayed out of sight, but he still wore his horns.

This was Joyce's family now—her future husband, his animated dogs and the babies they'd agreed to have.

Life with Kyle Prescott would never be boring.

She reached for his hand and linked her fingers through his, where they waited for another group of kids to climb the stairs. He leaned over to peck her cheek, and she realized how lucky they were.

Later that night, when the trick or treaters were gone and the pumpkin light was extinguished, they made love in her room, touching and kissing, whispering in the dark.

He roamed her body, and she reacted to his touch.

She arched to welcome him, to let him slide between her legs. He was hard and thick and desperately aroused.

But this was more than sex, more than an erotic joining. This was a man and a woman making a commitment, a vow that left her breathless.

Moonlight shimmered through the window, sending silvery streaks across the bed. This was the first time they'd made love without protection, without a veil of latex between them.

Flesh to flesh, she thought.

She ran her fingers up and down his spine. He moved inside her, a rhythm so deep, so real, she couldn't think beyond needing him, beyond accepting him as her mate.

She looked up at him, this man she was going to marry, this man who fought to change the world. She could feel the power of who he was, of what he believed in.

Together they would make a difference. Together, their limits were boundless.

Joyce didn't believe in fairy tales. She didn't believe in knights who swept ladies off their feet. But she believed in warriors who made compromises.

He lowered his head to kiss her, and their tongues tangled, the intensity of their lovemaking getting stronger.

Wilder.

They rolled over the bed, fever raging in their blood. Beautiful, sweet, reckless heat. It was part of them, part of what fueled their attraction.

But she couldn't imagine it any other way.

She craved the fire he ignited; she thrived on it, anxious for every sensation. He did exquisite things to her, making her heart pound gloriously in her breast, making her climax in his arms.

And when he spilled into her, she held him, knowing she would love him forever.

* * * * *

BEYOND BUSINESS

by
Rochelle Alers

ROCHELLE ALERS

is a native New Yorker who lives on Long Island. She admits to being a hopeless romantic, who is in love with life. Rochelle's hobbies include travelling, music, art and preparing gourmet dinners for friends and family members. A co-founder of Women Writers of Colour, Rochelle was the first proud recipient of the Vivian Stephens Career Achievement Award for Excellence in Romance Novel Writing. You can contact her at PO Box 690, Freeport, NY 11520-0690, USA, or roclers@aol.com.

Dedicated to Oliver Lewis—the first jockey of any
race to win the Kentucky Derby.

The children of those who serve you
will dwell secure, and their descendants live
on in your presence.
—Psalms 102:28

One

"**P**lease state your name," came the computer-generated voice through a speaker mounted on a post. A pair of electronic iron gates emblazoned with a bold letter *B* and closed-circuit cameras marked the entrance to the fabled Blackstone Farms.

Leaning out the driver's side window, Renee stared up at the camera. "Renee Wilson." Within seconds the gates opened and then closed behind her as she drove through.

New state, new job and a new beginning, she mused, driving past acres of white rail fences, stone walls and verdant landscaped grassland.

She smiled and returned the wave from a man sitting atop a tractor hauling bundled hay, sat up straighter and rolled her head from side to side. She was stiff—neck, shoulders and lower back. She'd made the trip from Louisville, Kentucky, to Staunton, Virginia, in a little more than eight hours, stopping only twice to refuel her car and eat.

"Yes," she whispered softly. She *had* made the right decision to accept the position as the administrative assistant for Blackstone Farms. Living and working on a horse farm would be a new experience for someone accustomed to the pulsating kinetic energy of Miami. And as much as she loved the south Florida city, with its personality and colorful residents, Renee knew she could not have remained there.

She had not wanted to risk running into her ex-lover who'd gotten her pregnant; a man who had conveniently neglected to tell her that he was married, she thought bitterly.

Slowing at a section where the road diverged into four directions, she followed the sign pointing the way to the main house. A towering flagpole with the American flag flying atop a black-and-red one lifted in the slight breeze.

It was late October, and trees were displaying their vibrant fall colors. The odor of wet earth lingered in the crisp autumn air from a week of thunderstorms that had left the Appalachian and Shenandoah Mountain regions saturated and lush.

Renee maneuvered her sedan behind a pickup truck in the driveway leading to Sheldon Blackstone's house. She had been interviewed and hired by his son Jeremy, who would eventually become her boss upon his father's retirement at the end of the year.

She turned off the engine, scooped her handbag off the passenger seat and pushed open the door. Her shoes had barely touched the ground when a tall figure loomed in front of her. Startled, she let out a soft gasp at the same time her head jerked up.

A pair of light gray eyes under curving black eyebrows in a deeply tanned olive-brown face pinned her to the spot. The afternoon sunlight glinted off streaks of red and flecks of gray in a full head of black wavy hair. Her breathing halted, her heart pounded erratically and a lack of oxygen made her feel light-headed. There was no doubt he was Sheldon. The resemblance between father and son was uncanny. But there was something in the elder Blackstone's gaze that unnerved her.

Recovering and letting out a soft exhalation of breath, she extended a hand. "Good afternoon. I'm Renee Wilson."

Sheldon Blackstone stared at the small hand before he shook it, her fingers disappearing in his larger grasp. He wondered how the woman with the delicate features in a nut-brown face and blunt-cut, chin-length hairdo would react once he informed her that she would have to live with him instead of in the bungalow she had been assigned.

Sheldon forced a smile he did not feel. "Sheldon Blackstone."

Renee eased her hand from his firm grip. "My pleasure, Mr. Blackstone."

Sheldon angled his head while raising an eyebrow. "Please call me Sheldon. Around here we're very informal."

The smile softening Renee's lush mouth deepened the dimples in her cheeks. "Then Sheldon it is, but only if you call me Renee."

His smile became a full grin. He found her dimpled smile enchanting. "Renee it is." Cupping her elbow, he led her toward the large two-story white house trimmed in black with an expansive wraparound porch. "I have something to tell you before you settle in."

Renee glanced at his distinctive profile. High slanting cheekbones, an aquiline nose, penetrating light gray eyes and a square-cut jaw made for an arresting visage. She stopped on the first step. "Jeremy told me everything about the position during the interview, including my duties and benefits."

Sheldon turned and stared down at her. "It's about your housing."

Renee closed her eyes for several seconds. She prayed the Blackstones would not renege on their promise to provide her with resident housing or onsite child care.

"What about it?"

Sheldon crossed his arms over his broad chest. "The bungalow assigned to you is uninhabitable. Unfortunately, lightning struck the roof, setting it afire. After we put the fire out, it rained. I had a contractor assess the damage yesterday, and he said he'll have to gut it before it can be renovated."

Renee's eyes widened with this disclosure as she curbed the urge to bite down on her lower lip as she usually did when upset or frustrated. "Are you saying I can't live *here*?"

Sheldon dropped his arms and reached for her elbow again. "Let's go inside and discuss your options."

She froze, her eyes widening again. She only had one option—if she couldn't live at Blackstone Farms she'd have to get into her car and drive back to Kentucky. And while Sheldon Blackstone wanted to discuss housing options she wanted to tell him that she was a thirty-five-year-old single woman, without a permanent residence *and* pregnant with the child of a lying man who had reconciled with his wife.

"Please, Renee, hear me out. Let's go into the house," Sheldon said in a deep, quiet voice.

She stared at him for several seconds before nodding. "Okay, Sheldon."

Renee would listen to what he had to say, but felt uneasy. Why, she asked herself, couldn't she find a man she could trust; they say one thing and do the complete opposite. It had begun with her father. Errol

Wilson had been an alcoholic, liar, gambler and a philanderer.

She dated from time to time, and although she had offered a few men her passion, she refused to give any her love. But everything had changed when she met Donald Rush. She offered him everything she'd withheld from every other man, and in the end he, too, had deceived her. With the others she had been able to walk away unscathed with her pride and dignity intact, but her luck had run out. It wasn't until after she'd moved out of Donald's house and spent two months with her brother and his family that she discovered she was pregnant with a married man's child.

Renee followed Sheldon up the porch and into the house. An expansive entryway was crowded with a breakfront and beveled glass curio cabinets. Many of the shelves were filled with trophies, mementoes and faded photographs of black jockeys from the mid-nineteenth century to the present. She walked through a formal living room and into another large room with a leather seating arrangement. Streams of sunlight poured in through mullioned floor-to-ceiling windows.

Sheldon pointed to a club chair. "Please sit down." He waited for Renee to sit before taking a matching love seat several feet away. He crossed one denim-covered knee over the other. He didn't know what it was, but something told him that the woman Jeremy had interviewed and subsequently hired to computerize the farm's business records would not make it through her three-month probationary period. He'd read her résumé and although she'd been office manager for one of the most prestigious law firms in Miami, it did not compare to living and working on a horse farm. He wondered how long would it take for her to tire of smelling hay and horseflesh.

He doubted whether he would have hired Renee despite her experience and exemplary references, but that decision had been taken out of his hands. She would eventually become Jeremy's responsibility once he assumed complete control of running Blackstone Farms. The final transfer of thirty years of power would take effect January first.

His gaze moved slowly from her professionally coiffed hair to a yellow silk tunic, and down to a pair of black wool crepe slacks and leather slip-ons with a renowned designer's logo. Everything about Renee Wilson screamed big-city sophistication.

"As I said before you won't be able to live in your bungalow for a few months," Sheldon began in a quiet tone. "However, I'm prepared to open my home to you until the repairs are completed."

Renee sat forward on her chair. "I'll be living with you?" She'd vowed never to live with another man, even temporarily; but she also had to remind herself that Sheldon Blackstone would be her boss for the next two months, not her lover.

The beginnings of a smile crinkled Sheldon's

eyes. There was no doubt his suggestion had shocked her. "This is a big house. We won't be bumping into each other. I have a housekeeper who comes in several times a week to clean and do laundry. You'll have your own bedroom with a private bath, and a makeshift office has been set up for you on the back porch. If you don't want to take your meals in the main dining hall, or have them delivered, you may use the kitchen. If you prefer cooking for yourself, just let me know what you'll need and I'll order it from the head chef."

Despite her consternation, Renee affected a smile. "It seems as if you've thought of everything." Sheldon, flashing a rare, open smile, nodded. "My living here with you won't pose a problem for your…" Her words trailed off.

Sheldon uncrossed his legs, clasped his hands together and planted his booted feet firmly on the parquet floor. "Are you referring to another woman?" Renee's averted gaze answered his question. "That will not be a problem for either of us," he continued. "There are two Mrs. Blackstones—my sons' wives, Kelly and Tricia." Her head came up. "My wife died twenty years ago, and I've never been involved with *any* woman who either lived or worked on this farm."

Renee let out an inaudible sigh. "Well then, I'll accept your offer."

Sheldon hadn't lied to Renee. There were no other women in his life, hadn't been in months. He had married at seventeen, become a father at eighteen, was widowed at thirty-two and now at fifty-three he planned to retire at the end of the year.

His retirement plans included fishing, traveling and spoiling his grandchildren. He wasn't actively seeking a woman to share his life, but if one did come along who shared similar interests, then he would consider a more permanent relationship—a relationship that was certain not to include marriage. He'd failed once as a husband and didn't want to repeat it.

He hadn't lived a monkish existence since burying his wife, but at no time had he ever advertised his liaisons. All of his encounters were always conducted off the farm. No one, and that included his sons, knew any of the women who shared his bed after he'd become a widower.

"There is a slight problem," Renee said as Sheldon pushed to his feet."

"What's that?"

"I've ordered furniture and it's scheduled to be delivered here today."

"It arrived earlier this morning," he informed her, "and I took the responsibility of having everything stored at a warehouse in Richmond."

Renee sighed in relief and rose to her feet. "Thank you."

She'd sold the entire contents of her Miami condominium before moving into Donald's palatial

Miami Beach oceanfront home, and the day she left him she'd walked away with only her clothes and personal items.

Sheldon smiled at the petite woman whose head came to his shoulder. "Let me show you to your room."

"I need to get my luggage from my car."

He extended his hand. "Give me your key and I'll get it."

Opening her handbag, Renee handed him the key. A slight shock rippled up her arm as her fingers made contact with Sheldon's. She stared up at him to see if he'd felt the same reaction, but his expression was reserved.

Slipping the key into the pocket of his jeans, Sheldon escorted Renee to a curving staircase leading to the second floor. Her fingertips trailed over the mahogany banister. Their footsteps were muffled in the carpeted hallway.

Sheldon walked past three bedrooms, stopping at the last one on the right. "This one is yours. It has its own sitting room and private bath."

Renee moved beyond Sheldon and into a large, sun-filled space, feeling as if she had stepped back in time. A massive mirrored pale green armoire, the only color in the near-white bedroom, was the room's focal point. An elegant antique, white, queen-size iron bed provided the perfect complement for the armoire.

She made her way to a door in a far corner. A bathroom with an old-fashioned claw-foot bathtub, yellow floral wallpaper dotted with sprigs of leaves and berries picked up the pale green hues of an upholstered chair in a corner. Antique wall sconces added the perfect finishing touch. She left the bathroom and reentered the bedroom, noting that the bathroom's wallpaper was repeated in the sitting room.

She smiled at Sheldon as he rested a shoulder against the open door, arms crossed over his chest. His pose reminded her of a large lounging cat. "It's perfect."

He flashed an open smile. He'd thought Renee would consider the bedroom too old-fashioned. After all, she had lived in one of the country's most cosmopolitan southern cities.

He straightened from his leaning position. "I'll bring up your luggage." He turned to leave, then stopped. "Would you like something to eat or drink? Just for tonight, dinner will be served an hour later than usual."

Renee glanced at her watch. It was after four, and she was scheduled to eat again at six. Her obstetrician had recommended she eat five small meals instead of three big ones. She had just begun her second trimester, and she had gained an average of two pounds each month.

"What time is dinner?"

"Tonight it will begin at seven."

There was no way she would be able to wait three hours before eating again, not unless she wanted a pounding headache or a fainting spell.

"I'd like a fruit salad and a glass of milk."

Sheldon's expression stilled and grew serious. "Are you a health-food fanatic?"

Renee flashed a bright smile. "I decided a couple of months ago to eat healthy. No fast foods, gooey snacks or anything with additives or preservatives."

Light gray eyes studied her intently. "Perhaps you living with me will help me reconsider some of my dietary choices." His only weakness was ice cream— lots of ice cream.

"You look quite fit to me." The words were out of Renee's mouth before she could censor herself.

Sheldon gave her a direct stare. His last physical indicated he was in excellent health for a man his age. He stood six-one and weighed one-ninety, and with a break in the hot weather he'd begun the practice of leaving his truck in the driveway and walking more.

Sheldon and Renee regarded each other with a waiting that hadn't been there before. Again, Renee felt uneasy, as if she were a specimen under a powerful microscope. She did not know the owner of Blackstone Farms and she did not want to come to know him—at least not beyond an employer-employee relationship.

She would live in Sheldon's house until her bungalow was habitable, organize and computerize years of paperwork that had been done manually and come spring she hoped to deliver a healthy son or daughter. She refused to plan beyond the time her child would go from the farm's infant center to its pre-school and subsequently to the day school.

Sheldon blinked as if coming out of a trance. "I'd better go and get your bags."

His deep, soothing voice shattered the silence between them, and Renee nodded in agreement. She stood in the same spot until pressure on her bladder forced her to retreat to the bathroom.

When she returned to the bedroom she spied her bags. Two sat on the floor next to a closet, while the largest rested on a whitewashed wooden bench at the foot of the bed. Sheldon had carried up all three bags in one trip where it would have taken her at least two, maybe three.

There was no doubt he was physically fit; he was tall, broad-shouldered with a trim waist and hips. It was the first time she'd encountered a man whose magnificent physique matched his face. Sheldon Blackstone was drop-dead gorgeous.

Slipping off her shoes, she decided to shower before eating. She would have to forego what had become a regularly scheduled afternoon nap. There were times when she'd felt so exhausted that she could not keep her eyes open, but thank goodness up till now she hadn't experienced morning sickness.

The reality that she was to become a mother had changed her outlook on life. Everything she did and every decision she made was predicated on the tiny life growing inside her.

There had been a time when she was forced to give up her dream to graduate from law school. After her father drank himself into an early grave, she went to work to help supplement her mother's meager income. But her dream of graduating college was delayed for more than a decade. It had taken her six years as a part-time student, but she did it. She now held a degree in pre-law.

Renee closed her eyes and smiled. *Live for today, and let tomorrow take care of itself.* That had been her mother's mantra, and it was now hers.

Two

Sheldon drove past the area where a large white tent had been erected for the evening's pre-race festivities. Dozens of tables were covered in white linen; folding chairs, swathed white organza tied with either black or red satin ribbon, represented the farm's silks.

It had been several years since Blackstone Farms had hosted a pre-race gala. This year was different because Ryan and Jeremy had decided to enter Shah Jahan in the International Gold Cup race.

The thoroughbred had become the farm's racing secret, along with its jockey. Seeing diminutive Cheryl Carney astride the magnificent black colt never failed to make Sheldon's heart stop whenever horse and rider crossed the finish line. Cheryl's uncle and head trainer, Kevin Manning, had clocked Jahan at one minute, fifty-nine and one-fifth seconds for a mile and a quarter—the distance run by three-year-olds in the Kentucky Derby. The record was one-fifth second faster than Secretariat's fastest winning time in Derby history.

Sheldon took a right turn and headed for the stables. He maneuvered into a space between his sons' SUVs. He left his truck and walked into the veterinarian's office.

"Isn't it a little early for celebrating?" he asked at the same time Ryan and Jeremy touched glasses filled with an amber liquid.

Dr. Ryan Blackstone smiled at his father. He lifted his glass. "Not early enough. Jeremy has good news for you."

Jeremy shifted on his chair and smiled at his father. "Tricia and I just got back from the doctor. She's pregnant."

Sheldon's smile matched his youngest son's. He pumped his fist in the air and howled, "Boo-yaw! Give me some of that sissy stuff you're about to drink. Once you come over to my place I'll give you a shot of my special blend."

"No, Pop!"

"Oh, hell no."

Jeremy and Ryan had protested in unison.

"I know someone at ATF whom I'm certain would

like to test your so-called special blend," Jeremy teased with a wide grin.

Frowning, Sheldon shook his head. "I can't believe my boys have gone soft on me."

Ryan reached for the bottle of bourbon in a cabinet behind his desk and poured a small amount into a glass for Sheldon. His dark gray eyes crinkled in amusement. "You can keep that special blend. I'd rather drink something that doesn't double as paint thinner or drain cleaner."

Sheldon's expression softened. He was proud of Jeremy and Ryan. It hadn't been easy trying to raise his two adolescent boys after Julia died. That time had been a low point in his life because he'd worked around the clock to keep the horse farm solvent while attempting to provide emotional support for his grieving children.

Ryan had become a veterinarian. He'd returned to the farm to start his practice. It had taken Jeremy fourteen years, a four-year stint in the Marine Corps and a brief career as a special agent for the Drug Enforcement Administration before he'd settled down on the farm. After recuperating from an injury he'd sustained several months before during an undercover mission in South America, Jeremy had reconnected with his childhood sweetheart, Tricia Parker. Now he and Tricia would give Sheldon his third grandchild.

The three men touched glasses. Ryan and Jeremy

took furtive sips while Sheldon tossed back his drink in one swallow. He set the glass down on the desk.

"Next time buy something that doesn't taste like Kool-Aid."

Ryan frowned from under lowered lids. "There's nothing wrong with this bourbon."

Sheldon rolled his eyes at Ryan and straddled a corner of the large desk. "Renee Wilson arrived about an hour ago," he said without preamble.

Jeremy sat up straighter. "How did she take the news that she would have to live with you until her place is renovated?"

Sheldon shrugged a shoulder, the gesture quite elegant for a man his size. "I suspect she wasn't too happy about it, but she didn't show it."

Leaning back in his chair, Ryan propped his booted feet on his desk and stared directly at his father. "Jeremy told me you cussed a blue streak when he suggested she live with you."

Sheldon glared at Jeremy. "You talk too much."

Jeremy returned the glare. "Well, you did, Pop. You said words I hadn't heard since Ryan and I were kids." There had been a time when he'd used foul language because he'd heard his father use it. He paid for the infractions whenever his mother washed his mouth with lye soap. But that ended once Julia Blackstone passed away. Jeremy stopped cursing and Sheldon stopped talking. Days would go by before he would utter a single word.

"Would you like to hear a few more?" Sheldon asked.

Jeremy held up a hand and shook his head. "No, thank you. What do you think of Renee?"

"If you're asking me whether she's qualified for the job, only time will tell."

A flash of humor glinted in Jeremy's smoky gray eyes. "Personally I think she's rather cute."

Sheldon gave his youngest son an incredulous stare. "Is that why you hired her? Because she's cute?"

Jeremy sobered quickly. "No. I hired her because she's qualified. In fact, her skills are exceptional. So much so that I wonder why she'd leave a position where she earned twice what we are going to pay her to live on a horse farm."

"Only time will tell," Sheldon responded. *Perhaps she's hiding from something or someone,* he added silently. "Is Jahan ready for tomorrow?" he asked, deftly changing the topic.

He did not want to think about Renee Wilson, because like Jeremy, he, too, found her cute—very cute and quite sexy. The last woman he'd found that cute and sexy he'd married....

"He's as ready as he will ever be," Ryan answered, bringing Sheldon's thoughts back to the present. "Cheryl had him on the track with three other horses a little while ago, and for the first time he didn't seem so skittish around them. In fact he was very calm once he was led into the gate."

Sheldon stood up. "Make certain Kevin knows he's not to race him without blinkers." Kevin Manning had been Blackstone Farms' head trainer for the past fifteen years.

"We have everything under control, Pop," Ryan said curtly.

Sheldon recognized the thread of irritation creeping into Ryan's voice. Ryan thought he was being controlling again. "I'm going back to the house to get ready. I'll see you later." Leaning over, he patted Jeremy's shoulder. "Congratulations, son."

Jeremy raised his glass in a salute. "Thanks, Pop."

Sheldon glanced at his watch as he climbed the porch steps. He had an hour to ready himself before the residents from neighboring farms arrived for the social event that usually preceded a premier race.

He walked into the house, and felt her presence immediately. It had been a long time, since Jeremy and Ryan moved into their own homes less than a quarter of a mile away, since he'd shared his roof with another person.

He headed for the staircase, but then hesitated when he heard voices. Retracing his steps he walked towards the rear of the house. A slow smile softened his mouth. Renee lay sprawled on a chaise, asleep. A pair of blue sweatpants and an oversized T-shirt had replaced her tailored attire. The radio on a table blared a popular love song.

Soft lighting from a floor lamp flattered her delicate features. Sheldon moved closer until he stood directly over Renee. Her face, relaxed in sleep, appeared so peaceful, angelic.

Who are you? Why are you here? The two questions came to his mind unbidden.

He reached out and touched her shoulder. Her eyes opened and she came awake immediately. Her gaze widened until he could see the dark centers in a pair of heavily lashed eyes that were the color of rich golden sherry. Why hadn't he noticed their odd color before?

Smiling, Sheldon straightened. "I'm sorry to wake you, but you need to get ready for tonight's party."

Renee sat up and combed her fingers through her mussed hair. "What party?"

The lingering effects of sleep had lowered her voice until it was a velvety purr. Why, he asked himself again, hadn't he also noticed the sultriness of her voice? But he knew the answer even before his mind had formed the questions. It was because he did not want to be reminded that he missed female companionship. He had become so accustomed to living alone that he'd let loose with a string of virulent expletives he hadn't uttered in years the moment Jeremy suggested their new employee live with him until her bungalow was repaired.

"Blackstone Farms is hosting a pre-race party.

One of our thoroughbreds will be racing for the first time tomorrow afternoon."

Renee swung her sock-covered feet to the floor. "How often do you host these parties?"

"It's been two years since we hosted the last one. But if Jahan wins, then we'll hold a post-race celebration Sunday afternoon."

She stood up. "Do you expect him to win?"

"There is no doubt he'll win, although the odds are 12-to-1 against him."

"I know nothing about betting on horses."

"Don't worry, I'll show you."

She shook her head. "That's okay. I'd rather not."

"Are you opposed to gambling?"

Renee gave Sheldon a long, penetrating stare. A momentary look of discomfort crossed her face and filled her eyes. "Yes, because my father was an alcoholic and a gambler. A very lethal combination. He had a wife and children who needed his support."

The moment Renee had mentioned her father she was unable to conceal her vulnerability, and Sheldon's protective instincts surfaced without warning. He wanted to take her in his arms and hold her until her pain eased. However, he would not act on his impulse, because he doubted whether she would accept the gesture.

"There's nothing wrong with gambling or drinking, if done in moderation," he countered gently.

"Moderation wasn't in my father's vocabulary."

"You don't gamble or drink." His question was a statement.

"I drink occasionally."

Sheldon smiled. "If Shah Jahan wins tomorrow, will you share a glass of champagne with me?"

Renee shook her head. "I can't."

He sobered. "You can't or you won't?"

"I can't," she repeated.

"Does it have anything to do with you working for me?"

It should only be that easy, Renee thought. She hadn't disclosed her physical condition to Jeremy during her interview, yet knew it was only a matter of time before her pregnancy became evident.

"It has nothing to do with our employee-employer status." He raised a questioning eyebrow once she paused. "I am going to have a baby."

Her explanation hit Sheldon in the face with the force of a stone propelled from a slingshot. "You're pregnant?"

She nodded. "I've just begun my fourth month."

His gaze swept over her chest before dropping to her belly as if he could see under the cotton fabric to see her expanding waistline. "What about your husband?" The farm's employment application had been revised to exclude age and marital status.

Renee was hard-pressed not to laugh at Sheldon's shocked expression. "I'm not married. My baby's father was already married."

"You slept with a married man?" he asked, his tone coolly disapproving.

Pulling back her shoulders, Renee faced him down. "I didn't know he was married. Not until I came home early from a business trip and found a woman in my bed with the man whom I thought I would eventually marry."

A myriad of emotions crossed Sheldon's handsome face. "Does he know about the baby?"

"No." The single word was emphatic.

"Are you going to tell him?"

"No," she repeated.

"He has a right to know that you're carrying his child."

Renee took a step closer to Sheldon, close enough to detect the lingering scent of his aftershave, close enough to see the stubble of an emerging beard on his angular jaw.

"That's where you're wrong. He forfeited that right when he conveniently neglected to tell me he'd married a Las Vegas showgirl when he'd attended a trade show convention there. I'd left Florida before I knew I was pregnant, and I have no intention of returning or contacting him. I don't need him for child support, so that lets him off the hook financially."

Sheldon saw a different woman than the one who had stepped out of her car only a few hours before. Under the delicate exterior was an inner strength that was not apparent at first glance.

She had come to Blackstone Farms to work and live, yet had not come alone. Now he understood why she sought out a position that offered on-site child care. A knowing smile touched his mobile mouth as he recalled the number of babies born to longtime employees who were now a part of the farm's extended family. His daughter-in-law Tricia had been a Blackstone Farms baby.

"I'll call the contractor Monday and have him add another bedroom to your bungalow."

Renee looked at Sheldon in astonishment, her jaw dropping. "Why?" The query came out in a breathless whisper.

Her reaction to his offer amused Sheldon. "Every child needs his or her own room, a place to call their own."

A dimpled smile curved her lush mouth. "You're right. Thank you, Sheldon."

He gave her a direct stare. "Your thanks may be a little premature, because I'm a hard taskmaster, Renee. You'll only have three months to bring Blackstone Farms into the twenty-first century. Everything, and that includes payroll and purchase orders, has been done manually for thirty years. And that translates into thousands of pieces of paper. Jeremy wants the farm's revenue and expenses computerized before he takes over in January.

"If you need someone to assist you on a temporary basis, just ask. More importantly, if you don't understand something, ask questions." His expression softened, his gaze as tender as a caress. "I may bark a lot, but I've never been known to bite."

Within minutes Renee recognized a maddening hint of arrogance in the owner of Blackstone Farms, but there was something in his manner that soothed rather than agitated her. There was no doubt they would be able to live and work together.

"I'll make certain to remember that."

He smiled again. "Good. Now, if you'll excuse me I have to get ready for a party."

She returned his smile. "I'll be ready by seven."

Renee still saw the broad shoulders under a pale blue denim shirt as she leaned over to turn off the radio. The enclosed back porch was the ideal workspace. Screened-in floor-to-ceiling windows faced the southeast. There would be an abundance of light during daylight hours. The area where she sat on the chaise had a wrought-iron table with seating for two, an entertainment center and an adjoining half bath. She could work, eat and relax without leaving the porch.

She would take the weekend to settle in, acquaint herself with the layout of the farm and its residents, before she began the task she'd been hired to do Monday morning.

Nightfall had descended on Blackstone Farms like a translucent navy-blue veil when Sheldon stepped out onto the porch to find Renee sitting on the rocker waiting for him.

His eyes widened in appreciation as she rose gracefully to her feet. She had pinned her hair atop her head, adding several inches, and a pair of three-inch black pumps added further to her diminutive height. A black dress and matching jacket pulled her winning look together. A pair of magnificent diamond earrings adorning her lobes supported Renee's claim that she could support her child on her own.

Sheldon forced himself to concentrate on her face and not her legs. A light breeze stirred the perfume on her body, and he froze. The fragrance had been Julia's favorite.

Renee saw his startled look. "Is something wrong?"

"No," he said a little too quickly. "You look very nice."

A wave of heat washed over her face, settling in her cheeks. "Thank you. So do you." Sheldon's dark suit looked as if it had been tailored expressly for his tall frame.

He moved closer, extending his arm, and he was not disappointed when Renee curved a hand over the sleeve of his suit jacket. "Thank you very much."

Renee was certain Sheldon could feel her trembling. There was something about the man that disturbed her—in every way, and she knew an attraction to him would be perilous to her emotional well-being. She hadn't missed the smoldering flame of

awareness in the gray orbs when he'd stepped out onto the porch. The flame had flared to life before he'd
successfully shuttered his gaze.

Sheldon looked good, smelled good and felt even
better. Her hand rested lightly on his sleeve, yet she
felt the power in his arm as hard muscle flexed under her light touch.

"Aren't you going to close the inner door?" she
asked as he escorted her off the porch.

Sheldon covered her hand with his free one,
squeezing her fingers gently. "My door always stays
open until I retire for bed. The same goes for everyone who lives on the farm. That is one of the few
mandates everyone is expected to follow."

She glanced up at him as he led her to a luxury sedan parked in the driveway behind his pickup truck.
"What are the others?"

"One is that you leave the key to your vehicle in
the ignition in case it has to be moved in an emergency, and the most important one is all residents must
check in with one another during violent weather."

Sheldon opened the passenger side door and she
slid onto the leather seat, mentally filing away the
mandates. There was no doubt her life on the farm
would be vastly different from the one in Miami.

Her mouth went suddenly dry as she watched
Sheldon remove his jacket and hang it up on a hook
behind his seat. Suddenly everything about him
seemed so much larger, broader. He sat down and

turned on the ignition and automatic seat restraints lowered over their chests and waists.

Turning his head, Sheldon stared at Renee. "Is the belt too tight for you?"

She met his gaze, the lights from the dashboard illuminating his eyes. "It's fine, thank you."

She was relieved that she had revealed her pregnancy; however, she did not want Sheldon to make allowances for her because of her condition.

Sheldon shifted the car into gear and backed out of the driveway. Within minutes they arrived at the area where tiny white bulbs, strung over fences, around branches of trees and the poles holding up a massive white tent, sparkled like flawless diamonds. He maneuvered into a parking space. Taped music flowed from large speakers set around the party perimeter in anticipation of an evening of dining and dancing under the autumn sky.

Sheldon slipped into his jacket, then came around the car to assist Renee, his right hand going to the small of her back. She stiffened slightly before relaxing her spine against his splayed fingers.

"I want to introduce you to my daughters-in-law before it gets too crowded," he said close to her ear. Lowering his arm, he reached for her hand, holding it gently and protectively in his warm, strong grasp.

Renee followed Sheldon as he led the way across the tent to a table where two women sat laughing hysterically. Sheldon cleared his throat and their heads came up at the same time.

Both were pretty, but the one with dark slanting eyes in an equally dark brown face was stunning. Her short curly hair was cut to complement her exquisite features.

Sheldon released Renee's hand, reached out and gently pulled Tricia Parker-Blackstone from her chair. Lowering his head, he kissed her cheek. "Congratulations. I'm so happy for you and Jeremy."

Smiling broadly, Tricia hugged Sheldon. "Thank you, Pop."

He held her at arm's length. "How are you feeling?"

"Not too bad. The nausea comes and goes."

He noticed the direction of Kelly and Tricia's gazes. Shifting, he extended a hand to Renee. He wasn't disappointed when she placed her hand in his. "Kelly, Tricia, I'd like for you to meet Renee Wilson, our new administrative assistant. Renee, these are my daughters, Kelly and Tricia. Kelly is headmistress of Blackstone Farms Day School and Tricia is the school's nurse." The three women exchanged handshakes.

Kelly Blackstone had draped a red silk shawl over a flowing black tank dress. She smiled at Renee. "It looks as if you came on board at the right time. Blackstone Farms is renowned for hosting the best pre-race party in Virginia's horse country."

The words were barely off Kelly's lips when a booming voice sliced the night. "Hey, Blackstone! I heard that you have a wonder horse better than the legendary Affirmed." A tall, florid-faced man with tousled silver-blond hair nodded to Tricia and Kelly. "Ladies."

Renee watched Sheldon's expression change, become somber. It was obvious he wasn't too fond of the middle-aged man.

"Someone has been lying to you, Taylor," Sheldon said quietly. "I'm certain you've seen the odds."

Kent Taylor, owner of Taylor Stables, stared boldly at Renee. "That's only because no one outside Blackstone Farms has seen him run."

"You'll see all you'll need to see tomorrow afternoon," Sheldon countered.

When it was obvious Sheldon wasn't going to introduce Renee, Kent Taylor's too-bright grin faded. "Are you saying I should put some money on Shah Jahan?"

"No, I am not." Sheldon's voice was a dangerously soft tone, his southern drawl even more pronounced. "I suggest you bet on something that is a sure thing."

Kent sobered. "Now that sounds like a challenge to me."

A mocking smile crinkled Sheldon's eyes. "That's why we have horse races, Taylor."

Kent nodded in agreement. "Tonight I'm going to enjoy your food and liquor. Sunday afternoon I'll return the favor when I host the post-race victory celebration."

Sheldon's face was marked with loathing as his closest neighbor turned and walked away with an exaggerated swagger. He did not know why the man always attempted to turn the sport of horse-racing into a back-alley brawl.

Kelly grunted softly under her breath. "Now I see why he's been married so many times. No normal woman would be able to tolerate his overblown ego for more than a week."

Tricia waved a hand in front of her face. "He smells as if he's been sampling his own liquor cabinet before he got here."

Within minutes of Kent Taylor's departure Ryan and Jeremy arrived, carrying plates for their wives.

"Taylor just passed us, talking trash as usual," Ryan said, as he set a plate on the table in front of Kelly.

"He's a blowhard," Sheldon spat out.

Jeremy, leaning on a cane, extended his free hand to Renee. "Hello again, and welcome to Blackstone Farms."

She shook his hand before repeating the gesture with Ryan. Sheldon's sons had inherited his dramatic good looks and commanding manner.

Sheldon's arm moved up and around Renee's shoulders. He lowered his head and asked, "Hungry?"

Her head came up, her mouth within inches of his. "Starved."

Smiling, he winked at her. "Good. Come with me."

Renee lay on her side in the darkened bedroom, smiling. She was tired, but too wound up to sleep.

Her first day at Blackstone Farms had become a memorable one. She'd attended her first pre-race party, met people whom she would get to know in the coming weeks and she'd found herself drawn to a man whose roof she would share until her own house was ready to move into.

She closed her eyes, a whisper of a sigh escaping her parted lips. Renee remembered, before sleep claimed her, the power in Sheldon Blackstone's arm whenever it circled her waist. There had been nothing sexual in the gesture, even though his touch communicated comfort and protection: two things she would need in the coming months.

Three

When Renee had gotten up earlier that morning she did not know she would become a participant in a spectacle resembling a fashion show rather than a horse race. She'd called her brother to let him know she had arrived safely, then waited another hour before calling her mother. Her mother had remarried two years before and had relocated to Seattle, Washington, with her new husband and stepchildren.

The weather was picture-perfect for a horse race. A bright blue sky with a few puffy white clouds, temperatures in the midseventies, moderate humidity, no wind and a slightly damp track from an early morning shower set the stage for Virginia's annual International Gold Cup.

She sat in a private box at the Great Meadow racetrack with Sheldon, Ryan, Kelly, Jeremy, Tricia and Kevin Manning, the trainer. Those in the grandstand representing Blackstone Farms had pinned red and black boutonnieres to their lapels.

Renee felt Sheldon's muscled shoulder as she leaned into him. "Why didn't you tell me I'd have to walk the red carpet to get to your box?" Many of the women occupying the private boxes were decked out in haute couture and expensive jewelry.

Sheldon gave Renee a sidelong glance. She had worn her hair down and the ends curved sensuously under her jaw, framing a rounded face that had enraptured him from first glance.

"There was no reason to say anything to you," he said close to her ear. "You have exquisite taste in clothing, and your natural beauty is a refreshing alternative to these plastic women with their designer labels, baubles and surgically altered features and bodies. Some of them have nearly bankrupted their husbands and boyfriends because they view aging as a terminal disease."

Renee did not have time to react to Sheldon's compliment as the voice blaring through the public address system garnered everyone's attention. The horses competing for the International Gold Cup were being led into position at the starting gate.

She peered through a pair of binoculars at the horses. A shiver of excitement coursed through her as she spied Cheryl Carney's petite figure in black-and-red silks atop the magnificent black stallion.

An eerie hush descended over the track as jockeys settled their horses. After several anxiety-filled minutes the gates opened and the horses and riders shot forth.

Renee was on her feet like the others in the box, mouth gaping, heart pounding, legs trembling. Shah Jahan streaked around the track in a blur, his hoofs seemingly never touching the earth. Jeremy and Ryan were shouting at the top of their lungs while Sheldon pounded the railing of the box with both fists. Kevin stood paralyzed, eyes closed, hands fisted, praying silently.

Halfway around the track it was evident the other horses would never catch Shah Jahan. Recovering her voice, Renee screamed along with everyone else. Cheryl and Jahan raced across the finish line eight lengths ahead of the second-place winner, and Renee found herself lifted off her feet and her mouth covered with an explosive kiss that sucked oxygen from her laboring lungs.

Her arms came up of their own volition and curled around Sheldon's neck. She lost herself in the man *and* the moment. Without warning the kiss changed from shared jubilation to a soft, gentle caress and then to an urgent exploration that left her mouth burning with a fire where she literally swooned in Sheldon's arms. Somehow she found a remnant of strength to pull away. Her head dropped to his shoulder as she inhaled to clear her head and slow down her heartbeat.

"Sheldon." She'd whispered his name.

"Yes?" he gasped as he buried his face in her fragrant hair.

"Please, Sheldon," Renee pleaded, "let me go."

Slowly, deliberately he did let her go. Sheldon stared over Renee's head, his gaze meeting and fusing with Ryan's.

A smile inched up the corners of the veterinarian's mouth as he winked at his father. "We did it, Pop."

Sheldon set Renee on her feet and nodded. "Yes, *you* did."

Jeremy leaned over and pounded Sheldon's back. "We've just broken the track record!"

The words were barely out of his mouth when the employees of Blackstone Farms pumped their fists, shouting, "Boo-yaw!" The grandstand reverberated with their victory cry.

The chanting continued as Sheldon leaned over and handed Ryan two betting slips. "Take care of these after you and Jeremy stand in for me in the winner's circle." Kevin had left the box, heading for the winner's circle.

Ryan shook his head. "We can't, Pop. We're not the owners."

"Today you are," Sheldon countered. "You and Jeremy better go join Kevin and Cheryl."

Jeremy stared at his father. "You're kidding, aren't you?" He had expected Sheldon to leave the box and pose for photographers and talk to reporters from major cable sports channels, magazines and newspapers.

Sheldon shook his head. "No, I'm not."

"You can't, Pop!"

His eyes darkened like angry thunderclouds. "Please don't tell me what I can or cannot do." His expression changed like quicksilver, softening as he lowered his chin, smiled at Renee and reached for her hand. "Renee and I will meet you back at the farm."

Those in the Blackstone box stood numbly, watching as Sheldon led Renee away.

Jeremy stared at Ryan. "What's up with them?"

Ryan shook his head at the same time as he shrugged a broad shoulder under his suit jacket. "Beats the hell out of me, little brother."

Kelly looped her arm through Ryan's. "Stay out of it, darling."

He gave her a questioning stare. "Do you know something I don't?"

Kelly pressed a kiss to his smooth cheek. "I'm pleading the Fifth." She had noticed Sheldon staring at Renee, a look she was more than familiar with whenever Ryan looked at her.

Ryan opened his mouth again, but she placed her fingertips over his lips. "They are expecting the

Blackstones to join their winning horse and jockey in the winner's circle."

Ryan grasped his wife's hand and followed Jeremy and Tricia out of the box. He shook his head, grinning broadly. "Pop and a woman," he whispered to Kelly. "I suppose there is hope for the old man after all."

Sheldon helped Renee into his car before rounding the sedan to sit behind the wheel. His decision not to talk to the media was based upon his initial opposition to enter Shah Jahan in the International Gold Cup race. He'd felt the thoroughbred wasn't ready to compete, but Ryan and Jeremy had overruled him and therefore the victory was theirs.

He started up the car and left the parking area, heading for the interstate. Once he set the cruise control button, he chanced a quick glance at Renee. She sat motionless, eyes closed and her chest rising and falling gently in an even rhythm. He returned his gaze to the road in front of him before risking another glance at her flawless face. Being pregnant agreed with her. She was exquisite, her skin glowing like brown satin.

He recalled the violent expletives he'd spewed after Jeremy suggested Renee live with him until her bungalow was ready. He guarded his privacy with the zealousness of a leopard secreting his kill from marauding scavengers. He did not want someone to monitor his comings and goings. Ryan had become accustomed to his declaration of "I'm going to be away for a few days." He had made it a practice of spending two or three days each week at his mountain retreat, but that would change because of the petite woman sitting beside him.

A smile stole its way across his face as he recalled the taste and softness of her mouth and soft fullness of her breasts when he kissed her. The action had begun impulsively before it changed into a deliberate, purposeful need to possess her mouth and more. The *more* wasn't sleeping with her—that he could do with other women, but an inclination to take care of her.

Why Renee, he did not know. But in the coming months he was certain he would find out.

A slight smile played at the corners of Renee's mouth as she turned her head slightly and stared from under lowered lids at the man sitting beside her. He had discarded his suit jacket and tie, and unbuttoned the collar to his crisp white shirt. He was so virile and masculine that she forced herself to glance away.

The memory of his kiss still lingered along the fringes of her mind. The initial joining of their mouths was shocking, unexpected. But everything had changed once she kissed him back with a hunger that had belied her outward calm. The caress of his lips and the solid crush of his body had sent spirals of desire through Renee that she hadn't wanted to acknowledge, because Sheldon was her boss—a man who wore his masculinity like a badge of honor.

"Where are we going?" she asked after seeing a road sign indicating the number of miles to Staunton. The farm was in the opposite direction.

"Somewhere to celebrate." Sheldon winked at Renee when she gave him a questioning look. "Do you like ice cream?"

"Does Don King need a hair transplant?"

There was a moment of silence before deep, rumbling laughter filled the sedan. Those who were familiar with Sheldon Blackstone would have been stunned by the sound, because it had been nearly twenty years since they'd heard his unrestrained laughter. He hadn't laughed out loud since he'd become a widower.

Renee found Sheldon's laughter infectious. She joined him, and within seconds they were laughing so hard he was forced to pull over onto the shoulder of the road.

Sheldon was still smiling as he rested an arm over the back of the passenger seat. Sobering, he gave Renee a long, penetrating look and marveled that she could laugh given her circumstances. She'd walked away from a position, one in which she'd been paid well, to work on a farm because a man she'd lived with had betrayed her.

Life had dealt her two losing hands when it came to men; first her father, then her lover. Had Renee been unlucky in love or had she unconsciously fallen in love with a lover with the same failings as her father?

In another five months she would deliver a baby and he wondered whether Renee would change her mind and contact her ex to inform him that he had become a father?

The questions bombarded Sheldon as his expression changed, growing tight with a realization he did not want to think about. There was something about Renee Wilson that reminded him of his late wife, something that evoked emotions he hadn't felt since he was seventeen.

An hour after he'd been introduced to Julia he'd known he wanted to marry her. But he didn't want to marry again. The truth was he wouldn't risk his heart again to the devastation he'd felt when Julia had died. He had failed Julia as a husband and he'd long ago vowed that he would never make that mistake again. He could not propose marriage to Renee as he had with Julia, but he intended to offer her and her child his protection as long as she was a resident of Blackstone Farms. He would do no less for any employee.

He removed his arm from her seat, put the car in gear and headed for downtown Staunton.

Sheldon escorted Renee into Shorty's Diner. The popular restaurant on Richmond Road had become a favorite with locals and tourists. All stainless steel with neon lights and colorful glass, it was an exact replica of a 1950s jukebox. They were seated at the last remaining table and given menus.

Sheldon watched Renee as she looked around. "It's not fancy, but the food is good."

"Fancy doesn't always mean good," she countered. "I once ate at a Miami Beach restaurant, which will remain nameless, whose construction costs exceeded three million dollars. The food was horrific."

"Are they still open?"

"Unfortunately, yes. People go there because the owner paid off the food critic, and right now it's the place to go to be seen. The paparazzi hang around every night, hoping to get a glimpse of the celebrities who congregate there."

Reaching across the table, Sheldon placed a hand on Renee's, tightening his hold when she attempted to extract her fingers. "Do you miss Miami?"

She closed her eyes and shook her head. When she opened them she gave him a direct stare. "No, I don't. Once I decided to leave I knew I'd never go back."

He eased his grip, but did not release her hand. "What do you want?"

A slight frown furrowed her smooth forehead. "What do you mean?"

"What do you want for yourself? Your future?"

Renee could feel Sheldon's sharp eyes boring into her. His gaze was penetrating, but there was also something lazily seductive in the look. It had only taken twenty-four hours to feel the seductive pull of his spell. And if she hadn't needed a job or a place to live she would've driven away from Blackstone Farms and its owner minutes after coming face-to-face with him. Yet there was something in the light gray eyes that communicated that she could trust him to protect her and her child.

"I want to complete my probationary period without mishap, move into my own bungalow, go to law school and give birth to a healthy son or daughter. Not necessarily in that order," she added with an enchanting, dimpled smile.

A network of attractive lines fanned out around Sheldon's luminous eyes. "I certainly can help you with your probationary status. I'll tell Jeremy to waive your probationary clause."

"You can do that?"

Sheldon removed his hand. His strong jaw tensed. "I can. Besides, you don't need any added stress in your life at this time."

Renee was hard-pressed not to kiss him. A warm glow flowed through her as her features became more animated. "Thank you, Sheldon."

He angled his head and gave her a sensual smile. "You're welcome, Renee." There was a pulse beat of silence before he asked, "Are you hungry?"

She shook her head. "No. I can wait for dinner."

He closed the plastic-covered binder. "Then we'll have some ice cream."

Renee and Sheldon returned to Blackstone Farms to find Ryan sitting on the porch waiting for them. He'd changed out of his suit and into a pair of jeans, boots and a cotton V-neck sweater. He rose to his feet, his expression grim. He handed Sheldon a large manila envelope.

"I thought you should see this before it's aired later on tonight on ESPN. There's no doubt it will also appear in the *Virginian-Pilot*."

Renee turned to make her way into the house, but Ryan reached out and touched her arm. "You should also see this, Renee."

She hadn't realized her heart was pumping wildly until she saw the photograph of her and Sheldon locked in a passionate embrace in the box at Great Meadow. The picture was taken at the exact moment she'd put her arms around his neck. The kiss had only lasted seconds, but the image of her kissing the owner of Blackstone Farms would last forever.

"Who gave this to you?" Sheldon had spoken to his son, while his gaze was fixed on Renee's shocked expression.

"Eddie Ray."

Sheldon shifted his attention on Ryan. "Are you certain it's going to be televised?"

Ryan nodded. "Eddie freelances for several tabloids and he loves uncovering scandals."

"There is no scandal," Sheldon retorted. The scowl marring his handsome face vanished as he stared at Renee. "I'm sorry to have put you in a compromising position."

Renee's smile belied her uneasiness. "Don't beat up on yourself. Neither of us can undo what has already been done."

She peered closely at the photograph. Only her profile was discernible, but the diamond studs Donald had given her as a graduation gift glittered in her lobes. Biting down on her lower lip, she prayed no one would recognize her in the arms of the man who owned Virginia's most celebrated African-American horse farm—especially Donald Rush.

She had left Florida believing Donald would never follow her; but what if he linked her to Sheldon Blackstone of Blackstone Farms and uncovered that the child she carried was his? Despite his deception, would he be vindictive enough to wage a legal battle for custody? There was no way she could win against a man who had amassed millions of dollars as a toy manufacturer. Unshed tears glistened in her eyes.

"I have to go inside." She had to get away from Ryan and Sheldon before she embarrassed herself.

Sheldon watched the screen door open and close behind Renee's departing figure. He waited a full minute, then let loose with a diatribe that included what he wanted to do to Eddie Ray.

Ryan slipped his hands into the pockets of his jeans, rocking back on his heels. "Folks outside the farm are going to want to know who the mystery woman is."

"Who she is is none of their damn business!"

"There's already been talk, Pop."

"What about?" Sheldon snapped angrily.

"About you and Renee. You were all over her last night like white on rice, and today at the track the two of you looked like a…" His words trailed off.

"We looked like what?"

Ryan ignored his father's angry glare. "A couple."

"Is that how you see us, Ryan? As a couple?"

The veterinarian gave a sheepish grin. "From what I've seen of the two of you—yes."

Sheldon put the photograph into the envelope and thrust it at Ryan. "Go home to your wife and children," he drawled. Turning, he pushed open the screen door and walked into his house.

He had to talk to Renee and reassure her that he would do everything in his power to protect her from salacious gossip. Horse farms had all of the characteristics of a small town. Any rumor was a prerequisite for scandal. Climbing the staircase to the second floor, he made his way along the hallway. Her bedroom door stood open. He rapped lightly. There was no response; he knocked again, then walked in.

Renee sat on a chair in the sitting room, her bare feet resting on a matching footstool. Although her eyes were closed, he knew she was not asleep.

"Renee?"

Her eyes opened and she stared at him as if he were a stranger. Her lower lip trembled as she smiled through the moisture shimmering in her gold-brown eyes. "I'm okay," she lied smoothly.

The truth was she wasn't okay, because if Donald saw the photograph he would know the identity of the woman in Sheldon Blackstone's arms.

Sheldon did not believe Renee. She looked delicate, vulnerable. He moved closer, reached down and pulled her gently off the chair. He gathered her to his chest, resting his chin on the top of her head.

"What are you afraid of, Renee?"

She tried to slow down her runaway heartbeat. "What makes you think I'm afraid?"

"You're trembling."

The possibility that Donald would attempt to contact her at Blackstone Farms held her captive with fear. "I don't want him to find me," she sobbed against Sheldon's chest.

Cradling her face between his palms, he kissed her eyelids, his tongue capturing the moisture streaking her cheeks. "Don't cry, baby." She quieted as he comforted her, his hand moving over her spine. "Who is he, princess?"

She sighed softly. "His name is Donald Rush."

"What does he do?"

"He's a successful toy manufacturer."

Easing back, Sheldon anchored a hand under her chin and raised her tear-stained face. "You will be safe here. No one, and I mean no one, can come on-to the property without being detected. And if he comes after you, then we'll have a surprise for him."

"What?"

"He'll be shot for trespassing."

Renee smiled despite her anxiety. "I hope it won't come to that."

"The decision will be his. Enough about Donald Rush." A frown settled into his features. "Now, we have to talk about you and me."

Her eyes widened. "What about us?"

"Ryan reports there's been gossip about us being a couple."

Her mouth dropped open. "But we're not," she said, recovering her voice.

"*We* know that. But, what's going to happen once your condition becomes evident?"

Pulling out of Sheldon's loose embrace, Renee walked over to a window and stared down at the leaves of a towering tree that had turned a brilliant red-orange. She turned and met his gaze.

"You think they'll believe I'm carrying your baby?"

Sheldon closed the distance between them. "I'm certain some people will believe that."

"What are we going to do, Sheldon?"

He crossed his arms over his chest. "Let them believe whatever they want."

She raised her eyebrows. "You don't care?"

"No. I stopped listening to gossip a long time ago."

"What do you propose?" Renee asked.

"Let me take care of you," Sheldon said without hesitating.

Renee's mind was spinning in bewilderment. Why was Sheldon giving her double messages? He'd said they weren't a couple—and they weren't. Then in the next breath he'd offered to take care of her.

"How?"

"Live here with me until the spring and become my hostess at all social events on and off the farm."

Her eyelids fluttered, her emotions spun out of control and she tried to digest his proposition. Not only would she work for Sheldon, but she would also live with him beyond the time he had projected her bungalow would be ready for occupancy. She would also become an actress whenever she stepped into a role as his date at social functions.

"Will this arrangement be on a strictly business level?"

Sheldon studied Renee thoughtfully for a moment. His eyes drank in her delicate face, unaware of the smoldering invitation in their silvery depths.

"It would be if I were your boss," he said in a deep, quiet voice.

She blinked once. "But you are my boss."

"Effective midnight, October thirty-first, I will officially retire as CEO of Blackstone Farms."

"But that's next week." There was no mistaking the shock in her voice.

Sheldon nodded. "I can't ask you to host a party for me if I'm your boss. That would be slimy *and* unethical."

Let me take care of you. His words came rushing back, and Renee stared at the man who within twenty-four hours had offered her what neither her father nor Donald had or could: his protection.

Tilting her chin in a defiant gesture, Renee gave him a challenging look. "You didn't answer my question, Mr. Sheldon Blackstone. Business or pleasure?"

He leaned in close, close enough for his breath to caress her cheek. "That decision will have to be yours, Miss Renee Wilson."

Renee felt in control for the first time since viewing the photograph. Sheldon was so compelling that her heart fluttered wildly in her breast. His nearness was overwhelming, presence potent.

Smiling, she said softly, "Strictly business."

Sheldon nodded, dipped his head and brushed his mouth over hers. He pulled back. "Business it is."

Renee stood, rooted to the spot as Sheldon turned and walked out of her bedroom. Once she realized what she'd agreed to, she floated down to the armchair and rested her bare feet on the tapestry footstool.

Living at Blackstone Farms would give her a

chance to heal as she prepared for a new life for herself and her unborn child. However, she had to be very careful, because she had no intention of permitting herself to succumb to Sheldon Blackstone's intoxicatingly sensual spell.

Four

The televised footage of the International Gold Cup and the image of her kissing Sheldon were both aired on ESPN, compounding her anxiety that Donald might recognize her.

Renee existed in a state of fear, believing that Donald would show up at Blackstone Farms demanding to see her. One day became two and eventually a week before she was finally able to relax.

She found the cooler morning and evening temperatures a welcome respite from Miami's sultry heat and humidity, and the task of bringing Blackstone Farms into the electronic age challenging. It had taken a day to set up a system for an electronic payroll procedure and two more to program a database for purchase orders. Her respect for Sheldon increased appreciably once she realized the amount of money needed for a horse farm's viability. And despite the glitter and glamour of pre- and post-race parties the behind-the-scenes work was ongoing: feeding, grooming and exercising thirty-four thoroughbreds, mucking out stalls, daily medical checkups for lameness and other equine maladies and the repair of paddocks and posts.

A knock on her office door garnered her attention. Swiveling on her chair, she saw Sheldon's broad shoulders filling out the doorway. Dressed in a pair of jeans, boots and pullover sweater, he presented a formidable figure in black.

She gave him a bright smile. "Good afternoon."

Sheldon winked at her. "Good afternoon. I came to tell you that Kelly has recruited us to help make jack-o'-lanterns."

It was Friday, Halloween and an official Blackstone Farms school holiday. The faculty and staff had organized a read-a-thon for students, in grades four to six, reading from the works of Mary Wollstonecraft Shelley, Bram Stoker, Edgar Allan Poe and J.K. Rowling.

Renee raised her eyebrows. "I've never made a jack-o'-lantern."

Sheldon studied Renee. He'd found her fresh-scrubbed face and her hair piled haphazardly atop her head innocently alluring. The image of her in his bed and her hair spread over his pillow popped into his head and popped out just as quickly. He did not want to lump her into the category of the other women who'd shared his bed, but would never share his life.

He had deliberately avoided her because he needed to know whether he was attracted to her because of her feminine sensuality or because he really liked Renee Wilson.

Even though he had kept his distance, he still could not stop thinking about her. It was October thirty-first, the day he intended to announce his retirement. After today, he intended to openly pursue her, hopefully satisfying his curiosity.

"It gets easier after you mutilate your first dozen or so."

The dimples in her cheeks deepened as her smile widened. "What happens to the ones that don't make it?"

"They become pies."

She wrinkled her nose. "How very convenient. Give me a minute to save these files."

Sheldon watched Renee shut down her computer and put her desk in order. If he had had any doubts as to her qualifications they were quickly dashed once she convinced Jeremy to set up the farm's payroll account with a local bank that offered service-free accounts to new depositors. Actual payroll checks would be replaced with electronic transfers, thereby eliminating the need for paper.

Renee turned off the desk lamp and stood up. "Where are we going to create these masterpieces?"

"The school's cafeteria." Sheldon glanced down at her feet. She had on a pair of sensible low-heeled boots. "Do you feel up to walking?" The school was a quarter of a mile from his house.

"I don't mind walking, but I will need a jacket." The oversized cotton knit tunic was perfect for moderate afternoon temperatures, but Renee doubted whether it would be adequate after the sun set.

Extending his hand, Sheldon closed the distance between them. "If it gets too cool for you I'll get someone to drive you back."

"What about you?"

"The cool weather doesn't bother me."

Renee placed her hand in Sheldon's, smiling when he squeezed her fingers gently. There were calluses on his palms, indicating he was certainly no stranger to hard work.

Waiting until they had stepped out into the bright early afternoon sunlight, Renee asked, "How did you get into the horse-racing business?"

A faraway look filled his eyes as he pondered the question, contemplating how much he wanted to tell Renee about his past. He decided to be forthcoming.

"I hadn't planned on racing horses. My father was a tobacco farmer, as was his father before him. They grew and harvested some of the finest tobacco in the state, but that ended when my mother died from lung cancer. She had a two-pack-a-day cigarette habit that literally consumed her. As she lay dying she made Dad promise two things: marry her and stop growing tobacco."

"Did he marry her?"

Sheldon nodded. "Yes, but it was not what you would consider a legal union."

Renee glanced up at his distinctive profile. "Why not?"

A muscle in his jaw tensed. "My mother worked for him."

A tense silence enveloped them as they walked. "Your father was white and your mother black," Renee stated after a prolonged silence. Sheldon's eye color, hair texture and features were characteristic of someone of mixed blood.

The tense lines in his face relaxed, and Sheldon nodded again. "Virginia's miscegenation law would not permit them to marry."

"But you say they were married."

"There was no license nor any record of the marriage at the courthouse. A black minister who swore an oath of secrecy performed the ceremony. James Blackstone buried his wife, and three months later harvested his last tobacco crop.

"Dad took his life savings and bought twenty-two horses. It's ironic that he knew nothing about breeding horses, but told everyone he was a quick learner. And he was right. He made huge profits selling horses to farmers and for riding.

"He wanted me to go to college, then eventually take over from him. But I told him I didn't want to be a horse breeder. We argued constantly. After one particularly hostile exchange, I drove to Richmond and enlisted in the army."

"How old were you?"

"Seventeen. I know it broke Dad's heart because he knew I would be sent to Vietnam. I went to South Carolina for basic training, met a girl there, fell in love and married her before I was shipped out. I was assigned to Special Forces and trained as a sniper."

Renee remembered his comment about shooting trespassers. "Did you and your father ever reconcile?"

"Yes. After Julia wrote and told me she was pregnant, she went to live with Dad."

"Why didn't she stay with her folks?"

"They felt she had disgraced them by marrying out of her social circle."

Renee's delicate jaw dropped. "You're joking?"

"I wish," Sheldon drawled. "Julia's family, the Grants, believe they are the black elite, aristocrats of color."

Sheldon released Renee's hand, curved an arm around her waist, picked her up and moved quickly off the road. Within seconds a pickup truck sped past them.

She leaned into Sheldon; her heart pounded in her

chest as he set her on her feet. She hadn't heard the truck. "You must have ears like a bat."

He smiled down at her. "If you live here long enough you'll be able to hear a frog croak a mile away."

Tilting her chin, Renee met his amused gaze. "I like living here. I thought it would be boring and much too quiet after living in Miami."

"I'm glad you like living here, because I like you, Renee."

"Thank you. It makes it easier to work together if we like each other."

His light gray eyes captured her warm gold-brown ones. "I don't think you understand my liking."

"What is there to understand, Sheldon?" she argued softly. "You *like* me."

Tightening his hold on her waist, he pulled her gently under a copse of trees. "I don't think you understand how much I like you, Renee. Maybe I should show you." Lowering his head slowly, deliberately, he brushed his lips against hers.

Renee clung to him like a drowning swimmer as his warm, moist, demanding mouth called, and she answered the call. This kiss was nothing like the one they'd shared in the box at Great Meadow. It was persuasive, coaxing. A fire she had not felt in a long time flared to life, and standing on tiptoe she opened her mouth to his probing tongue. Curving her arms under his shoulders, she communicated silently that she liked him, too—a lot.

She had spent a week telling herself that she had not been affected by Sheldon's kiss, that she did not find him attractive and that their agreement to pose as a couple was preposterous.

She had told herself that women gave birth to babies every day without a husband or a man in their lives, yet with each month bringing her closer to motherhood she knew that was not the kind of life she wanted for herself. She wanted someone with her whenever she went for her checkups; someone to massage her aching back and legs because she wasn't used to carrying the extra weight; someone with her in the delivery room to share her joy once she brought her son or daughter into the world.

She wanted that and so much more, but refused to think of the more.

Sheldon couldn't get enough of Renee. He kissed her mouth, the end of her nose, her eyes and then moved to the hollow of her fragrant throat. Nothing mattered except the woman in his arms.

He smiled when Renee giggled softly. "What are you laughing at?" he whispered in her ear.

"You," she whispered back. "I think you've made your point."

As he eased back, his gaze caught and held hers. "I don't think I have."

Her smile faded, and the pulse in her throat fluttered erratically, making swallowing difficult. "What are you talking about?"

Sheldon pressed a kiss to her ear. "I'm a little rusty when it comes to the dating game, so you're going to have to help me out before we make our debut as a couple."

Renee anchored her palms against his chest, pushing him back. "When?"

"Next month. I've committed to attend the wedding of a friend's daughter."

She rested her hands on her hips. "Next month," she repeated. "Tomorrow is next month."

"It's three weeks from now."

"Three weeks will give me enough time to shop for something to wear. My body is changing rapidly." He reached for her, but she moved out of arm's reach. "If you need me to act as your date or hostess you're going to have to let me know well in advance, because I'm extremely busy. After all, I do work nine-to-five, and I also have to have time to see my obstetrician."

The mention of an obstetrician sobered Sheldon as if he had been doused with cold water. Although Renee's body hadn't displayed the obvious signs of her pregnancy he was always cognizant that she was carrying another man's child—a man from whom she was hiding.

He nodded. "I'll give you the dates and events of my social commitments. I'll also take you to Staunton tomorrow so you can shop for whatever you need. Does this meet with your approval, princess?" he teased.

She affected an attractive moue, curtseying gracefully. "Yes, your highness."

Laughing, Sheldon reached for her hand and they returned to the road. "Look," he said, pointing upward.

Renee squinted up at a large bird flying in a circle. "Is that a hawk?"

"Yes. There was a time when we didn't see too many of them. But since it's illegal to kill them they've made a comeback."

Sheldon waved to two men in a truck going in the opposite direction, the cab of the pickup loaded with fencing to replace the worn posts along the undeveloped north section of the property, property he had deeded to his grandchildren.

He had purchased the two thousand additional acres because of rumors that a developer wanted to erect half a dozen subdivisions on the site. New homes meant an influx of people, cars and pollution that would impact on the natural beauty of the horse farms with stately manor homes, miles of forests divided by hedges, white rail fences and stone walls. He had joined the other farm owners whose mission was to halt the encroachment of development in the region.

Renee walked into Blackstone Day School's cafeteria to a flurry of activity as a group of women carved faces into pumpkins, while Kelly and Tricia Blackstone filled cartons with already carved specimens wearing funny and grotesque cutout expressions.

The school that had begun as an early childhood care center was expanded to include up to grade six. The children from Blackstone Farms and many others from neighboring farms had become recipients of a superior education taught by a staff of highly qualified teachers.

Kelly glanced up, flashing a smile when she spied her father-in-law and Renee. "Thank you guys for coming."

"How many do you have left?" Sheldon asked.

"About sixty."

Renee stared at the small round pumpkins lining the stainless steel countertop. Their stems, tops and seeds had been removed. "How many have you carved?"

Kelly wiped the back of her hand over her forehead. "I lost count after a hundred and thirty."

Sitting on a stool, Renee picked up a small knife with a wicked-looking curved blade. She stared at Ryan's wife. It was the first time she noticed the absence of a southern drawl in her beautifully modulated voice.

"Why do you carve so many?"

"You'll see why after they're lighted," Kelly said mysteriously.

Renee's curiosity was piqued. "Do you light them with candles?"

Kelly nodded. "Tea lights."

Sheldon sat down next to Renee and picked up a marker. "How artistic are you?"

She wrinkled her nose. "Not very," she admitted.

He handed her the marker. "Draw your face, then I'll show you how to use the knife."

Renee drew two hearts for the eyes, a circle for a nose and a crooked grin for the mouth. She gave Sheldon her pumpkin and within seconds he'd cut out a face sporting a silly-looking expression.

"Very, very nice, princess," he crooned.

"Thank you," she whispered back.

They spent the next two hours making jack-o'-lanterns. This year's jack-o'-lantern production differed from the prior ones. Only ten pumpkins would be turned into pies.

Renee sat at a table in the dining hall with Sheldon, Jeremy and Tricia, totally amused by the number of children outfitted as hunchbacks, werewolves, pirates, skeletons, vampires, princesses, clowns and a popular wrestler. It was the first time school-age children and their parents from the other horse farms had come for the Halloween holiday celebration.

The dining room staff had prepared a buffet feast reflecting the holiday: dem rattlin' bones spareribs; tombstone taters: baked potatoes with bacon, grated cheddar cheese and sour cream; creepy crawlers: shrimp served with a Cajun sauce in a spicy mayonnaise; deviled eggs; devil's food cake and peanut butter cupcakes. A large bowl was filled warm nonalcoholic apple cider.

Sheldon stood up, waiting until the babble of

voices became a hush, followed by complete silence. His silvery gaze swept over those whom he had come to regard as his extended family. They were hard-working, loyal people who were directly responsible for the farm's success.

A melancholy expression flitted across his features. "I'd like to welcome our neighbors to Blackstone Farms' annual Halloween celebration, hoping you'll enjoy yourself enough to come again next year. I say this because I will not stand here next year to meet and greet you because I'm retiring—tonight." His announcement was followed by gasps.

Ryan leaned back in his chair at a nearby table and stared at Jeremy; their expressions mirrored confusion. Sheldon nodded to Jeremy before repeating the gesture with Ryan.

Sheldon knew he'd shocked his sons with the announcement that he was stepping down two months early. He'd decided not to tell Ryan and Jeremy because he was certain there would be a confrontation. He'd spent the past year dropping hints that he wanted to retire because he'd tired of the day-to-day responsibility of running the farm, while they'd spent the past year denying the inevitable.

"I've waited thirty years for this day, and I'm blessed to have two sons who will accomplish feats I can only dream about. Jeremy, Ryan, I love and trust you to continue Blackstone Farms' quest for the Triple Crown."

Kevin pumped his fist, shouting, "Boo-yaw! Boo-yaw! *Boo-yaw!*"

The Blackstone victory cry reverberated throughout the dining hall as others joined in. Sheldon held up a hand until the room grew quiet again.

"Ryan and Jeremy will share equal control of the farm. Jeremy will be responsible for finance and personnel, and Ryan will provide day-to-day oversight." He had selected Jeremy as the chief fiscal officer because he'd earned a business degree from Stanford. Turning to Jeremy, he extended his hand. "Now, please get up and say something profound."

Renee watched Jeremy lean over and kiss his wife before coming to his feet. He'd brushed his rakishly long black hair off his face, revealing tiny diamond studs in his pierced lobes. There was no doubt the next generation of Blackstones would march to the beat of their own drum.

Jeremy flashed a crooked smile as everyone applauded. He gave Sheldon a quick glance. "My father asked that I say something profound. To tell you the truth I really can't come up with anything except to say that hopefully twenty years from now I can stand here and pass the torch to my nephew Sean."

Five-year-old Sean waved his fist the way he'd seen his father, grandfather and uncle do. "Boo-yaw, Uncle Jeremy." The room erupted in laughter.

Placing two fingers to his forehead, Jeremy saluted Sean. "Boo-yaw to you, too, champ. I know everyone wants to eat and celebrate the holiday, so I leave you with this. Shah Jahan and Cheryl will accomplish what no other horse has done in decades. They *will* win the Triple Crown." The Boo-yaws started up again as people came over to the table to wish Jeremy the best.

Looping her arm through Sheldon's, Renee asked, "Who or what is Boo-yaw?"

Sheldon covered the small hand on his arm. "He was our first champion." He had been their first Derby winner and the last race Julia attended. A week later she'd died in his arms.

He smiled down at her. "After we eat we'll take a hayride."

She glanced up at him from under a fringe of thick lashes. "I hope you don't think I'm going to roll around in the hay with you."

Throwing back his head, Sheldon let loose with a peal of laughter. The room went suddenly quiet as everyone turned and stared at him. He sobered quickly, returned their stares until their attention was refocused elsewhere. Renee tried to suppress a giggle, but she was unsuccessful. Burying her face against Sheldon's shoulder, she laughed until her sides hurt.

Curving a hand around her neck, Sheldon whispered, "I'm going to get you for that, Renee."

"I'm so-o-o-o scared, Sheldon," she said, still laughing.

"You should be," he countered. His hand trailed down her spine, coming to rest on a rounded hip. She went completely still as her gaze widened. "Now, say something else," he threatened softly.

The warmth of his hand penetrated the fabric of her slacks, and Renee was hard-pressed not to squirm in her chair. She met his gaze as he looked at her as if he were photographing her with his eyes. He had stoked a gently growing fire she was powerless to control.

She had left Florida because of one man, and had come to Virginia to start over. It had only taken a week and she found herself falling under the spell of another man who made her want him in spite of herself.

The very air around them seemed electrified with a waiting, a waiting for the next move. Sheldon's nearness made her senses spin as his potent energy wrapped around her in a sensual cocoon that made her want to take off her clothes and lie with him.

A hint of a smile softened her mouth as she fluttered her lashes. "Please get me something to eat before I faint on you."

Sheldon removed his hand, stood up and pushed back his chair in one motion. She watched him as he cut the line. Three minutes later he returned to the table and set a plate on the table in front of her. "What do you want to drink, princess?"

"Milk. Please make certain it's fat-free and ice-cold."

Sheldon flashed a saccharine grin, then left to do her bidding. He didn't know whether he was good for Renee, but knew for certain she was good for him.

She made him laugh, something he hadn't done in years. And she made him look forward to his retirement with the expectation of a young child opening gifts on Christmas Day.

Yes, he thought, he was going to enjoy being a couple.

Five

Hundreds of lighted jack-o'-lanterns lined the roads of Blackstone Farms like an airport runway; a full moon, the second in the month, silvered the countryside in an eerie glow added to the magic of the night.

The cool night air seeped through the fibers of Renee's bulky pullover sweater, and she snuggled closer to Sheldon, sharing his body's heat. She had taken her first hayride in a horse-drawn wagon. The driver stopped, dropping off and picking up passengers along a northbound route; children gathered on padded mats in the schoolyard, crowded around a large oil drum from which blazed a bonfire, listening to ghost stories while eating cotton candy, popcorn and candied apples.

She sat on the grass with Sheldon and stared up at the star-littered sky. "The moon looks close enough to touch." Her soft voice whispered over Sheldon's throat.

Sheldon pressed his mouth to her hair. "The second full moon in any month is called a blue moon. However, Native Americans have named every full moon in the calendar."

"What are the names?"

"January is full wolf moon, February full snow moon and March full worm moon."

"What do they call October?"

"Full hunter's moon."

"How do you know so much about Native American folklore?"

"Growing up my best friend was a Delaware Nanticoke boy. His family moved to Virginia the year he turned four."

"Where is he now?"

There was a moment of silence before Sheldon said, "He died in Vietnam."

Shifting, Renee put an arm around his neck and rested her head on his shoulder. She was sorry she'd asked because each time she questioned Sheldon about someone the subject of death surfaced: his mother, his wife and now a childhood friend. His life was filled with the loss of loved ones while hers had been filled with disappointment.

"I'm sorry." The two words, though whispered, sounded unusually loud.

"I'm not sorry you're here," Sheldon mumbled in her hair.

A smile lifted her mouth. "Why?"

"Because you make me laugh, Renee."

"Are you saying I'm funny or silly?"

A chuckle rumbled in his chest. "No. It's just that you're good for me. You remind me that life shouldn't be so serious."

"I'm glad I can make you laugh."

Sheldon tightened his hold around her waist. "What do you want from me?"

Renee refused to acknowledge the significance of his query. Did he actually want her to tell him what she wanted from him as a man? That she wanted to trust a man enough to protect her and her child?

Could she tell Sheldon that the more time she spent with him the more confused she became? That her feelings for him intensified each time he touched or kissed her.

"I want a friend," she said instead. "Someone I can confide in, someone who will laugh and cry with me in the good and not so good…." Her words trailed off as she realized how vulnerable and needy she must sound to Sheldon.

His warm breath caressed her parted lips as he lowered his head and tasted her mouth.

"What do you want from me, Sheldon?" Her query was a shivery whisper.

Sheldon pulled her closer. "I want to be your best

friend, I want to protect you *and* your child and I'd like you to live with me."

"But I am living with you," she countered.

"No, Renee, we are sharing a house."

Strange and disquieting thoughts swirled through Renee, his words not registering on her dizzied senses. "You want sex?"

A low, rumbling laugh bubbled from his throat. "Why do you make it sound so sordid?"

"Because I tell it like it is?"

Sheldon sobered. "You've misunderstood me, Renee. I've been widowed a long time, and until meeting you I had no idea how lonely I've been." His lips came coaxingly down on hers. "I want companionship, princess."

Parting her lips and swallowing his breath, Renee kissed Sheldon leisurely, lingering and savoring his scent, the feel of his firm mouth. There was no mistaking the hardness he pressed against her. She smothered a groan and bit down on her lower lip. The urge to roll her hips against him was so strong that it frightened her.

Her hands came up and cradled his face, thumbs sweeping over the elegant ridge of his cheekbones. He was offering her everything she wanted and needed, everything except marriage. But even without a promise of marriage she wondered whether she could trust him?

"I don't know, Sheldon." *I don't know if I can trust you,* she added silently.

He placed a forefinger over her lips. "You don't have to give me an answer. Come to me when you're ready."

"What if I'm never ready?"

"Then we'll remain best friends."

Renee lowered her hands, curving her arms under Sheldon's shoulders. They sat motionless, holding each other until the sound of the approaching wagon propelled them off the ground for the ride back to the main house.

The sound of tires crunching gravel drowned out the cacophony of nocturnal sounds serenading the countryside. A knowing smile curved Sheldon's mouth as he waited for his late-night visitors. Renee had retired to bed, but he hadn't been able to sleep. His mind was too active, too wound up after he'd bared his soul to Renee. He left bed, pulled on a sweatshirt over a pair of jeans, then came downstairs to sit on the porch.

Vulnerability, something he hadn't experienced in years, had slipped under the barrier he had erected to keep all women at a distance. The women who knew him were aware that he would offer them his passion, but never his heart. However, in the span of a single week a woman had unknowingly woven her way into his life and into his heart.

Sheldon sat forward on the rocker. The sound of doors closing was followed by booted footfalls on the porch steps. "What took you so long?"

Ryan climbed the stairs and sat on the glider, leaving his brother to take the chaise. "You were expecting us?"

Sheldon gave Ryan a long, penetrating stare. "But of course."

"Are you all right, Pop?"

Sheldon shifted his attention to Jeremy. "I'm fine," he countered sharply. "Why would you me ask that?"

Jeremy ignored his father's clipped tone. "You announced your retirement without giving us prior warning."

"I told you I was retiring at the end of the year. But with Jahan's win I decided to push it up."

Clasping his hands between his knees, Ryan leaned forward. "Are you sure that's the reason, Pop?"

Sheldon's jaw tightened as he glared at Ryan before pinning his angry gaze on Jeremy. "What's going on here?"

"Jeremy and I...we thought that something might be wrong and you were trying to conceal it from us."

Realization slowly dawned. Sheldon closed his eyes and shook his head. This scene was a repeat of one that had occurred twenty-one years before. He'd sat down with his sons and told them their mother was ill—terminally ill. Julia had discovered a lump in her breast, but refused to go to a doctor until it was too late. She'd waited until after Boo-yaw's Derby victory to tell her husband that she was dying. Her excuse was that she hadn't wanted to bother him.

It had been the first and only time he'd raised his voice to his wife. His tirade ended with him weeping in her arms because he hadn't been there for Julia when she needed him. That had been the first and last time he'd let anyone see him cry.

Sheldon opened his eyes. "There's nothing wrong with me."

Jeremy's dove-gray eyes narrowed. "Are you sure, Pop?"

"Do you want to see the results of my latest physical?"

"No, Pop." Jeremy reached over and patted Sheldon's shoulder. "I'm just glad you're okay."

"Me, too," said Ryan. "Sometimes it's hard to tell with you because your moods run hot and cold."

Jeremy winked at Sheldon. "I've noticed lately that you're running more hot than cold. Does a Miss Wilson have anything to do with that?"

There was a long pause before Sheldon said, "Yes."

Ryan moved off the glider and thumped his father's solid back. "Good for you."

"Boo-yaw!" Jeremy said in a loud whisper.

A flash of humor crossed Sheldon's face before his expression changed, becoming somber. "Thank you for worrying about your old man."

Jeremy swung denim-covered legs over the side of the chaise and stood up. "You're not old, Pop. We just don't want anything to happen to you. Tricia and I would like to give you at least three grandchildren before we turn forty."

Sheldon nodded his approval. "What about you, Ryan?"

"Kelly and I talked about having one more."

Sheldon nodded again. "Six grandchildren. I like the sound of that."

"Good night, Pop," Ryan and Jeremy said in unison as they prepared to take their leave.

"Good night," Sheldon said in a quiet voice. He felt as if a weight had been lifted from his chest. He'd even surprised himself after admitting to Jeremy and Ryan that he was attracted to Renee; he'd never disclosed his involvement with a woman to them before. He suspected his sons believed he had been celibate for the past two decades. That meant for twenty-one years he had successfully kept his private life private. All of that would change in a month once he attended the wedding with Renee, he thought with a wry smile.

Sheldon and Renee left the farm Saturday morning for Staunton. On the way they shared a gourmet brunch at the Frederick House, a small hotel with a tearoom in the European tradition.

Sheldon left her at a specialty boutique, promising to return in an hour. The one hour became two as she tried on undergarments, tunics, slacks and dresses that artfully camouflaged her fuller breasts and expanding waistline.

She finally emerged from the dressing room to find Sheldon sitting on a delicate chair reading a newspaper. His head came up slowly. Smiling, he stood up.

"Are you ready?"

Her gaze met his. "I have to pay for my purchases."

He took her arm. "I already paid for them. They'll be delivered to the farm Monday."

Renee tried escaping his firm grip, but his fingers tightened like manacles. "I don't need you to pay for my clothes."

"Let's not argue *here,*" he warned in a dangerously soft tone.

"No. Let's not," she retorted between her teeth. Seething, she followed him through the rear of the boutique and into the adjacent parking lot. "I don't need or want you to pay for anything for me."

Sheldon opened the passenger side door to his pickup truck, caught her around the waist and swung her up to the seat. He glared at her, then closed the door with a solid slam.

Once it became apparent that he wasn't going to respond to her protests, Renee crossed her arms under her breasts and stared out the windshield. Sheldon took his seat beside her, turned on the engine and shifted into gear. The silence inside the vehicle swelled to a deafening pitch.

She did not want Sheldon to believe she was destitute. Although she'd lived with Donald she also had retained her independence. She paid her own bills, and when Donald offered to give her one of his many cars, she had refused it. In the end she was able to walk away with what had belonged to her and her dignity.

"I have to make a stop." Sheldon's voice broke the silence five minutes later. He pulled into a parking space at a supermarket.

"I'll wait here for you," Renee mumbled.

He shrugged a shoulder. "Suit yourself." He left the truck and made his way into the store. She was still pouting when he got into the truck and handed her a large paper sack.

"You can repay me for *that* if you want to."

Renee peered into the bag. It held two half-gallon bottles of fat-free milk. "Very funny, Sheldon," she said, biting back a smile.

"Think of it as a peace offering."

"How can it be a peace offering when we haven't had a fight?"

Suddenly his face went grim. "And we won't. We may not agree on everything, but one thing I will not do is fight with you." He had made it a practice never to argue with a woman. It was not his style.

"Why did you pay for my clothes?"

"Because I asked you to go out with me, not the other way around. Does that answer your question?"

There was a pulse beat of silence before Renee nodded. "Yes, it does."

His expression softened. "Good."

Resting his right arm over the back of her seat, he trailed his fingertips over the nape of her neck. "How would you like to hang out with me for the rest of the day?"

Renee shivered as much from the feathery stroking motions on the sensitive skin as from the gray orbs boring into her with a silent expectation. It was easy, too easy, to get lost in the way he was looking at her. She studied his face, feature by feature, committing them to memory while curbing the urge to trace the shape of his black curving eyebrows, the bridge of his aquiline nose and firm mouth with her fingers.

Desire, want and need swooped at her innards, and she shuttered her gaze quickly before he read her licentious thoughts. Sheldon Blackstone was the first man she'd met who made her want him just by staring.

"Okay, Sheldon. I'll hang out with you." She heard his audible sigh. It was apparent he'd been holding his breath.

Leaning closer, he pressed a kiss to her forehead. "Thank you."

Sheldon took the sack with the milk off her lap and put in a space behind the seats, then drove out of the supermarket's parking lot, heading in a westerly direction.

* * *

Renee woke up ninety minutes later surrounded by towering pine trees. The truck had stopped. Her lids fluttered as she peered through the windshield at the forested area.

"Where are we?"

Sheldon got out and came around to assist her. "Minnehaha Springs."

Dry leaves and pine cones crackled under their booted feet. "Are we still in Virginia?"

"Yes. But we're only fifteen miles from the West Virginia state line." Wrapping an arm around her waist over a lightweight jacket, Sheldon led Renee toward a house erected in the middle of a clearing. "Let's go inside the cabin, because once the sun sets the temperature drops quickly."

Renee glanced up at a structure that looked more like a chalet than a cabin. She waited as Sheldon unlocked the front door and touched a panel on the wall. Within seconds the entire first floor was flooded with golden light. She walked in, staring at a stone fireplace spanning an entire wall.

Sheldon reached for her hand. "This is where I hang out whenever I need to get away from the farm."

Her stunned gaze swept over a space that was comparable to the health spa she had frequented in South Beach. Ceiling fans, track lighting, skylights, gleaming wood floors, white-on-white furnishings, floor-to-ceiling windows and a wrought-iron staircase leading to a second-story loft provided the back-drop for a space that invited one to enter—and stay awhile.

"It's beautiful."

"It's peaceful," Sheldon countered. "Wait here while I get the milk from the truck, then I'll give you a tour."

The house contained three bedrooms. The master bedroom and bath took up the entire loft. There were two other bedrooms on the first floor. The larger had an adjoining bath with a massive sunken tub, free-standing shower and a steam room. A full, function-al kitchen, living/dining area and a family room completed a space constructed for maximum living, dining and relaxing comfort.

Renee sat in the kitchen on a tall stool, munching on raw carrots, washing them down with milk and watching Sheldon as he rubbed ground spices onto the steaks he had taken from the freezer and quick-ly defrosted in the microwave.

Her gaze moved leisurely over his tall, slender body. He moved around the kitchen slicing and sautéing foods as if he'd performed the tasks on a daily basis. Then she remembered his mother had been a cook.

"Are you certain you don't want me to help you?"

He gave her a sidelong glance before he focused his attention to the temperature gauge on the stove-top grill. "Don't you know how to sit and relax?"

"I sit all day."

Drying his hands on a towel, Sheldon closed the distance between them and hugged her. "After you have your baby you'll look back on this moment and wished you'd taken advantage of it."

Renee went completely still. It was the first time Sheldon had made reference to her having a baby since the day of the race. She found it odd that he was willing to be seen with her in public when there was certain to be gossip once her condition became evident.

Tilting her chin, she stared up at him staring down at her. "You're probably right."

"I know I'm right. It's not easy for a woman to balance work and motherhood. That's the reason I set up the farm's child-care center. Some of the mothers wanted to go back to school to either begin or resume careers, but couldn't find anyone to watch their children. With Tricia as the school's pediatric nurse most of them don't have to miss days if their children aren't feeling well. It will be even easier for you because you work on the farm."

"Having on-site child care was the reason I accepted the position."

Sheldon wanted to tell Renee that he was glad she had been hired. Once he'd acknowledged his growing attraction for her he thought about her unborn child, asking himself whether he wanted to become involved with a woman with a baby when his youngest son, at thirty-two, was going to make him a grandfather for the third time. He had taken early retirement at fifty-three to kick back and relax, not play surrogate father.

The questions had bombarded him when he least expected them, and the answer was always the same: yes. Yes, because Renee made him laugh—something he hadn't done in a long time. And yes, because she unknowingly had elicited from him a profound longing for a woman he hadn't felt in years. What amazed him was that she hadn't flirted with him as some women did. She had just been herself. He had found her strong, independent, but whenever the topic of her ex came up she exhibited a vulnerability that made him want to do everything in his power to protect her.

Sheldon reached up and wiped a residue of milk from her top lip with his thumb. "Did you drink a lot of milk before you got pregnant?"

Dimples winked in her flawless cheeks as she gave him a warm smile. "No. Instead of craving potato chips and pickles like other women, I have an insatiable thirst for milk."

"Milk is a lot healthier than chips and pickles." He kissed the end of her nose. "When are you scheduled to go to the doctor?"

A slight frown appeared between Renee's eyes. "Next Friday. Why?"

"I'll go with you."

She stared, complete surprise on her face, as an

unexpected warmth eddied through her. She wanted
to ask Sheldon why, but the word was lodged in her
constricted throat.

Renee nodded her consent, not trusting herself to
speak. He was offering her what she wanted, someone to accompany her when she went for her checkups. Her sister-in-law had gone with her the first three
times, and she hadn't been able to ignore the rush of
envy when she saw women in various stages of confinement with the fathers of their unborn children
holding their hands or rubbing their backs. Afterward, she chided herself for being weak and needy.

Wrapping her arms around Sheldon's waist, she
rested her cheek over his heart and counted the
strong, steady beats. Unbidden tears filled her eyes
and overflowed as she cried without making a sound.

Sheldon felt moisture soaking his shirt. He moved
his hand over Renee's back in a comforting motion.
"Shush, princess. Everything is going to be all right."

His attempt to console made her cry harder and
Renee clung to him like a swimmer floundering in a
dangerous undertow. She had tried telling herself she
could go through nine months of pregnancy and deliver a baby alone, but when she least expected it her
armor cracked, revealing her vulnerability and leaving her with a feeling of helplessness.

She pressed a kiss to his strong neck. *Live for today, and let tomorrow take care of itself.* Her mother's mantra echoed in her head. Right now Sheldon

had offered her everything she needed for emotional stability. She needed to focus on the present instead of agonizing over whether their relationship would work out in the future.

"I'm ready, Sheldon," she whispered in his ear.

Sheldon froze, his breath stopping in his chest. When it resumed he was certain Renee could feel his heart beating. "Are you certain?"

"Very certain."

Pulling back and staring at her tear-stained face, Sheldon's heart turned over when he saw pleading in her eyes. "I don't want you to come to me because you're feeling vulnerable." His gaze softened. "I can't and won't take advantage of you."

"I am ready," Renee repeated. She pulled her lower lip between her teeth to stop its trembling.

Leaning forward, Renee pressed her mouth to his, kissing, lingering and savoring the taste and touch of his firm mouth. He kissed her back in a series of slow, feathery kisses that set her nerves on edge.

Mouths joined, Sheldon tightened his hold on her body. What had begun as a tender joining segued into a hungry, burning desire, the sparks igniting like brilliant showers of embers flung heavenward. Her sensitive nipples tightened, ached; her breasts grew heavy, swelling against the fabric of her bra.

"Please," she moaned as if in pain.

Sheldon tore his mouth from hers, laser-gray eyes glittering like quicksilver. He knew if he did not stop now he wouldn't be able to. He wanted Renee just that much. His chest rose and fell heavily as if he had run a grueling race.

"Okay, baby. I'll stop." He did not recognize his own voice.

She grabbed the front of his shirt in a punishing grip. Her eyes had darkened with her rising desire. "Don't you dare stop!"

He cradled her head between his large hands. "You know what this means, don't you?" She inclined her head. "If we make love, then there will be no turning back." She nodded again. "Tell me *now* what you want from me."

Renee closed her eyes, shutting out his intense stare. "I want you, Sheldon."

"For what?" he whispered against her lips.

"To protect me and my baby."

He nodded. "I can do that. What else, darling?"

"Become my best friend."

Lowering his head, he nuzzled her neck, inhaling the sensual, haunting scent of Shalimar. "I can do that, too. What else, princess?" Renee opened her eyes and something in her gaze gave Sheldon his answer.

"I want you to be the last man I sleep with."

He swept her off the stool, reached over, turned off the grill and walked out of the kitchen. His long, determined strides took him across the living room, up the staircase and into the bedroom he had never shared with a woman. Whenever he brought a woman to the cabin in the woods they always slept together in one of the first-floor bedrooms. The loft had become his monastery—a private sanctuary—until now.

Shifting Renee's slight weight, he walked to the bed, lowering her to the mattress. The light from the emerging near-full moon cast a silver glow on every light-colored surface. He made his way to the adjoining bath before returning to lie next to her; holding her hand, he stared up at the shadows on the ceiling.

There was only the sound of measured breathing as seconds ticked to minutes. Sheldon pulled her over his chest with a minimum of effort. He met her gaze in the diffused moonlight. "I can make love to you without being inside you."

She willed the tears pricking the back of her eyelids not to fall. Why, she asked herself, did tears come so easily now when in the past she hardly ever cried? Sheldon had scaled the wall she had erected to keep all men out of her life and her heart with a quiet gentleness she hadn't encountered in any man she knew—in or out of bed. He had asked how to proceed because of the child in her womb.

She exhaled audibly. "What I had with Donald is over. Any love I had for him died the moment I walked out of his life. There will never be three people in our bed, and this will be the last time I mention his name to you."

Combing his fingers through her hair, Sheldon cradled her head and kissed her with a passion that threatened to incinerate her. Reversing their positions, he supported his weight on his arms while at the same time he pressed his middle to Renee's, communicating his desire for her.

Slowly, methodically he undressed her, his mouth mapping each inch of flesh he bared. Trailing his tongue over her warm, scented flesh, he committed her smell to memory. The throbbing between his legs increased, yet Sheldon forced himself to go slow, slow enough to give Renee the pleasure he was certain she would wring from him.

The buttons on her blouse gave way and he stared mutely at the swell of flesh spilling over her bra's delicate fabric. Reaching around her back, he released the clasp and slipped off the bra. His breathing quickening, he swallowed a groan. Her breasts were as full and firm as ripe fruit.

Renee felt the heat from Sheldon's gaze as he eased her slacks down her hips and legs. Her panties followed, leaving her naked to his hungry gaze. The pads of his thumbs swept over her swollen nipples, sending pinpoints of exquisite pleasure to the pulsing between her thighs.

Eyes wide, breathing heavily, Sheldon sat back on his heels. "Sweet heaven, princess. You are beautiful," he whispered reverently.

His mouth replaced his hand, suckling her, and she rose off the mattress, her breasts heaving. She wanted to touch Sheldon, taste him the way he was touching and tasting her. Tears filled her eyes again as he lowered his head and trailed soft kisses over her slightly rounded belly. She crooned his name again and again while mouth and tongue worshipped her.

Renee sat up, her hands going to the buttons on his shirt. She managed to undo two, but was thwarted when he brushed her hand aside and accomplished the task in one sweeping motion; buttons were ripped from their fastenings.

Sheldon went to his knees, unsnapped the waistband on his jeans and pulled down the zipper in a motion too quick for the eye to follow. His jeans, briefs and socks lay in a pile with hers on the floor beside the bed.

He slipped the latex sheath over his aroused flesh and extended his arms. He wasn't disappointed when Renee moved into his embrace. Holding her, breathing in her scent, filled him with a sense of completeness. It was as if he had waited twenty years for a little slip of a woman to come into his life, a woman who would change him forever.

Why Renee and not some of the other women he had slept with?

What was so different about her that he had willingly pledged his future to her?

He prayed silently he would discover what it was before he got in too deep.

Supporting his back against the headboard, he cupped Renee's hips, lifting her high enough to

straddle his thighs. "Put your legs around my waist."
She complied, lowered her forehead to his shoulder,
her breath coming in short, quick pants. "Are you
comfortable?"

"Yes," she gasped.

All of Renee's tactile senses were on high alert:
the mat of chest hair grazing her sensitive breasts,
heavy breathing against her ear and the hardness between her thighs. She moaned, then bit down on her
lower lip to stifle another one as her flesh stretched
to accommodate Sheldon's sex.

She rocked her hips against his, setting the pace.
Each push, stroke, moan, groan and gasp of air became part of a dance of desire that sucked them into a vortex of sensual delight that had no beginning,
no end.

Renee was drawn to heights of passion she had
never known; her body vibrated with the liquid fire
scorching her brain and nerve endings. Her lips quivered in the intoxicating desire she had not felt in
months.

Sheldon could not stop the groans escaping his
parted lips as flames of desire swept over him with
the ferocity of a tornado touching down and sweeping up everything in its violent wake. He tried thinking of anything but the woman in his embrace, and
failed—miserably.

Cradling her hips, he increased their cadence, their
bodies moving faster and faster until the swirling ec-

stasy escalated and erupted in a tidal wave that swept them away to a private world of erotic enchantment.

Renee collapsed against Sheldon's moist chest, her breath coming in deep surrendering moans. Filled with an amazing sense of completeness, she closed her eyes.

Sheldon loathed having to withdraw from Renee. Their lovemaking had become a raw act of possession. He belonged to her and she belonged to him.

Easing her arms from under his shoulders, he laid her gently on her side before he covered her moist body with a sheet and lightweight blanket. He sat motionless and stared at her, then moved off the bed and made his way to the bathroom.

He stood under the warm spray of the shower recalling what Renee wanted from him. He had been forthcoming when he told her he would protect her and her child. That he'd done with his sons.

However, he knew he could never promise Renee marriage, because despite his success as a father and businessman, he had failed as a husband. That was a failure he would not chance repeating.

Six

Renee lay in the drowsy warmth of the large bed reliving the pleasure and satisfaction she'd shared with Sheldon. His lovemaking—the warmth of his body against hers, his protective embrace and the touch of his lips on hers had left her aching and burning for more.

Even with spiraling ecstasy that had nowhere to go, she'd prayed for it to continue until she was sucked into a vortex that held her prisoner for an eternity.

Reaching over, she turned on a lamp, looking for her clothes. They weren't on the bed or floor. She left the bed and went into the bathroom. The bathroom was more than twice the size of her first apartment. A free-flowing master bath opened into a dressing area with built-in drawers and closets tucked into an alcove. She opened a drawer and took out a T-shirt with the logo of Tuskegee University. Sheldon revealed he had not attended college, and she wondered which of his sons had attended the historically black college.

Opening the cabinets below the vanity, she discovered a plethora of grooming supplies. Twenty minutes later she'd brushed her teeth, showered and moisturized her body. She pulled on the T-shirt, walked out of the bedroom and descended the curving staircase.

Renee hadn't stepped off the last stair when she saw Sheldon, his back to her, setting the table in the dining area. Light from an overhead chandelier created a halo around the damp black hair clinging to his head. He'd changed into a pair of jeans and a black cotton sweater. She smiled. Like her, he had elected to go barefoot.

"Are you certain you don't want my help?"

Turning slowly, Sheldon stared at Renee. She wore the T-shirt Ryan had given him after he'd returned from his alma mater as a visiting professor. The sleeves reached below her elbows and the hem below her knees. His gaze lingered on her shapely legs and bare feet.

A slow smile crinkled his eyes and deepened the slashes in his lean jaw. He moved toward her.

Cradling her face, he dipped his head and brushed a light kiss over her parted lips.

"I'm certain. I wanted to set the table before coming up to get you. Are you hungry?"

She wrinkled her nose and nodded. "Starved. I'm sorry I'm not dressed for dinner, but I couldn't find my clothes."

"I put them in the wash." He kissed her again. "They're now in the dryer." With an arm around her waist, he led Renee to the table. He waited until she'd pulled the hem of the shirt under her hips, then pushed the chair under her.

Sharing dinner with Sheldon was a surreal experience for Renee. He started a fire in the fireplace, dimmed all the lights except in the dining area and tuned on the stereo to a station that featured love songs.

He had prepared a four-course meal beginning with lobster bisque and a salad of tomato and mozzarella topped with freshly grated Parmesan cheese. A grilled steak complemented baked potatoes and blanched snow peas. She'd refused dessert because she had eaten too much at one sitting.

Smiling across the table, she closed her eyes and sighed audibly. "You can cook for me any time."

"Is that what you want me to do? Cook for you?"

Her eyes opened and she sat up straighter. "No, Sheldon. That's not what I want you to do. I wouldn't mind if you cook for me on occasion and I'll do the same for you."

"You cook?"

She affected a frown. "Of course." Her mother had taught her to cook, and by the age of fifteen she could prepare an entire meal by herself.

"No, princess." His voice was low, soothing. "I look forward to cooking for you."

The distinctive voices of Kenny Rogers and Sheena Easton singing "We've Got Tonight" came through speakers hidden throughout the first floor.

Sheldon pushed back his chair, rounded the table and extended his hand to Renee. "Come dance with me. This is one of my favorite songs."

She hesitated. "I can't."

"Why?"

Renee stared over his head rather than meet his questioning gaze. "I don't have on any underwear."

A hint of a smile played around his mobile mouth. "By the time I go and get your underwear the song will be over. But, if you feel uncomfortable, then I'll take off my underwear."

She shot up from the chair and grabbed his hand. "No. Don't. Please."

Sheldon led her out to the middle of the living room, chuckling softly. "I just want you to feel comfortable."

Renee moved into his embrace. "I'm comfortable," she said a little too quickly.

He pulled her close to his body, spinning her around as he sang, "We've got tonight. Who needs tomorrow? Let's make it last."

She closed her eyes, listening to Sheldon sing. Was he saying that he only wanted right now—tonight and not tomorrow?

She wanted to tell Sheldon that tonight was all they had, because tomorrow was not promised. Sinking into his comforting embrace, she rested her head over his heart. The strong, steady beats kept time with hers. The song ended, but they did not pull apart. There was no need for words. Their bodies had communicated without words and what their bodies shared had nothing to do with business.

The clock on the fireplace mantel chimed the half hour as Sheldon and Renee climbed the staircase in the house at Blackstone Farms. It was one-thirty. He'd wanted to stay over until Sunday night, but she complained about having a sore throat.

"I think I'd like to sleep in my own bed."

Sheldon's stoic expression concealed his disappointment. They'd made love but would not sleep together. He nodded. "I'll see you in the morning."

Renee forced a smile. Every time she swallowed she felt as if her throat was on fire. "Good night." Rising on tiptoe, she kissed his cheek. She walked the length of the hallway and into her bedroom. She undressed quickly and slipped into bed.

* * *

Renee woke Sunday morning chilled to the bone. She could not stop her teeth from chattering. It was obvious she had come down with something.

It was ironic that *something* was the reason she'd gotten pregnant. A paralegal at the law firm had died from bacterial meningitis and everyone who had come in contact with her was prescribed a powerful antibiotic. Unknown to Renee, the antibiotic interacted with her low-dose contraceptive, decreasing its potency.

There were times after she'd relocated to Kentucky when she wondered what if Donald hadn't been married. Would he have offered marriage once she told him he was to become a father? The what-ifs had haunted her until she went for a drive, parked along the bank of a small river and screamed at the top of her lungs. The action was enough to purge her what-ifs and lingering angst.

Renee forced herself to leave the bed long enough to brush her teeth and take a hot shower. She made it back to bed on wobbly knees and went back to sleep.

Sheldon walked into the dining hall and saw Jeremy and Tricia sitting at a table with her grandfather, Gus Parker. Tricia motioned for him to join them.

Leaning over, he kissed her cheek. "Good morning."

"Good morning, Pop." Her dark eyes sparkled. "Grandpa has some wonderful news."

Sheldon sat next to his longtime friend. Augustus Parker had come to the farm as a groom two weeks after Sheldon purchased his first thoroughbred, and retired as assistant trainer some thirty years later.

"What's the good news, Gus?"

Tall, thin and nearing eighty, Gus affected a mysterious smile. "I'm getting married." He and his first wife Olga were married for forty-seven years before she died twelve years ago.

Sheldon's shocked expression gave way to a wide grin as he pumped Gus's hand. "Congratulations. Who is the lucky woman?"

"Beatrice Miller."

"Your nurse?" Sheldon asked.

"My ex-nurse and soon-to-be wife."

Tricia rested a hand on her grandfather's shoulder. Gus had suffered a heart attack and been hospitalized in late summer, but had recovered enough to give her away in marriage to Jeremy Blackstone. It was apparent the middle-aged visiting nurse not only helped heal the older man's heart; she'd softened it as well.

"When is the big day, Grandpa?"

"I'm leaving that up to Beatrice."

"Do you plan to move off the farm?" Sheldon asked.

Gus shook his head. "No. I wouldn't even consider leaving now that I'm going to become a great-grandfather." He winked at his granddaughter. "Beatrice told me she would love to fill in for Tricia as school nurse once she goes out on maternity leave."

Tricia stared at Gus. "I'm not going out on maternity leave, Grandpa. The baby is due the first week in July. School is over by that time. I'll have two months to bond with the baby, then I'll see it every day at the school's infant center."

Sheldon thought about Renee and her baby. She'd told him she was in her fourth month, which meant she would probably deliver sometime in March. Although she would not have worked for Blackstone Farms long enough to make her eligible for maternity leave, he would ask Jeremy to allow her some time off.

He glanced down at his watch. It was nearly noon and Renee had not put in an appearance. If she did not come to the dining hall before he'd left it, he would bring her breakfast favorites to the house.

Sheldon rapped on Renee's bedroom door, listening for movement on the other side. He tried the knob, turning it slowly. The door opened silently and he walked over to the bed. She lay on her side, eyes closed. He touched a bare shoulder, then jerked his hand away. She was burning up!

Guilt attacked him. He thought she'd refused to share his bed because she hadn't felt comfortable sleeping with him at the farm. Reaching for the cell phone on his waistband, he dialed Jeremy's number. The call was answered after the second ring.

"Tell Tricia I need her to come and check on

Renee. She's burning up with fever." Ending the call, Sheldon walked into the bathroom, wet a towel with cold water, then retraced his steps.

Jeremy and Tricia found Sheldon sitting on the side of Renee's bed, dabbing her face and neck with a cloth.

Tricia met her father-in-law's worried gaze. "Let me take her temperature."

Sheldon rose from the bed. He stood with his back to the window, watching intently as Tricia took Renee's temperature and blood pressure.

"Last night she complained of a sore throat," he said in a quiet voice.

Tricia glanced at Sheldon over her shoulder. "At least half a dozen kids have also come down with sore throats. The doctor tested them for streptococcus."

A frown appeared between Sheldon's eyes. "Did any of them have it?"

"No. All of the cultures came back negative."

"I can't take antibiotics," Renee said in a croaking voice.

Tricia met her gaze. "Why not?"

Renee closed her eyes. It hurt her to talk or swallow. "I'm pregnant."

Jeremy and Tricia turned and stared at Sheldon, whose impassive expression did not change with Renee's admission. They exchanged a knowing look. It was apparent the elder Blackstone knew about Renee's condition.

"I want her tested for strep throat," Sheldon ordered softly.

After tucking her stereoscope and blood pressure equipment into a small black leather case Tricia stood up. "You want the doctor to come out here today?"

"Call him, Tricia. *Now.*" Sheldon could barely control his annoyance. The farm's on-call physician was paid a generous retainer to come at a moment's notice.

Jeremy was more than familiar with his father's explosive temper. He had challenged him countless times as an adolescent, and had always come up the loser.

"I'll call the doctor, Pop." Turning on his heels, Jeremy walked out of Renee's bedroom.

Tricia, more than anxious to follow her husband, said, "Make certain she drinks lots of water to avoid dehydration. I'll wait downstairs for Dr. Gibson."

Renee lost track of time, but she remembered hearing the doctor tell Sheldon she had contracted a virus, and with bed rest, a light diet and plenty of fluids she should feel better in three to five days.

She slept for hours, waking to find Sheldon hovering over her while urging her to drink from the glass he held to her lips. Milk and blended fruity concoctions were added; these she sipped through a straw. What she did not remember was Sheldon washing her body as if she were a small, helpless child. Early one morning she woke up to find him asleep on the chair in the sitting room.

* * *

Renee sat up in bed Tuesday afternoon alert and ravenous. The first thing she noticed was that she wasn't wearing a nightgown, but a man's T-shirt; the second was the woman coming out of the bathroom with a pail filled with cleaning supplies. Even though she'd met Claire Garrett at the pre-race party, she'd only seen the housekeeper once before. She heard the hum of her vacuum cleaner, but failed to catch a glimpse of the tall elusive woman.

The third thing she noticed was the most shocking: her stomach. She'd lost her waistline the month before, leaving her belly slightly rounded; however, now it protruded above her pelvis.

Claire smiled, her bright green eyes sparkling like emeralds. "I'll let Sheldon know you're up."

"Thank you." The two words came out in a low husky tone. Her throat no longer hurt, but whatever she'd picked up had affected her vocal cords.

Renee returned Claire's smile as she swung her legs over the side of the bed. Her feet touched the cool bare floor and she shivered. It wasn't even winter and she felt cold. It probably would take her some time to get used to the change of seasons.

Walking into the bathroom, she filled the tub with water, added a capful of bath salts, the scent of vanilla wafting in the air. She brushed her teeth, rinsed her mouth with a mint-flavored mouthwash and washed her face, then stepped into the tub. Sighing, she rested her head on a bath pillow and closed her eyes.

"Do you need me to wash your back?"

Sitting up and splashing water over the sides of tub, Renee spied Sheldon lounging in the doorway, smiling broadly. A swath of heat cut a path from her face to her toes.

"No...no thank you."

Sheldon could not move, not even to breathe. The sight of her full breasts and the timbre of her husky voice rendered him temporarily paralyzed. The increasing heaviness between his thighs was akin to pain, a pain he did not want to go away.

"Does your throat still hurt?"

Sinking lower in the water, she shook her head. "No. But I sound like a foghorn."

He fixed his stare on her dewy face, smiling. "All foghorns should sound so sexy."

Sheldon knew he had to leave the bathroom *now*, or he would strip off his clothes and join Renee in the bathtub. "I'll see you downstairs."

He knew his feelings for the woman living under his roof were intensifying with every minute he remained in her presence. Sitting and watching Renee sleep while he waited for her body to heal had taken him back twenty years. Then he'd sat by another woman's bedside, waiting and watching her die. While the events in his life had changed in two decades, he hadn't—not until now.

In the past, he'd slept with other women because of sexual frustration. However, it was different with Renee because he did not need her as much as he wanted her. A wry smile tilted the corners of his mouth. It was time he opened himself to accept whatever life offered.

Seven

"Is this your first one?"

Sheldon pulled his gaze away from *The Washington Post* and looked at the red-haired man sitting on his right. A slight frown furrowed his smooth forehead. "First what?"

"Baby?"

His frown vanished. "No."

"Which one is it?"

As promised, Sheldon had accompanied Renee to her obstetrician the following week.

"This one will be the tenth," Sheldon replied, deadpan.

The man's face paled, leaving a sprinkling of

freckles over his nose and cheeks before a bright pink flush eased its way up from his neck to forehead. "You're kiddin', dude?"

Nodding and hoping not to burst into laughter, Sheldon continued the charade. "Nope. I have nine sons. We keep trying because we're hoping for a girl."

"Holy…" The redhead's words trailed off.

Sheldon went back to reading his newspaper.

Renee walked into the waiting room at the same time he finished reading the business section. He placed the newspaper on a coffee table and rose to his feet. Her dimpled smile was as bright as a spotlight.

When she had come to Blackstone Farms he never would have suspected she was carrying a baby. Now three weeks later, a hint of a belly was apparent under her khaki-colored tunic.

He closed the distance between them, putting an arm around her waist. "How are you?"

She snuggled closer to his side, her arms circling his waist. "Wonderful. It's a girl!"

Lowering his head, Sheldon pressed a kiss to her forehead. "Congratulations."

The moment she had informed him she was pregnant and intended to raise her child alone he'd hoped for a girl. He'd been a single father, and there were times when his teenage sons tested the limits of his patience *and* sanity.

He'd found girls quieter, less aggressive than boys. The difference between his three-month-old granddaughter Vivienne and Sean at the same age was like night and day. Vivienne was content to coo and play with her fingers and toes, while Sean had demanded to be picked up whenever he wasn't sleeping.

"When's your next appointment?"

"A month from now."

"Is everything okay?"

"I'm fine, Sheldon. Let's get out of here," Renee said quietly. Seeing some of the women in their last days of confinement was a blatant indicator of what awaited her.

Sheldon escorted Renee through the waiting area, stopping only to tap the inquisitive man on his shoulder. "We can stop now. It's a girl."

He glared up at Sheldon. "What if it was going to be another boy?"

Leaning closer, his gray eyes giving off sparks like streaks of lightning, Sheldon bared his straight white teeth. "Then I'd keep trying, *dude*."

Waiting until they were out in the parking lot, Renee placed a hand on Sheldon's arm. "Did I miss something back in the doctor's office?"

Sheldon opened the pickup's passenger-side door. "He asked me how many children I had and I told him nine." He bit back a smile when Renee's delicate jaw dropped. "I said we were going to keep trying until we got a girl."

Resting her hands on his chest, Renee shook her head. "You're bad, Sheldon Blackstone."

He moved closer, trapping her between his body and the truck's door. "How bad, princess?"

Tilting her chin, she stared up at him through her lashes. "Very, very bad, your highness."

Sheldon dipped his head. "Is that a good bad or a bad bad?"

Closing her eyes against his intense stare, she shook her head. "I don't know." The sultry hoarseness in her voice floated around them like a low, lingering fog.

"What would I have to do to help you make up your mind?"

Renee opened her eyes. "I'll leave that to your imagination."

Without warning, she found herself swept up in a strong embrace and seated in the truck. She did not have time to catch her breath when Sheldon got in beside her, put the vehicle in gear and drove out of the parking lot.

"Where are you going?" Renee asked as Sheldon parked the truck behind a gourmet shop.

Leaning over, he kissed her cheek. "How would you like to share a late afternoon picnic dinner with me?"

She ran the tip of her tongue over her lower lip, drawing his gaze to linger there. "Where?"

He raised an eyebrow. "Front porch, back porch, your bedroom or mine. It's your call."

Renee thought of his choices, then said, "How about outdoors?" The early frost had come and gone, and the Indian summer temperatures topped out in the low seventies during the daytime hours.

Sheldon regarded Renee for a minute. She was totally unpredictable, a trait he liked because he knew she would never bore him. "Outdoors it is."

Renee lay on a blanket in the same spot where she'd lain with Sheldon on Halloween. They sampled the most delectable foods, emptied a bottle of sparkling water, then fell asleep in each other's arms.

The sun had begun its descent and the air had cooled considerably when she stirred, her face pressed to Sheldon's solid chest, one leg sandwiched between his.

"Sheldon?"

He opened his eyes at her sultry query. "Yes, baby?"

"I want you to be bad."

There was a pulse beat of silence. "How bad?"

There came another pause. "Naughty."

Cradling her body with one arm, Sheldon rolled Renee over on her back. "Here?"

She nodded. "Yes."

"I can't protect you, because I didn't bring any condoms with me."

Renee giggled like a little girl. "It's too late for that, Sheldon. Remember, I'm already pregnant."

She was pregnant and he was disease-free. He had used a condom with her the first time because he didn't want Renee to think he was cavalier when it came to sleeping with women.

Sitting back on his heels, he reached down and pulled off his waffle-knit pullover. His gaze fused and locked with Renee's as he removed boots, jeans and boxers. He followed her gaze as it moved downward.

The first time they'd made love it had been in the silvered glow of a full moon, and now it was in the fading shadows of the setting sun. He had tasted and touched her like a sightless man, but this time everything she claimed would be presented for his viewing.

A cool breeze rustled the leaves on an overhead tree, leaves falling and littering the blanket like colorful confetti. Shifting, Sheldon removed Renee's shoes and striped trouser socks. He unbuttoned her tunic, his breath catching in his chest. Leaning over, he pressed a kiss to her distended belly.

"You're beautiful, princess."

Renee closed her eyes. "I'm fat, Sheldon."

Reaching for her hand, he placed it over her stomach. "You're filled with life, darling. Don't you realize how special that is?"

She opened her eyes, seeing unspoken pain glowing in his eyes and recalling the loved ones he'd buried. "Yes." Her voice was barely a whisper. "This baby is special."

He removed her tunic, bra and panties with a skill and familiarity indicating he had performed the action innumerable times.

Renee did not have time to ponder his statement when she found herself naked to his penetrating gaze.

Extending her arms, she welcomed Sheldon into her embrace. She did not feel the full effect of his comforting weight because he'd supported it on his arms.

Under a darkening autumn sky with all of nature as their audience, they began a dance of desire that needed no dress rehearsal.

His eyes smoldering with liquid fire, Sheldon feasted on the woman who made him look forward to the next day, the woman who made him laugh without trying to be funny and the woman who made him want to be inside her every day, hour, minute, second.

He brushed featherlike kisses around her mouth. Her lips parted of their own volition, and his tongue entwined with hers like pieces of molten steel. He did not kiss her mouth, but devoured it before moving down to the scented column of her neck, lingering at the base of her throat.

Traveling southward, he tasted one breast, then the other. She gasped as if in pain and rose off the blanket when his teeth closed on a nipple, worrying it gently before giving the other equal attention.

Renee was mindless with the divine ecstasy wrung from her. The pulsing between her legs thrummed faster, harder, and she was afraid it would be over before he claimed her body. She reached for his hair, fingers tightening in the heavy strands.

"Please do it, Sheldon," she begged hoarsely. "Take me, *now!*"

He complied, easing his sex into her warm, pulsing flesh. The turbulence of her passion swept Sheldon up in a flood tide of the hottest fire, clouding his brain. He was lost in the flames threatening to devour not just a part of him, but all that he was and he had hoped to become.

Then it came upon him like the whispered feet of a cat out of the darkness of the night. Feelings, emotions, sensations he had locked away when he'd buried Julia surfaced. The love he'd had for one woman, the love he was unable to offer another, trickled through the chasm in his heart, bursting forth, rushing and sweeping him up in its turbulent wake of realization as he surrendered all to the woman in his arms.

Renee welcomed the powerful thrusts, meeting each one with her own. Her hands were everywhere: in his hair, trembling over his broad shoulders, tunneling through the thick mat of hair on his chest. She wanted to yield to the burning sweetness that held her prisoner, but knew it was only a matter of seconds before she was forced to surrender to the raging passion lifting her higher and higher until she floated beyond herself. Her breath came in long, surrendering moans, and she gave in to the ecstasy.

The sounds escaping Renee's parted lips became Sheldon's undoing. Lowering his head, he growled in her ear as the explosions erupted in his lower body. The aftermath left him gasping and fighting for his next breath. It was a full two minutes before he was able to move, collapsing heavily to the blanket.

Renee rolled over on her side and rested her head on his shoulder. He pulled her close, offering his body's heat. "Don't go to sleep on me, darling," he whispered in her hair.

"I can't move."

"You don't have to."

Renee lay motionless while Sheldon pulled on his clothes, then dressed her. During the short ride to the house, she managed to doze off. It wasn't until hours later that she remembered sharing a shower with Sheldon and his request to share her bed.

Around three o'clock she woke up and made her way downstairs for a glass of milk. She returned to the bedroom, finding Sheldon sitting up and waiting for her. There was no mistaking the concern in his gaze.

"Are you all right?"

Renee got into bed, straddled his lap, wiggling until she found a comfortable position. "I just went down to get a glass of milk."

"You shouldn't do that," he crooned in her ear.

"Do what?"

"Sit on me."

A sensual smile touched her mouth. "And why not?"

"Because you'll find yourself on your back and me inside you…"

Her explosive kiss cut off his words. It was her

turn to gasp as Sheldon gathered the hem of her night-gown, pushing it above her waist. He lifted her with one arm and joined their bodies, making them one.

Instinctively, her body arched toward him. The crisp chest hair teased and tantalized her sensitive nipples and she welcomed the erotic sensation. Writhing, she moved closer, rocking up and down, back and forth over his hardness. Why, she asked herself as she came down to meet Sheldon in a moment of uncontrolled passion, couldn't she get enough of him? What spell had he cast over her that made her temporarily forget everything—even her name?

Sated, she collapsed against Sheldon, her lower lip trembling from the ebbing raw sensuality coursing through her. She did not know if the increase in her libido was from her being pregnant or from the real-ization that she was falling in love with Sheldon Blackstone.

In the six weeks Renee lived at Blackstone Farms, she had changed. The most apparent change was her body. Anyone who saw her knew she was carrying a child, and despite Sheldon's reassurance that he found her more beautiful than when she'd first come to the farm, there were times when she felt clumsy and misshapen.

Since they'd begun sleeping together it was al-ways in her bed, because despite their intimacy she felt something was missing in their relationship.

Each time she opened her arms to Sheldon the love she felt for him deepened. Each time he brought her to the pinnacle of desire she feared blurting out how much she had come to love him.

She had asked Sheldon for friendship, a confidant; his proposition included companionship and a promise to protect her and her child. Falling in love was not a part of their agreement—that went beyond business.

Late the next afternoon Renee mounted the porch, opened the door and walked into the main house. Heat greeted her as she went through the entryway and up the staircase.

The door to Sheldon's bedroom was slightly ajar and she heard him singing loudly. A knowing smile softened Renee's vermilion-colored lips as she walked to her bedroom. At first she'd found it odd that although she and Sheldon lived together, they rarely encountered each other during the day. It was only at night whenever Sean did not come for a sleepover with his grandfather that they slept together.

A strapless periwinkle-blue silk gown with an empire waist and slip lay across the bed; the matching quilted jacket hung from a padded hanger in the armoire.

Twenty minutes later Renee slipped her feet into a pair of sapphire-blue silk heels and walked over to the full-length mirror on the door of armoire. She did not recognize the woman staring back at her. Her hair had been pulled off her face and pinned into a chignon at the back of her head. The style was sophisticated without being too severe.

A slight gasp escaped her as another image joined hers in the mirror. Sheldon stood behind her, resplendent in formal dress. He wore a tailored tuxedo, white spread collar dress shirt and dark blue silk tie with an aplomb she hadn't seen on many men. Close-cropped raven hair brushed off his forehead and fell in layered precision against his scalp. The heat from his body and the tantalizing smell of his aftershave made her heart beat a little too quickly.

Sheldon placed one hand over the silk fabric artfully concealing her belly; the other circled her neck. His thumb caressed the skin over the nape of her neck as Renee's gaze met his.

His impassive expression did not reveal what he was feeling at that moment, what lay in his heart. He had deliberately avoided Renee because he'd found himself caught in a web of desire that held him captive. Each time he encountered her he was sucked into a force field, making him helpless and vulnerable. These were familiar emotions he had not wanted to experience again.

Renee shivered as Sheldon's forefinger toyed with the diamond stud in her right ear. Closing her eyes, she rested her head against his shoulder. The shiver became a noticeable shudder as he trailed kisses along the column of her neck.

"You look incredibly beautiful, smell delicious and taste scrumptious," he murmured against her velvety flesh.

Renee drank in his strength. "If we don't leave now, we're going to be late," she said not too convincingly.

"We won't be late, princess," he whispered, nuzzling her ear. "Thank you, darling."

She melted against his stronger body, her breath coming quickly. "For what, honey?" The endearment slipped out of its own accord.

"For being you, Renee." Sheldon's hands went to her upper arms and he turned her in his embrace. His hands came up and he cradled her face. His gaze widened, the gray orbs missing nothing. "I never thought you'd be able to improve on perfection, but you have. I'm going to be the envy of every man tonight." Her professionally coiffed hair and makeup highlighted her best features.

Renee reached for his hands, pulling them down. "Is that why you asked me to go with you and paid for this dress? To show me off like one of your prize thoroughbreds?"

A warning cloud settled into Sheldon's features, his expression a mask of stone. "Is that what you think, Renee?"

"Yes."

He shook his head slowly. "You don't know, do you?"

Her waxed eyebrows lifted. "Know what?"

Without warning his expression changed, his eyes brimming with tenderness and passion. "I adore you."

Renee's body stiffened in shock, complete surprise on her face. Sheldon had given her everything she wanted, but she never suspected deeper feelings would become a part of their plan. She wanted to tell Sheldon she adored and loved him, too, but his confession caused the words to wedge in her throat.

"Thank you," she whispered, recovering her voice.

Inclining his head, Sheldon forced a smile, successfully concealing his disappointment. It was apparent she did not share his sentiment.

Threads of doubt nagged at him. Was she still in love with her ex?

"Are you ready?"

She nodded. "Yes."

Eight

Renee walked out of the chapel, her hand resting on Sheldon's sleeve. She had given him several sidelong glances as the bride and groom exchanged vows, wondering whether he had relived the moment when he'd married his young bride; however, his solemn expression had not changed.

Sheldon covered the small hand on his arm. Renee's fingers were ice-cold. "Are you all right?"

"Yes. Why?"

"Your hand feels cold."

"This is one time when I'm not cold." The temperature inside the mansion was comfortably set for the expanse of bared skin in low-cut and backless gowns.

The number of carats glittering from throats, wrists and ears of the other women present in the grand ballroom stunned Renee. The guests were Virginia's aristocracy, with a few Washington senators and other politicians in attendance. The wedding was touted as the wedding of the year, linking heirs to two of the largest and the most profitable horse farms in the state.

Sheldon found their table and seated her. Leaning down, he pressed his mouth to her ear. "What can I get you to drink?" Guests were quickly lining up at several bars set up around the ballroom.

Renee opened her mouth to say milk, but changed her mind. "Sparkling water with a wedge of lime."

Sheldon chuckled softly, his gaze straying from her mouth to the swell of breasts rising and falling above her revealing décolletage. "Does this mean that I'm going to have to be the designated driver tonight?"

"Hello again, Renee." A familiar voice interrupted their interchange.

Renee glanced over her shoulder. Kent Taylor leered at her chest, a lopsided grin on his face. His attention was temporarily averted when Sheldon grabbed his hand and shook it, while pounding his back.

"When are you racing Kiss Me Kate again?"

The high color in Kent's face deepened. He still had not recovered from his horse coming in second at the International Gold Cup. "I don't know." He eased his fingers from Sheldon's firm grip. "I hope you don't mind if I ask your lady for a dance later on tonight."

Sheldon's cold smile would've chilled most men, but Kent was too inebriated to notice. "I do mind."

Nonplussed, Kent blinked a few times, hoping he hadn't heard what he thought he heard. Shrugging a shoulder, he turned and walked away.

"He's worse than a swarm of mosquitoes," Sheldon mumbled under his breath.

Renee's eyes narrowed. "I hope you're not going to growl at every man who asks to dance with me. I came here tonight to have a good time."

Sheldon hunkered down beside her chair, cradled the back of her head and pressed his mouth to hers. "And you will have a good time."

Her dimples winked at him. "You promise."

His smile matched hers. "I promise."

She did have a good time as she danced with Sheldon. A band whose repertoire included more than four decades of familiar tunes replaced a string quartet that played during the meal and many toasts.

Excusing herself, Renee whispered to Sheldon that she was going to the ladies' lounge. Making her way across the marble floor of the ballroom, she felt as if every eye was directed at her. Whenever Sheldon introduced her, he only offered her first name. Of course that made her more mysterious and others more curious.

Fortunately, she did not have to wait on line in the opulent bath and powder room. In the stall, as she adjusted her dress, she heard someone mention her name.

"Who is she?" came a soft drawling female voice.

"I don't know." This feminine voice was lower, more dulcet than the other woman's. "I thought you knew who she was. After all, you went to Sheldon's pre-race party."

"I don't remember her," the first woman admitted in a hushed tone.

"Where on earth do you think Sheldon picked her up?"

"I don't know. Maybe he joined some dating service, or he could've picked her up in one of those so-called gentlemen's clubs. You can find anything there."

"What do you mean anything?"

"Women who dance topless and swing around poles."

"Are you saying she's a whore?"

"She doesn't really look like a whore. But, one can never tell nowadays."

"The cut of her dress is a little deceiving, but I think she's in the family way."

"Bite your tongue, Valerie Marie Winston. I can't imagine Sheldon waiting until he's a grandfather to start making babies again."

"Bite your own tongue, Susanna Caroline Sullivan.

You see what she looks like. The good Lord was certainly smiling on her when He handed out bosoms."

Renee could not move. If she left the stall, then the women would know she was eavesdropping on their conversation. But she also did not intend to hide behind the door indefinitely.

"No one has seen Sheldon with a woman since Julia died. Maybe he was having a problem with you-know-what," Valerie continued.

"Where have you been?" Susanna chided. "There are drugs for men with that kind of *problem.*"

Renee had heard enough. Sliding back the lock, she left the stall. The shocked expression on the women's faces was priceless. It was impossible to tell their ages. They were the surgically altered women Sheldon had mentioned: perfect noses, collagen-enhanced lips, facelifts and expertly dyed ash-blond hair.

Smiling, she washed her hands and accepted a towel from the bathroom attendant. It was apparent Valerie and Susanna thought the woman so insignificant they could gossip in her presence. Opening her evening purse, she left a bill in the plate on the countertop before she faced the elegantly dressed women who had taken a sudden interest in powdering their noses.

Renee cradled her breasts, her gaze meeting and fusing with wide-eyed stares in the mirror. "Yes, these are mine. And to set the record straight, Sheldon Blackstone doesn't have that particular *problem.*"

Head held high, back ramrod-straight, Renee

strutted out of the rest room, staring down anyone whose gaze lingered longer than was sociably polite.

She found Sheldon sitting with several men as she neared their table. Vertical lines appeared between his eyes when he saw her tight-lipped expression. He stood up, the other men following suit.

Rounding the table, Sheldon cupped Renee's elbow. "What's wrong?"

"I want to leave," she whispered.

"Now?"

Renee had clenched her teeth so tightly that her jaw ached. "Yes, Sheldon. Now."

Sheldon saw something in Renee's eyes that had never been there before, and he wondered what had set her off. He nodded to the other men. "Gentlemen. We'll continue our conversation another time."

"Give me a call next week, Blackstone, so we can get together."

"Will do," Sheldon said to a tall, lanky man who bore an uncanny resemblance to Abraham Lincoln.

He led Renee out of the ballroom and retrieved her jacket from the cloakroom. They waited, staring at each other in silence while a valet brought his car around.

Five minutes into the return drive to the farm, Sheldon broke the swollen silence. "What's the matter, Renee?" She told him everything, including the full names of the two women who had indirectly called her a whore.

"If this is a taste of what I'm going to have to confront every time we go out together, then I want out of our agreement. They know nothing about me, yet they have the audacity to call me a whore."

Signaling, Sheldon maneuvered the car to the shoulder of the road and stopped. He shifted into park. His eyes glittered like particles of diamond dust in the diffused light of the dashboard. "You know who you are, and I know who—"

"You know nothing about me," Renee countered, cutting him off. "You've slept with me, Sheldon, yet you know nothing about me." She willed the tears filling her eyes not to fall.

His eyes widened. "Is what you've told me about yourself a lie?" he asked in a dangerously soft voice.

Averting her head, she stared out the windshield. The rapid pumping of her heart echoed in her ears, the roaring sound deafening. "When you introduced me to your high-born *friends* why didn't you give my full name? I'm not on the FBI's Most Wanted list. I'm also not one of those women who make their living as Amber or Bambi for 1-900-talk-dirty-to-me."

Sheldon shook his head. "It's not like that, darling."

"Oh, really? Let me tell you what it's like. I'm not going out with you again."

Sheldon gave Renee a long, penetrating stare. She did not understand, couldn't understand her impact on those who'd met her. The men were awed by her lush beauty, the women envious because she claimed what most of them hadn't had in a long time—natural beauty. He would not refute her accusations. Not now. Not when she was so visibly upset. He shifted into gear, then rejoined the flow of traffic.

He didn't know whether Renee had lied to him about her ex, but he was certain of one thing: he hadn't been entirely forthcoming when he admitted adoring her. The truth was that he *had* fallen in *love* with her. It was only the second time in his life that he'd found himself in love with a woman.

Renee sat at the workstation, staring out the window instead of printing an inventory schedule. She hadn't been able to concentrate for days. Her confrontation with Sheldon had caused a shift in her emotional equilibrium.

They'd returned home Saturday night, climbed the staircase and gone to bed—alone. She hadn't seen or heard from him in days, and it was over breakfast she overheard Ryan tell Jeremy that they would have to wait for Sheldon to return from his mountain retreat.

He had gone without her, and his promise to teach her to fish had been an empty one.

She felt a familiar flutter, closed her eyes and smiled. Her expanding waistline, viewing sonogram pictures and listening to the rapidly beating heartbeat with Doppler had all become insignificant since the first time she felt her baby move.

"Renee."

She swiveled on her chair. Jeremy stood in the doorway. He had come for his report. "Please come in. I just have to print out the schedule for you."

Jeremy sat in a chair near a desk, draping one leg over the opposite knee and studied Renee from under lowered lids. She'd changed since coming to the farm, and it wasn't only the changes in her body. She had become less reclusive, more open with the other farm residents.

He'd told himself to mind his own business; what went on between Sheldon and Renee was of no concern of his. The responsibility of running the horse farm, being a husband and impending fatherhood left little time for him to indulge in gossip.

Leaning forward, Jeremy studied the printed list Renee had tacked to a corkboard. It was a schedule of tasks and projected dates for completion. So far, it appeared as if she was ahead of schedule.

While Renee waited for the printer to complete printing more than thirty sheets, her cell phone rang. The sound startled her. It wasn't often her phone rang, and if it did it was usually her mother, brother or sister-in-law.

Reaching for the tiny instrument, she pushed the talk button. "Hello."

"Hey, Rennie."

She smiled. It was her brother. "Hey, yourself. What's up, Teddy?"

There was a pause before Edward Wilson's voice came through the earpiece. "This is not a social call, Rennie."

Knees shaking, she sank down to her chair and closed her eyes. "Is it Mama?" She had just spoken to her mother the week before.

"No," came his quick reply. "It's about Donald."

Renee sat up straighter, opened her eyes. "What about him?"

"He called here looking for you. He said he just got a divorce and he wants to marry you."

"What did you tell him?"

"I told him that I didn't know where you were."

"Thanks, Teddy."

"Don't thank me yet, Rennie. He says he knows you always spend Thanksgiving with us, so he plans to stop by to see if he can run into you."

"I can't come, Teddy. If he sees me then he'll know that I'm carrying his baby." Her voice had lowered when a pair of smoky gray eyes studied her.

"Then, don't come. Let me handle Mr. Rush. If he decides to get funky with me, then I'll just have to lock him up. I'll come up with a charge after I cuff the lying bastard."

Renee smiled. Her brother, a Kentucky state trooper, flew into a rage after she'd told him of Donald's duplicity.

"I'm going to miss you guys."

"We'll miss you, too. Let's plan to get together for

Christmas. I have a lot of time coming to me, so we'll come to Virginia. The kids have been bugging me about visiting Williamsburg."

"I would like to see it, too."

"Then that does it. We'll come by and pick you up Friday afternoon, and bring you back Monday night."

"Okay, Teddy."

"I'll call and let you know if the clown shows up here."

Renee pulled her lower lip between her teeth. "Please be careful. I've seen Donald lose his temper a few times and he was unbelievably rude."

"Don't worry about me. You just stay put."

"Okay. Love you, Teddy."

"Love you back, Rennie."

Renee ended the call, gathering the pages from the printer. She stapled and handed them to Jeremy, mindful her hands were shaking.

Jeremy took the papers without dropping his gaze. "Do you want to get together when you're feeling better?"

"I'm all right," she said a little too quickly.

"You're shaking."

"I'll be okay in a few minutes." She made her way over to her chair and sat down. Meeting her boss's questioning gaze, Renee drew in a deep breath before letting it out slowly. "The first page is an analysis covering the past three years."

Jeremy half listened to what Renee was saying, his mind recalling her telephone conversation. He knew Teddy was her brother, because when he'd called the Louisville area code and exchange, Teddy Wilson had answered the call, telling him he would give his sister the message.

He hadn't intended to eavesdrop on her conversation, but once she said, *"If he sees me then he'll know that I'm carrying his baby,"* all of his senses were on full alert. It was obvious Renee did not want the father of her baby to know her whereabouts.

There came a light knock against the door frame. "I'm sorry for interrupting." Jeremy and Renee turned to find Sheldon's broad shoulders filling out the doorway. He nodded to her. "Good afternoon."

Renee hadn't realized how much she'd missed Sheldon until now. She missed his drawling voice, deep sensual laugh and most of all the warmth of his embrace. She had come to depend on him more than she'd wanted to.

Tilting her chin, she smiled up at him. "Good afternoon, Sheldon."

Jeremy studied the myriad of emotions crossing Sheldon's face. His mother had died the year he turned ten; however, he'd been old enough to recognize the surreptitious glances between his parents. Unspoken glances that precipitated retiring to bed before their sons. And the look his father and Renee shared was one usually reserved for lovers.

Sheldon reluctantly pulled his gaze away from Renee and nodded at his son. "Jeremy."

"Hey, Pop. I'm glad you're back because I need to talk to you."

"I'll be in the den when you're finished here."

Jeremy turned to Renee. "Can we finish this another time?"

She blinked as if coming out a trance. "Of course."

Jeremy stood up and followed Sheldon, the remnants of Renee's conversation with her brother lingering in his head.

Sheldon entered the den and sat in his favorite chair, while Jeremy took a facing love seat. "What's up?"

Jeremy studied his father, seeing what he would look like in another twenty years, while hoping he would age as elegantly.

"Ryan and Kevin want to race Jahan at Santa Anita and Kentucky Oaks."

Leaning forward and clasping his hands between his knees, Sheldon caught and held Jeremy's gaze. "You don't trust their decision?"

"It's not that I don't trust them, Pop. It's just that I—"

"You don't trust them, Jeremy," Sheldon repeated emphatically, interrupting his younger son. "If you did then we wouldn't be having this conversation. Once I retired and turned complete control of running the farm to you, I'd hoped you wouldn't second-guess Ryan or Kevin's decision whether a horse is ready for a race.

"When you and Ryan decided to race Jahan for the International Gold Cup, I conceded because you, Kevin and Ryan overruled me by three-to-one. You've been overruled, Jeremy, so leave it at that."

For a long moment, Jeremy stared back at Sheldon. "Okay, Pop. I won't oppose them. But, there is something else I should tell you."

He repeated what he'd heard of Renee's conversation with her brother, watching Sheldon change before his eyes like a snake shedding its skin. An expression of hardness had transformed his father into someone he did not know—a stranger.

It was Jeremy's turn to lean forward. "Talk to me, Pop."

Sheldon's voice was low, quiet as he told his son what Renee had disclosed about her relationship with Donald Rush. "Are you familiar with the slug?" he asked.

"I know he is a pioneer in the computer game industry."

"Like those games Sean plays with?"

Jeremy nodded. "Yes. She doesn't want him to find her, Pop."

"And he won't. At least not here. If he steps one foot on Blackstone property he'll be shot on sight."

"What are you going to do? Hold her hostage?"

Sheldon shook his head. "No. I'll protect her. I want you to increase security around the property."

"Can you actually protect Renee from a man who

might sue for joint custody of a child he can prove is his?"

"No," Sheldon admitted.

"I know another way you can protect Renee without becoming her bodyguard or shooting her ex-boyfriend."

"How?"

Jeremy watched his father with hooded eyes that resembled a hawk. "Marry her." The instant the two words were uttered, he girded himself for a violent outburst, but when Sheldon sat staring at him with eyes filled with raw, unspoken pain he regretted the suggestion.

Lowering his head, Sheldon stared at the toes of his boots. "I can't do that."

"Why not, Pop?"

His head came up. "Why not?" he repeated. "Because I wouldn't be a good husband for her."

"Is it because she's carrying another man's baby?"

"No. I wouldn't have a problem raising her child as my own."

"Then, what is it?"

A melancholy frown flitted across Sheldon's taut features. "I wasn't there for Julia when she needed me. Your mother found a lump in her breast, and had a biopsy without my knowledge; when she discovered it was malignant she swore her doctor to secrecy."

Jeremy's eyes widened. "Why wouldn't she tell you?"

"Because she knew I never would've completed the circuit for Boo-yaw's Derby eligibility. She knew how much I wanted a Derby win."

"But, Pop. You can't blame yourself for something you couldn't control."

Sheldon buried his face in his hands. "The signs were there, son, but I was too caught up in my own world to notice them."

Moving to the opposite end of the love seat, Jeremy rested a hand on his father's shoulder. "What happened with my mother is over, and can't be undone. But now you have a second chance to make things right."

Sheldon's head jerked up. "What are you talking about?"

Rising to his feet, Jeremy turned to walk out of the room. He hesitated, but didn't turn around. "Look at what you have, and what you could hope to have."

Sheldon repeated Jeremy's cryptic statement to himself, refusing to accept the obvious. The minutes ticked off, the afternoon shadows lengthened, the sun dipped lower on the horizon. Dusk had fallen when he finally left the den.

Nine

Renee did not see the shadowy figure sitting on the top stair until she was practically on top of him. If she hadn't been daydreaming then she would have detected the familiar fragrance of sandalwood aftershave.

The telephone call from her brother had continued to haunt her although she'd told herself over and over that Donald wouldn't come after her. After all, she was just one in a string of many women he had dated or lived with—one of a lot of foolish women who thought they could hope to become Mrs. Donald Rush.

The only difference between her and Donald's

other women was that it had taken him more than a
year to get her to agree to go out with him. And once
she did, it was another six months before she agreed
to sleep with him. She thought he would give up his
pursuit, but he kept coming back. After eighteen
months Renee believed he was truly serious about
wanting a future together. She hadn't known that
during a wild, uninhibited week in Vegas he'd married a long-legged dancer.

"What are you doing here?" Her query came out
in a breathless whisper.

"I live here."

Renee felt heat sweep over her face and neck. "I
know you live here, Sheldon, but I didn't expect you
to be sitting on the steps." Light from hallway
sconces did not permit her to see his expression.

"I was waiting to talk to you." He patted his knees.
"Please sit down."

She shook her head. "I can't. I need to change for
dinner." His right hand snaked out, caught her wrist
and pulled her down onto his lap. Renee squirmed,
but she couldn't free herself. "Please let me go."

He buried his hair in her hair. "Indulge me, Renee.
Just for a few minutes."

Relaxing in his embrace, Renee luxuriated in the
muscled thighs under her hips and the unyielding
strength in the arms holding her in a protective embrace. Oh, she'd missed those arms around her; she'd
missed Sheldon.

"What do you want to talk about?"

"About what happened two weeks ago."

She stiffened before relaxing again. "What about it?"

Sheldon pressed a kiss to her fragrant hair. "I want to apologize if you feel I was not supportive of you."

"All I asked of you was to be a friend, to support me during the good and bad times, but I got a lover instead."

"I am your friend, darling—friend, lover *and* protector. I wanted to tell you to forget about Susanna and Valerie, but you were too upset for me to reason with you. They said what they said because they're jealous."

"They can't be jealous of me, Sheldon."

He pressed a kiss along the column of her neck. "They are, sweetheart. We have no control over what another person says or thinks, but if any of what they said about you in that bathroom gets back to me, then there's going to be hell to pay."

Covering the hands cradling her belly, Renee shook her head. "I didn't tell you so that you could fight with someone. I just wanted to let you know why I don't want to attend any more soirees with you."

"You don't have…" Whatever he intended to say died on Sheldon's lips when he felt movement under his hand. His expression changed, features softening. "When did she start kicking you?"

Renee smiled at Sheldon over her shoulder. "Last week. At first they were flutters, but they're much stronger now."

"She's a frisky little thing," he said with a broad smile.

"She sleeps all day, then wakes up and performs somersaults half the night."

"Does she keep you up?"

"Sometimes." Renee eased Sheldon's hands away from her belly. "I have to go get ready for dinner." She moved off his lap; he also rose to his feet.

"I'll wait downstairs for you."

"I'm not eating at the dining hall."

"You're going out?"

"Yes."

"Off the farm?"

"Why?"

Sheldon crossed his arms over his chest, deciding on honesty. "Jeremy told me about your telephone call."

"He had no right to tell you about a personal conversation."

"If it was so personal, then you could've either called your party back or asked Jeremy to leave the room."

Renee rolled her eyes at Sheldon. "One does not ask one's boss to leave the room to indulge in a personal telephone conversation during work hours. Besides, he shouldn't have told you my business."

"Jeremy told me because as long as you live and work here you *are* his business. You, thirty-five others, thirty-six including the child you're carrying, and half a billion dollars in horseflesh. Don't ever forget that, Renee.

"If you leave the farm, then you will be accompanied either by me or an armed escort. Security has already been tightened around the property. Now, I'm going to ask you again, Renee. Are you leaving the farm tonight?" He had enunciated each word.

There was a long, brittle silence as Renee struggled to keep her raw emotions in check. After ending the call with her brother she'd forced herself not to think about Donald. If he had divorced his wife in order to propose marriage, did he actually believe she would marry him now?

No. She could not and would not even if she were carrying quintuplets. Not when she had fallen in love with another man, a man who had become her friend, lover and protector.

"No, Sheldon. I'm not leaving the farm tonight."

Moving closer, he cradled her face and brushed a kiss at the corners of her mouth. "Shall I wait up for you?"

Renee wanted to tell Sheldon he was being controlling, but offered him a saucy smile instead. There was no doubt he wanted to make certain she was safe.

"Only if you wish. Perhaps when I return we can have a sleepover."

Throwing back his head, Sheldon laughed, the sound rich and full-throated. "I'm looking forward to it, princess."

Rising on tiptoe, she kissed his clean-shaven cheek, then made her way down the hallway to her bedroom. She had been invited to share dinner with Kelly, Tricia and Beatrice Miller, followed by a game of bidwhist.

Renee rang the doorbell to Kelly and Ryan's home, pushed open the door and walked into bright light, heat and mouthwatering smells.

Tricia appeared from the rear of the house, a bright smile softening her round face. "Hi. Come on back to the kitchen."

Renee noticed Tricia's curly hair was longer than when she'd been introduced to her. Thick black shiny curls fell over her ears and the nape of her neck. Tricia Blackstone was blooming—all over.

She walked into the kitchen and into a flurry of activity. Beatrice Miller stood at the cooking island slicing an avocado, while Kelly browned chicken cutlets in a frying pan. Kelly's daughter, four-month-old Vivienne, sat in a high chair, patting the chair's table as Tricia resumed spooning food into her bird-like mouth.

Beatrice, a petite woman with salt-and-pepper hair and smooth dark brown skin had a slender body that rivaled women half her age. A quick smile, soft drawling voice and a gentle manner made her the perfect companion for Gus Parker.

The four women, ranging in age from sixty to mid-thirties, shared a warm smile. "Thank you for coming," Kelly said.

Renee nodded. "Thank you for inviting me. Can I help with something?"

Kelly shook her head. "Not this time. The first time you're a guest. The next time you can do something more strenuous like set the table."

Renee could not stop the rush of heat flooding her face. "I'm pregnant, not physically challenged."

"Not yet," chorused Kelly and Tricia.

Kelly stared at Renee's belly. "By the time you're ready to deliver you won't be able to bend over to tie your own shoes."

"Stop teasing the child," Beatrice chided softly. "She's carrying rather nicely."

"When are you due, Renee?" Tricia asked.

"March third."

Tricia sucked her teeth. "I'm due the beginning of July and already I can't fit into my slacks."

Kelly stared at her sister-in-law. "I told you even before you knew you were pregnant that I dreamt you were holding three fish. And that means you're going to have triplets."

Tricia sucked her teeth again, this time rolling her eyes at Kelly. "You and your lying dreams."

Beatrice nodded. "You know the old folks say when you dream of fish you're going to hear of a pregnancy."

"I know for certain I'm having one," Renee said quietly.

"Girl or boy?" Beatrice asked as she sliced a ripe mango.

"Girl."

Kelly pressed her hands together. "Wonderful. Now Vivienne will have someone close to her age to play with."

"May I feed her?" The question was out before Renee could censor herself.

Tricia looked at Renee and smiled. "Sure."

"Where can I wash my hands?"

Tricia pointed to a door at the opposite end of the kitchen. "A bathroom is over there."

The three women exchanged knowing glances as Renee went into the bathroom. "She's going to need the practice before you, Tricia," Kelly whispered to her sister-in-law.

Renee returned, exchanging seats with Tricia. Vivienne Blackstone was a beautiful little girl. She'd inherited her mother's looks and her father's curly black hair; her eye color had compromised. It was gunmetal-gray.

Over a dinner of chicken piccata, linguine with roasted garlic and oil, a tropical salad of smoked chicken with avocados and mangoes, toasted Italian bread and lemon sorbet, followed by a lively card game, Kelly and Tricia became the girlfriends Renee had left behind in Miami. Beatrice provided the sage advice she occasionally sought from her mother.

Ryan and Sean had returned from the dining hall in time to put Vivienne to bed; they retreated to the family room to watch a movie, leaving the women to their card game.

"Where did you learn to play bidwhist?" Kelly asked Renee.

"I used to watch my mother and aunts. How did you learn?"

Kelly smiled. "From my mother. She and her sorority sisters used to get together and play Sunday afternoons when they were in college."

"How about you?" Renee asked Tricia.

"My grandmother taught me."

Beatrice stared across the table at Renee. "Do young people still play?"

"I don't think so. Some of the college students who worked part-time at the law firm where I worked talked about playing spades."

Tricia laid down a card. "That's too bad. I suppose we're going to have to keep the tradition going."

"You're right," Kelly concurred. "If Sheldon and his wild bunch can hang out at his cabin to play poker, smoke cigars and drink beer for their annual fall camping weekend, then I suggest we get together every other month for a bidwhist party."

Tricia stared at her grandfather's fiancée. "Did you smell cigar smoke on my grandfather when he got back this afternoon?"

Beatrice shook her head. "No. Gus swore he

didn't take one puff and neither did Sheldon, who told the other two guys that they couldn't smoke inside the cabin."

"They need to give up the cigars *and* the beer. It takes them two days to empty a keg," Tricia grumbled.

"Get out!" Renee gasped. "That's a lot of beer."

Kelly put down her cards and placed a hand on her hip. "Why don't you talk to your man?"

Renee's eyes widened. "Sheldon's not my man!"

Kelly lifted an eyebrow. "I didn't mention Sheldon's name. Gotcha!" she teased, pointing a finger at Renee.

Tricia peered over the top of her cards. "Is my father-in-law your man-n-n-n, Renee?" she drawled singsong.

"I'm not telling," Renee teased back, flashing a dimpled grin.

Leaning across the table, Kelly and Tricia exchanged high-five handshakes. "Boo-yaw!" they chorused in unison.

Renee laughed until her sides hurt.

She was still chuckling under her breath as she climbed the porch steps and found Sheldon sitting on a rocker waiting for her. He rose to his feet, extended his arms and she moved into his embrace.

Burying her face in the soft fibers of his sweater, Renee felt safe, safer than she had ever been in her life. Even safer than when she'd slept in the Miami

Beach mansion surrounded by gates, guard dogs and high-tech electronic surveillance equipment.

Easing back, she smiled up at Sheldon. "Are you ready for our sleepover?"

He returned her smile. "Yes, I am."

Renee did not have time to catch her breath as he lifted her off her feet and carried her into the house. Sheldon shifted her body, locked the door and then headed for the staircase.

Sheldon did not walk to the end of hallway, but stopped before they reached his bedroom, lifting a questioning eyebrow. Every time he and Renee made love he had come to her. The only exception had been their first encounter at the cabin. However, the day of reckoning could not be postponed forever. He had to know whether she wanted him in her life as much as he wanted her.

"Yours or mine?"

Renee did not know how, but she knew what Sheldon was feeling at that moment. The doubts, questions as to where they and their relationship were heading, and if what they shared went beyond sharing a bed and their passion.

Closing her eyes, she affected a secret smile. "Yours."

Sheldon lowered his head and pressed a kiss to the top of her head. In that instant all that made Renee Wilson who she was seeped into him, becoming a part of him.

It had taken three days away from her, three days where he and three of his best friends had gotten together for their annual fall camping weekend, to remind him what had been missing in his life.

The wild bunch, as they'd called themselves, had become longtime friends who left the farm to kick back for several days of male bonding. They fished, hunted, cooked, smoked cigars, drank beer, swapped war stories and talked about the women they'd loved and lost. These men had become the brothers Sheldon always wanted, but never had. They were his confidants and his conscience.

However, this year it was different, different because although he had brought women to the cabin, none of them had touched the part of him that ached for more than a physical release. None of them were able to make him look beyond the basic human need of food, shelter and clothes for the one thing every human being needed for ultimate survival and perpetuation of oneself: love.

He'd stopped trying to rationalize why Renee had come to him carrying another man's child beneath her heart. Why her and not some other woman, unencumbered by her past. And why did he feel so completely helpless whenever he thought about what she needed most: a husband. Jeremy's parting cryptic statement was imprinted on his brain: "look at what you have, and what you could hope to have."

He had enough money to last him well into old age, had transferred a horse-racing legacy to the next generation and had set aside ten thousand acres of prime property for his grandchildren. He had everything a man could ever hope for—everything but a woman to share his future and the dreams he had for the second half of his life. Every time he opened his mouth to say the two most blissful words a woman yearned to hear, they died on his lips.

He remembered his mother on her deathbed begging his father to "marry" her before she drew her last painful breath. And, although James Blackstone knew he was breaking the law and could have been sent to jail, he had married the woman whom he had loved.

Let go of the fear, his inner voice whispered. Renee wasn't Julia and he was no longer a thirty-two-year-old single father with two young sons who depended on him for their daily needs. *Marry her,* the voice continued. And if he did marry, Renee and her daughter would become Virginia Blackstones, a name with clout and influence.

Walking into the bedroom, he placed her on the king-size bed. The side of the mattress dipped with his weight as he sat beside Renee. A loud pop, followed by a brilliant shower of burning embers behind a decorative fireplace screen threw macabre shadows on the whitewashed ceiling and walls.

Leaning over, Sheldon quietly, seductively removed and then placed Renee's clothing on the bench at the foot of the large bed.

Renee did not open her eyes as she luxuriated in the gossamer touch of Sheldon's fingertips as he sculpted the roundness of her swollen belly before moving up to trace the outline of her engorged breasts. One hand slipped between her knees, moving upward and parting her thighs as it traveled toward the source of heat and the soft throbbing making it almost impossible for her to lie motionless.

Reaching for his hand, she held it against her moist, pulsing warmth, unable to stop the moans coming from her constricted throat. If Sheldon did not take her—quickly—it would be over within seconds. His finger searched and found her. It was his turn to groan when her flesh convulsed around his digit.

Pulling back, he sat on his heels and pulled the sweater over his head. Within seconds his slacks and underwear were pooled on the floor. Gently, he shifted Renee until her buttocks were pressed to his groin. He rested her top leg over his, then eased his swollen flesh into her, both moaning in satisfaction as their bodies melded as one.

I'm home, the scalding blood in Renee's veins sang. It wasn't the modest house where she'd grown up in a Miami suburb; it wasn't the shabby apartment where she'd lived with her mother and brother after her father's untimely death; it wasn't the small condominium apartment she'd bought after working two jobs to save enough money for the down payment; and it certainly wasn't the palatial beachfront mansion with views of the Atlantic Ocean and passing luxury yachts and cruise ships in the distance. Sheldon Blackstone was home and everything the word represented: love, safety, comfort and protection.

Closing her eyes, she tried concentrating on anything but the hardness sliding in and out of her body. Her heart rate skyrocketed along with the uneven rhythm of her breathing. She experienced extreme heat, then bone-chilling cold that made her teeth chatter. Sheldon had set a pace that quickened, slowed, then quickened again until she was mindless with an ecstasy that had become a mind-altering trip shattering her into millions of pieces before lulling her back to a euphoric state that left her weak and mewling as a newborn.

Sheldon clenched his teeth as he fought a hopeless battle. He did not want to let go—release the passion streaking along the edges of sanity. He wanted the whirling, swirling sensations to last—forever if possible. The passion Renee wrung from him hurtled him to heights of erotic pleasure he had never experienced before—not with any woman. He quickened his movements, mindful of the child kicking vigorously in her womb, then went completely still as he moaned and poured out his passions in a flood tide that made him forget everything.

They lay joined, waiting until their hearts resumed

a normal rate. Sheldon moved once to pull the sheet and blanket up and over their moist bodies, then as one they fell into a deep sated sleep.

Ten

Renee slipped out of Sheldon's bed early Thanksgiving morning, retreating to her old bedroom to shower. She hadn't slept there since the night of her bidwhist party with Kelly, Tricia and Beatrice.

Her daily routine had changed since she'd begun sleeping in Sheldon's bedroom. She retired earlier and woke up earlier. Weather permitting she usually took a morning walk. And what Sheldon had told her about additional security around the perimeter of the farm had become apparent whenever she spied a man sitting on horseback with a rifle resting in the crook of an arm or slung across his chest.

Dressed in a bulky sweater, stretch pants, boots

and a baseball cap, she set out on her walk. A haze hung over the valley like a diaphanous blue-gray veil. Although a national holiday it was not a farm holiday. Horses had to be washed, groomed and turned out into the paddocks for daily exercise.

Her early morning walks were now a part of her daily exercise regimen. The added weight had put pressure on her lower back, but since she'd begun walking it eased.

Forty minutes and a mile later, she stood in front of one of four barns where the thoroughbreds were stabled. Several grooms were hosing down horses. She spied Shah Jahan as he stood motionless under the stream of water sluicing over his ebony coat. She couldn't pull her gaze away from the long arching neck, noble head and the sleek powerful lines in half a ton of regal horseflesh. Jahan had raced twice since the International Gold Cup, and had come in first both times. The scorecard with Jahan's racing statistics read:

> *Owner: Blackstone Farms*
> *Trainer: Kevin Manning*
> *Sire: Ali Jahir Dam: Jane's Way*
> *Starts: 3 Wins: 3 Earnings: $1.2 million*

What had most people in the world of thoroughbred racing wagging their heads was the fact that Shah Jahan had yet to celebrate his second birthday.

Nodding to the grooms, Renee walked into the barn. The sounds of stalls being swept out reverberated in the large space. The sweet smell of hay masked the odor of sweat, manure and urine.

She stepped aside just in time to avoid a ball of black and white fur scampering around her feet. Leaning down, she picked up a tiny puppy. It wiggled and yelped as it struggled to free itself.

"To whom do you belong?"

"No one, Miss Renee."

Turning on her heel, Renee stared at Peter Mc-Cann, a teenager whose pleasant looks were neutralized by an outbreak of acne.

"Is he a stray?" she asked.

Peter nodded. "His mama whelped a litter about six weeks ago. Dr. Blackstone has already given away four. He's the only one left. Doc already gave him his shots."

Renee smiled at the large black eyes staring back at her. "What breed is he?"

"Mutt," Peter replied, deadpan. "His mama is part lab and sheepdog. Don't know about his papa. Lady Day must have snuck off the farm when she was in heat and found herself a man. She didn't come back until she was ready to whelp. Now that she's weaned this last one Dr. Blackstone plans to neuter her. He claims we have enough dogs to keep the horses company."

Sheldon had explained to Renee that most horse farms kept either dogs or goats as pets to keep the stabled horses, which are by nature social animals, company. She did not know why, but she felt an instant kinship with the puppy.

"I think I'm going to take him home with me."

"He's going to be a big one, Miss Renee. Take a look at his paws."

She looked at his paws. They were rather large for a small puppy. "If he's part sheepdog, then he'll adapt to staying outdoors."

"None of the farm dogs come inside, except when it snows. If you're going to take him home, then I'll get a leash for you. I'll also bring over some food after I finish up with my chores."

Renee gave him a warm smile. "Thank you."

It wasn't until after she had attached the leash to the collar around the puppy's neck that she thought about Sheldon. Would he even want a dog in his house? Had his sons grown up with pets?

She hadn't had a pet of her own since her mother was forced to sell their house and move into an apartment where the landlord had posted a sign prohibiting pets of any kind.

The puppy tired, stopped and sat down. Squatting, she picked up the dog, cradling it against her jacket. She'd just walked past Jeremy and Tricia's house when she saw Sheldon striding toward her. A sensual smile curved her mouth. He had a sexy walk. His back ramrod-straight, he swaggered, broad shoulders swaying from side to side.

Slowing her pace, she smiled, stopped and waited for him to approach her. He'd elected to wear a flannel shirt with jeans and a pair of worn boots.

She'd seen him dressed in a tailored suit, a tuxedo and jeans with a pullover sweater or cotton shirt, and she liked him dressed down best. The casual attire seemed to enhance his rugged handsomeness.

Her smile faded the moment she noticed his stern-faced expression. "Good morning."

Sheldon's gray eyes swept over Renee, lingering momentarily on the puppy cradled against her chest. "I thought because it wasn't a work day you'd stay in bed beyond daybreak."

"I enjoy getting up early and walking."

"Why don't you wait for me to walk with you." His tone was softer, almost conciliatory.

"I don't want to wake you up."

"Wake me up, Renee."

"Okay, Sheldon. I'll wake you up."

He pointed to the puppy. "What do you have there?"

"A pet."

He lifted both eyebrows. "A pet?"

"Our pet, Sheldon."

He crossed his arms over his chest. "Did I say I wanted or needed a pet?"

Renee shook her head. "No. But, if I'm going to live with you then he will become *our* pet." She peered up at him. "Don't you like animals?"

Sheldon gave Renee an incredulous look. "If I

didn't like animals why would I own a horse farm? I'm not opposed to you having a dog, but who's going to take care of him when we go away?"

"When are we going away?"

"I'd planned to take you to the cabin this weekend. You said you wanted to learn how to fish."

"Can't we take him with us, Sheldon? Please," she added when a frown appeared between his eyes.

The corners of his mouth twitched then inched upward as he tried and failed to bite back a grin. "Yes, princess. You can bring *our* pet to the cabin."

Moving closer, she wound her free arm around his waist, encountering a bulge in the small of his back. "Sheldon." His name was a weak whisper. He was carrying a handgun.

Grasping her hand, he pulled it away from his body. "It's all right, baby."

"It's not all right. I don't like guns."

"Neither do I," he countered. "But sometimes they are a necessary evil."

She took a step backward. "I don't want to see it."

"Walk ahead of me and you won't see it."

Renee moved in front of Sheldon. She could feel his gaze boring into her back. "I need a name for the puppy."

"Is it a boy?" She nodded. "How about Patch?"

"How did you come up with that one?"

"Because he looks as if he's wearing a black patch over one eye."

Renee stared at the sleeping puppy. So much for her being observant.

"Patch Blackstone. I like the sound of that," she said, peering at Sheldon over her shoulder.

"He's going to need food."

"Peter promised to bring some to the house."

Sheldon shook his head. Three months ago he lived alone. Now he had not only a woman but also a dog sharing his home. "Try to paper train him as soon as possible, because I don't want more work for Claire."

"I'll clean up after him."

"No, you won't."

"Why not, Sheldon? He's my pet and therefore my responsibility."

"You don't need to be on your knees cleaning up dog crap. I'll do it."

Renee's back stiffened. "No, you won't."

"If that's the case, then get rid of the damn dog." She stopped, spun around and walked back to face him. "I'm not going to argue with you, Renee," he warned in a deceptively soft voice.

There was something about Sheldon's expression that stilled Renee's tongue. His implacable expression was unnerving. "Nor I you," she said quietly.

Turning on her heel, she bit down on her lower lip until it pulsed between her teeth. How could she prove her point with a man who refused to debate?

The answer was she couldn't.

* * *

Renee sat next to Sheldon at a table in the dining hall. Each table's centerpiece was representative of the season: tiny pumpkins, gourds, sprigs of pine and pine cones. Orange and yellow tablecloths had replaced the usual white. Prerecorded taped music provided a nice backdrop for the various conversations from the diners.

She'd had a light breakfast because she wanted to save her appetite for Thanksgiving dinner. Within minutes Kevin Manning, his wife and their niece, Cheryl, joined them.

Nineteen-year-old Cheryl had become a racing celebrity. Barely five feet in height, she topped the scales at an even one hundred pounds.

Ryan Blackstone stood up, waiting for conversations to fade. He smiled, flashing sparkling white teeth under a neatly barbered mustache. "Good afternoon. Unlike my esteemed father and brother, I'll make this speech short and sweet, because I don't know about you but I'm hungry enough to eat a horse."

There came a round of hisses and boos when he mentioned horse. "Not any of our horses, of course." This was followed with applause. Ryan sobered. "But on a more serious note, I'd like to give thanks for so many things this year. I'm thankful for our families, immediate and extended. We also have to thank Kevin and Cheryl for their incredible successes. We are thankful and grateful for the new members of our farm family." He smiled at Renee and Beatrice.

"I'd also like to thank my brother for his hard work and unwavering support as we prepare for another generation of Blackstone Farms achievements. I'd like to thank my father for always being here not only for me but also for all of us. He's sacrificed a lot to make Blackstone Farms what it is today, and for that I'm certain he will be rewarded in ways he cannot imagine.

"Last year our mothers came to Sheldon because they wanted a safe environment for their children. That request gave birth to the Blackstone Farm Day School and Infant Center. This year some of you have asked for a place of worship, and your request has been taken under advisement. Sheldon has offered to give up five acres of land in the north end for the construction of an interdenominational church. The contractor laid the foundation two days ago, and we hope to have the project completed before spring."

Ryan paused as applause and whistles rent the air. He held up a hand. "Some of you may not be aware of it, but in another life one of our grooms served as an assistant pastor in a little church in Texas." He motioned to a table to his right. "Reverend Jimmy Merrell, I'd like for you to meet your flock and bless the food." There were gasps of surprise intermingled with applause.

Jimmy stood up and clasped his hands, everyone following suit. Renee folded her hands in her lap. She gave Sheldon a sidelong glance when his hand covered hers.

There were so many things to be thankful for this year: the child kicking vigorously inside her; the love of the man cradling her hand; the love and happiness her mother had found after so many years of pain and despair, and her brother for his love and support after she'd come to him when she needed him most.

The invocation concluded and the feasting began. Renee ate so much that she had to refuse dessert. She'd wanted to sample the pastry chef's renowned sweet potato pie, and in the end she had a slice wrapped up to take with her before she and Sheldon left for their weekend at the cabin.

Sheldon cradled Renee to his chest, staring into the flickering flames in the fireplace. A gentle smile touched his mouth. It was a perfect scenario: a man and woman in bed together while their dog slept on a rug in front of the fireplace.

He'd come to the cabin with Renee because he needed to be away from the farm…and alone with her. Here he hoped he would be able to face his fear and come to terms with his feelings for her. He had known there was something special about her from the very beginning, yet he could not have imagined he would fall in love with a woman carrying the fruit of her love for another man inside her.

Once he'd recovered from the shock that she was pregnant it had become insignificant. Kelly had married Ryan and had become mother to Sean, his son from a prior marriage. Kelly had legally adopted Sean the year before.

Sheldon closed his eyes, sighing softly. If he married Renee before the birth of her daughter, then she would automatically become a Blackstone.

"Have you thought of a name for the baby?"

Renee snuggled closer and wiggled her nose when the hair on Sheldon's chest tickled her. "I've thought of a few."

"Do you want to tell me, or it is a secret?"

"It's not a secret. I'm considering Virginia, because it was my grandmother's name. I also like Sonya and Hannah."

"They're all strong, traditional feminine names. Have you picked out ones for a boy, just in case?"

Pulling out of his embrace, Renee sat up. "I can't have a boy."

Sheldon noted the look of distress on her face. "Why not? Sonograms aren't always that accurate."

Tunneling her fingers through her hair, Renee held it off her face. "I don't want a boy, because..." Her words trailed off, locked in her throat.

Reaching for her, Sheldon pulled her up to sit on his lap. "Why not, Renee?"

She stared at him in the wavering light from the fireplace fire. "A boy needs a mother *and* a father. I know I can raise my daughter by myself, but not my son."

"I'll help you, darling."

She froze. "What?"

"I'll help you raise your son. I've made mistakes with Ryan and Jeremy, yet they've turned out all right. I'm very proud of them."

Renee shook her head. "No, Sheldon. I can't ask you to do that."

"Didn't you ask me to protect you and your baby?"

"Protect, not assume responsibility for raising it."

A weighted heaviness settled in Sheldon's chest as he digested Renee's statement. She would permit him in her life but not to share in it.

His life had come full circle. Julia had married him, borne his two sons, yet she had withheld a part of herself from him, had concealed her illness until it was too late.

Was he destined to repeat the same mistake? Had he fallen in love with a woman like Julia?

Now it was his turn to hide, hide his true feelings from Renee. He had fallen in love with her, would probably always love her, but it was something he would never reveal to her or anyone else.

He squeezed her shoulder. "Let's get some sleep because we're going to have get up early tomorrow to go fishing."

* * *

"Let's go, sleepyhead. Time to get up." Renee mumbled in her sleep, but did not wake up. Sheldon shook her harder. "Renee."

Her lids fluttered wildly as she opened her eyes. Where was she? She heard a soft yelping and came awake. Rolling over on her back she saw Sheldon leaning over her.

"What time is it?"

"Four," he whispered.

"Four o'clock in the freaking morning?"

Grinning, he nodded. "Let's go while the fish are biting." He nuzzled her ear. "Okay, princess. If I catch the fish you'll have to clean them."

Renee sat straight up. She hated cleaning fish. "No. Give me a few minutes and I'll be ready."

Sheldon sat down on the side of the bed, watching her as she walked to the bathroom. She was moving more slowly now. Cupping a hand over his mouth, he closed his eyes.

He had spent a restless night wondering whether he'd coerced Renee into living with him. Renovations on her bungalow were nearing completion, and he thought about giving her the option of moving out of his house and into her own.

But seeing her waddle across the room while massaging her lower back squeezed his heart. He couldn't leave her—not now. Not until after she delivered the baby.

* * *

Renee lay on a wooden bench in the bathroom, her legs covered with foam. Sheldon straddled the bench, razor in hand. He had offered to shave her legs.

He raised her foot to his thigh. "Relax, baby. I'm not going to cut you."

"I've always shaved my own legs."

Leaning forward, he laid a hand over her distended belly. "That was before, when you could bend down or lift your leg. Right now, you're at my mercy."

Staring up at the recessed lights, Renee nodded. "That's what I'm afraid of."

His right hand moved up her thighs and covered the furred mound. "You know I wouldn't take advantage of you."

She slapped at his hand. "I know nothing of the sort."

"Maybe if I shave a little higher the hospital won't charge you for that particular procedure once you go into labor."

"Stop it, Sheldon!" She laughed so hard that her stomach muscles contracted. "Now, I'm hurting," she said between guffaws.

"Where?"

"My sides and back."

Hovering over her, Sheldon smiled. "I'll give you a massage after I finish your legs."

Renee calmed down enough to remain still as he drew the blade over her legs.

Sheldon finished one leg, then did the other. Gathering her off the bench, he cradled her to his chest.

"I think you've gained a few pounds since yesterday."

Renee met his gaze. "Did you see how much I ate for Thanksgiving?"

He shook his head. "No, because I was too busy stuffing my own face."

"I hope the doctor won't put me on a diet after I weigh in."

"How much have you gained overall?"

"Twelve pounds." She'd doubled her weight gain since coming to the farm.

"That's not much."

"I know. But there are times when I feel like a beached whale."

"You look beautiful."

Tightening her hold on his neck, Renee kissed his stubbly jaw. "You're so good for a woman's ego."

He angled his head. "You are beautiful, Renee."

"Thank you. I'd like to cook for you tonight, Sheldon."

"Are you sure you know how to cook?"

She remembered another time when he'd doubted her culinary skills. "Stay out of the kitchen, and you'll see if I can. I'm going to check your refrigerator and freezer, and if you don't have what I need then you're going to have to drive me to the nearest supermarket."

He placed her on her side on a table in a steam room. "There are no supermarkets around here."

"Where do you buy your food?"

"I usually bring it from the farm."

"Like the keg of beer you and your buddies drink during your annual fall frolic."

"If I tell you something, will you promise not to tell anyone?"

Sheldon's expression was so serious Renee felt her heart stop before starting up again. "Yes."

"We usually drink a couple of six-packs, not a keg."

"Tricia said her grandfather brags about you guys emptying a keg in a couple of days."

Pulling over a stool, Sheldon sat down and gently kneaded the muscles in Renee's lower back. "The first year we got together we bought a keg. We emptied the keg by pouring out more than three quarters of the beer. I'm lucky if I can drink two beers in one sitting."

"Then it's all a lie?"

He pressed his mouth to her bare shoulder. "It wasn't a lie. When I said we emptied a keg everyone assumed we had actually drunk a keg of beer. We never bothered to clarify the misconception because that would destroy the wild bunch's mystique. Do you know how many guys want in our elite organization?"

Renee laughed again. "You guys are a fraud."

"And you better not tell," Sheldon threatened.

"I'll think about it."

"Renee!"

"Okay, Sheldon. I'll keep your secret."

Rounding the table, he hunkered down and kissed her until her lips parted to his probing tongue. The kiss claimed a dreamy intimacy that hinted of more as Sheldon gathered Renee off the table and carried her into one of the downstairs bedrooms. He lowered her to the bed, his body following; he supported his weight on his elbows.

Reversing their positions, Sheldon pressed his back to the headboard and brought Renee to straddle him, her back against his chest. Lifting her slightly, he entered her, covering her breasts with his hands. The coupling lasted minutes, but when they climaxed simultaneously it was to offer the other the sweetest ecstasy either had ever experienced.

Eleven

Renee stood at the cooking island, adding chopped fresh rosemary to a lemon marinade for the trout she'd planned to cook on the stovetop grill.

"Do you need me for anything before I go upstairs and wash my hair?" Sheldon asked as he walked into the kitchen. He had taken Sean with him to Staunton for a haircut.

She smiled at Sheldon. "No. I'm good here."

After sharing cooking duties over the Thanksgiving weekend, she and Sheldon continued the ritual once they returned to the farm. He had been so impressed with her cooking skills that he had begun making special requests.

He left the bed when she did, accompanying her on early morning walks, and returning to the house after stopping for breakfast at the dining hall. She had adjusted her work hours from nine-to-five to eight-to-four. Although she no longer required a nap during the day, she rarely slept soundly through the night. As soon as she got into bed the baby began her nightly aerobic workout.

She concentrated on whisking the marinade, then placed it on a shelf in the refrigerator. Removing a platter with two cleaned and filleted trout, she lightly salted them, added freshly ground pepper, wrapped two slices of bacon around each fish and tucked bay leaves inside the fold close to the skin of the fish.

Sheldon entered the kitchen as Renee was putting the finishing touches on the meal.

Renee took several steps, stopping inches from the man whom she had fallen in love with and rested her head over his heart. It was pounding a runaway rhythm. "Talk to me, Sheldon."

Reaching out and pulling her to his body, he rocked her gently. "I love you, Renee. I love you, yet I'm afraid of losing you."

Tilting her chin, she saw pain in his eyes before he shuttered his gaze. "Why on earth would you lose me?" she whispered. "I plan to be around for a long time."

He released her shoulders, cradling her face between his hands. "I want you in my life not for a few months or for a few years, but for always. I know I can be a good father to your baby, but I doubt whether I can be a good husband to you."

"Why, Sheldon?"

Lowering his head, he pressed his mouth to her ear, telling Renee about Julia, her illness and his selfish pursuit to make horse-racing history.

"I saw her grow weaker and weaker, but whenever I asked if she was all right she reassured me she was okay. And like a fool I believed her."

"It's not as if you didn't ask her, darling. She just chose not to tell you the truth."

"I should've insisted."

Renee shook her head. "That wouldn't have changed a thing. Not when you live with someone who chooses to conceal the truth."

Sheldon pulled himself from his past and back to the present. *Not when you live with someone who chooses to conceal the truth.*

Julia had deceived him, and Donald had deceived Renee. The difference was Julia was gone and Renee was here. He should ask her to marry him and claim her child as his own.

But could he risk it?

"Yes," he said softly.

Renee stared at Sheldon. "Yes, what?"

He blinked as if coming out of a trance. "Do you love me, Renee?"

A flicker of apprehension coursed through her.

Was Sheldon losing his mind? "What's going on with you?"

"Do you love me, Renee Wilson?" He'd enunciated each word as if she were hard of hearing.

Her lids fluttered wildly, keeping time with her runaway pulse. "Yes, I do, Sheldon Blackstone. I do love you."

"Will you do me the honor of becoming my wife?" She hesitated. "Yes or no, Renee?"

"Yes."

"And will you also permit me the honor to be a father to your daughter?"

As their gazes met, Renee felt a shock run through her. Sheldon was offering her what she had wanted all of her life: a man she could love *and* trust, a man who would protect her *and* her baby.

She bit down on her lower lip to still its trembling. "Yes, Sheldon." A delicious shudder heated her body when he dipped his head and kissed her. "Will this arrangement be strictly business?" she whispered against his mouth.

Lines fanned out around his incredible eyes. "Oh, it will be business, all right. I want to marry you before the end of year, turn one of the upstairs bedrooms into a nursery, then when Virginia, Sonya or Hannah Blackstone is at least six months old we're going to go on a belated honeymoon to somewhere exotic and make mad, passionate love to each other."

Giggling and snuggling as close as her belly would allow her, Renee curved her arms under his shoulders. "We don't have to go away to make mad, passionate love to each other."

Sheldon placed a hand over her middle. "Just once I'd like to make love to you without our daughter coming between us."

"Three months, then another six weeks. It's not that far off."

"You're right. I think I'm going to like having a daughter."

"I'm sure she's going to love having you for her father."

His hands moving up and down her back in a soothing motion, Sheldon rested his chin on the top of Renee's head. "I'm going to tell you now that I'm going to spoil her, Renee."

"That's okay as long as she doesn't become a brat."

"Let's have dinner, then we'll call Jeremy and Ryan and let them in on our good news. After that we'll call your folks."

"I think I'd like to have a Christmas Eve wedding."

"And you will, princess. You can have any and everything you want."

Renee knew there was something special about Sheldon Blackstone the instant she stepped out of her car to find him staring down at her. So special that she fell in love with him despite her vow never to trust another man.

Christmas Eve

White damask tablecloths, delicate china, crystal stemware, sterling silver, beeswax tapers in sterling holders and large pine wreaths decorated with white satin bows and white rosebuds at Blackstone Farms' dining hall set the stage for the nuptials between Renee Anna Wilson and Sheldon James Blackstone.

Rumors were circulating throughout Virginia's horse country that there was to be a wedding at Blackstone Farms, and for the first time in farm history no one deigned to confirm or deny the rumor.

Sheldon had selected Jeremy as his best man, Ryan and Sean as his groomsmen. Renee had asked her brother to give her away, her sister-in-law had agreed to be her maid-of-honor and Kelly and Tricia were her bridesmaids.

The farms' employees began filing into the dining hall at seven forty-five, sitting at assigned tables. A string quartet played Mozart concertos, then at exactly eight o'clock, the lights dimmed. Jeremy and Sheldon, dressed in formalwear, entered the dining hall. An eerie hush fell over the room as groomsmen with burgundy silk ties and bridesmaids in floor-length matching gowns followed the procession.

The distinctive strains of the wedding march began and Renee, clinging to her brother's arm, concentrated on putting one foot in front of the other as she made her way over the white carpet leading to where Sheldon waited in front of the stained-glass window. Her dress, an off-white, long-sleeved satin gown with an empire waist, was designed to artfully camouflage her swollen belly. She looked at her mother and smiled.

Edward Wilson tightened his hold on his sister's hand. "We're almost there, Rennie."

Edward had contacted Donald Rush after Renee informed him that she was marrying Sheldon, and told him that his sister had married. Donald offered his best wishes for her happiness, then abruptly hung up. The telephone call had closed the door on Renee and Donald's past.

Renee let out a soft gasp as she felt a strong kick. Her baby had awakened in time to celebrate her parents' wedding. She focused her attention on the Reverend Jimmy Merrell, who waited to perform his first wedding as the farm's resident minister.

After midnight, when Renee lay in the warmth of her husband's embrace, she recalled her wedding and the reception dinner that followed. The resident chefs had outdone themselves with a reception that included passed hors d'oeuvres, seafood, carving and Asian stations. A seated dinner menu offered soup, salad, blue lump crab cakes and entrées of rib-eye steak and free-range chicken breast.

Shifting to her right side, she placed her left hand

over her husband's chest, the light from a table lamp glinting off the precious stones in her wedding band.

Sheldon squeezed the tiny hand, whispering a silent prayer of thanksgiving for his wife and the child kicking in her womb. He had been given a second chance to be a good husband. This time he was certain he would get it right.

"Do you want to know something, Sheldon?"

"What, darling?"

"I just realized how lucky I am."

"Why?"

"I get to have a sleepover with my best friend every single night."

Chuckling softly, Sheldon kissed her forehead. "Merry Christmas, princess."

Renee kissed his shoulder. "Merry Christmas, my love."

This Christmas they would celebrate as husband and wife.

The next one would be as husband, wife, mother and father.

Epilogue

Eighteen months later

The photographer checked his light meter, then changed the lens on his camera.

"Renee, please move closer to your husband. Jeremy, you're going to have to hold two of your daughters."

The Blackstones had gathered in Renee and Sheldon's living room for a formal family photo session. In only a year and a half the family had increased by five.

Renee had given birth to a daughter whom she'd named Virginia.

Tricia and Jeremy had become the parents of identical triplet daughters who were feminine miniatures of their father.

Ryan and Kelly had welcomed their third child, a son, who was named for his grandfather, Sheldon James Blackstone the second.

Virginia squirmed to free herself from Renee's arms. "Poppa."

Sheldon reached over and took his daughter, bouncing her on his knee. The chubby little girl had become his pride and joy from the moment she came into the world, crying at the top of her tiny lungs. He'd kissed her, cut the umbilical cord and had claimed her as his own within seconds of her birth. Virginia may have looked like her mother, but there was no doubt she was his daughter.

"Let's do this now," Sheldon ordered the photographer.

The man held up a hand. "One, two, three. Hold it." A flash of light went off, startling the children. They'd barely recovered when another flash followed. This time they laughed, trying to catch the tiny white circles floating in front of their eyes.

The photographer got off one more shot, capturing the lively smiles and bright-eyed stares of the next generation of Virginia Blackstones.

* * * * *

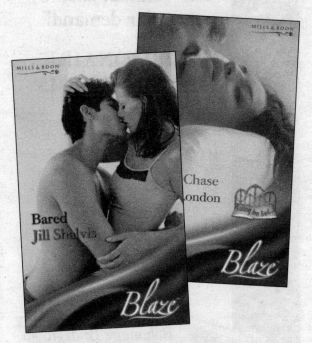

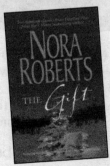

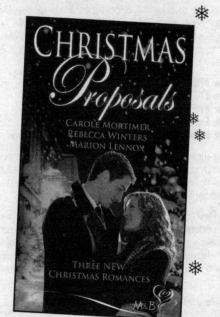

2 FREE

BOOKS AND A SURPRISE GIFT!

We would like to take this opportunity to thank you for reading this Silhouette® book by offering you the chance to take TWO more specially selected titles from the Desire™ series absolutely FREE! We're also making this offer to introduce you to the benefits of the Mills & Boon® Reader Service™—

- ★ **FREE home delivery**
- ★ **FREE gifts and competitions**
- ★ **FREE monthly Newsletter**
- ★ **Exclusive Reader Service offers**
- ★ **Books available before they're in the shops**

Accepting these FREE books and gift places you under no obligation to buy, you may cancel at any time, even after receiving your free shipment. Simply complete your details below and return the entire page to the address below. You don't even need a stamp!

YES! Please send me 2 free Desire volumes and a surprise gift. I understand that unless you hear from me, I will receive 3 superb new titles every month for just £4.99 each, postage and packing free. I am under no obligation to purchase any books and may cancel my subscription at any time. The free books and gift will be mine to keep in any case.

D6ZED

Ms/Mrs/Miss/Mr ....Initials ....

BLOCK CAPITALS PLEASE

Surname ....

Address ....

....

....Postcode.............................

Send this whole page to:
UK: FREEPOST CN81, Croydon, CR9 3WZ